ABOUT WHIT

Just when you get out…

Former Chicago cop Jack Daniels thought she'd left her former life behind. She'd traded her badge for a toddler, and her lifelong pursuit of heinous serial killers for a boring house in the suburbs.

…you're pulled back in.

Then Jack sees some pictures. Pictures of men who are supposed to be dead. And once again, against the fierce insistence of her husband, Phineas Troutt, Jack reluctantly straps on her gun and goes hunting. Hunting for the worst of the worst.

Jack treks across the Great Plains, searching for a modern slavery ring, on a collision course with three of the worst villains she has ever faced.

But Jack, and her irritating buddy Harry McGlade, will face them, and much more. Because they're prepared to go to hell and back to rescue an old friend.

The trick will be getting back in one piece. And—spoiler alert—they don't.

WHITE RUSSIAN by J.A. Konrath

What are you willing to lose?

WHITE RUSSIAN
A Jack Daniels Thriller

J.A. KONRATH

WHITE RUSSIAN
Copyright © 2016 by Joe Konrath
Cover art copyright © 2023 by Lynne Hansen

This book is a work of fiction. Names, characters, places and incidents are either products of the author's imagination or used fictitiously. Any resemblance to actual events, locales, or persons, living or dead, is entirely coincidental. All rights reserved. No part of this publication can be reproduced or transmitted in any form or by any means, electronic or mechanical, without permission in writing from the authors.

November 2017

WHITE RUSSIAN

2 ounces vodka
1 ounce coffee liqueur
1 ounce heavy cream

Pour vodka and coffee liqueur over ice into a rocks glass. Float cream on top.

SOMEWHERE IN THE USA

MANY YEARS AGO

Tara, half her husband's age and tanned the color of saddle leather, glanced at her Cartier watch. The diamond-tipped minute hand was creeping up on three o'clock. She was going to miss *Jeopardy*, and the accompanying pre-dinner martini. A double tragedy. To make this situation even more unpleasant, her post-lunch martini had almost worn off, and she was suffering the company of a worthless moron.

"It was just a hamster," Tara stated, letting her lack of interest seep into her inflection.

The teacher—young, plump, with one of those round faces that no gym could ever fix—wore an expression so serious it almost made Tara laugh. They were discussing a harmless behavior problem, not anything as serious as a death in the family. Or, god forbid, bankruptcy.

"I don't think you understand the gravity of this situation, Mrs.—"

"Do not call me Mrs. Tara is fine."

Christ, Tara hated being called Mrs. She hated it almost as much as she hated being a mother. But when you marry old money, certain things were expected. Tara could live with the stretch marks, the inconvenient pregnancy forever scarring her tight body. She could live with the quick, feeble attempts that passed for lovemaking, with a flabby, grey husband more than double her age. But why did she have to attend these damn parent/teacher meetings? The school refused to let the nanny substitute, for some bullshit reason. If they'd lived in a better school district, with a better class of people, no doubt the nanny would be allowed to take care of these petty disciplinary issues.

Tara crossed her legs, Dolce & Gabbana draping perfectly over thighs that could still turn heads. "I'll buy the school a new one. How much can the damn things cost? A few dollars?"

"The cost isn't the issue."

"Then, for god's sake, why am I here?"

The teacher's fat face sagged, her jowls jiggling. "This wasn't an accident. I believe the twins... they killed Fluffy intentionally."

Tara frowned, noting the big toe protruding from her Ferragamo sandals had a chip in the French pedicure. "I'm sure they were just playing with it."

"They took pictures."

"Don't be absurd."

The chubby fourth grade teacher reached into her desk with all the drama of the President pushing the button to launch a nuclear strike. She set something down in front of Tara.

Tara snorted. "That's a plate of spaghetti." She was about to add, "you stupid moron" but caught herself when the sauce and noodles rearranged themselves in her brain, registering as blood and guts.

Her stomach clenched and Tara quickly looked away. "The twins didn't do that."

"They were caught with blood on them."

"Maybe they found it that way."

"Blood on the bottoms of their shoes." The teacher appeared ready to cry. "From... stomping... on Fluffy."

Tara almost snorted again, because *Fluffy* was clearly no longer descriptive of the mangled rodent in the picture. *Flatty* was a better name.

"They could have stepped on it accidentally. And took pictures because they're curious."

"This isn't normal childhood curiosity."

Tara's hackles rose as naturally as if she'd been born entitled. "Are you telling me my children aren't normal? I didn't know you'd acquired a psychiatric degree since our last meeting."

The teacher slumped in her chair. "This isn't the first behavioral issue we've had. There's the hitting."

Tara made a show of rolling her eyes, a gesture that regularly put little people back in their place. "They were hitting each other. They're twins. That's how they play."

"A split lip and a black eye isn't playing. If they'd done that to another student, they'd be expelled."

"It's just sibling rivalry. And I don't need you telling me what's normal. We pay a shrink ten times your public servant salary to make that diagnosis."

The barb was intended to sting, but the teacher's face only registered concern.

"They won't respond to their real names," she continued. "They only answer to Tom and Jerry. Like the cartoon cat and mouse."

"Dr. Rabinowitz says it's a phase they're going through."

"And speaking gibberish? Making up words?"

"It's their own special language. A lot of twins do that. Most of them, in fact."

Tara wasn't sure if *most* was correct, but she'd heard it was common.

"There have been other incidents. Last week, I sat on a tack that someone placed on my chair."

Tara kept her expression neutral, but the thought of this overweight, untalented wage slave getting poked in her ass amused the hell out of her.

"Did you see the twins do it?"

"No."

"Did anyone else?"

The teacher hesitated, then said, "The other students...they're afraid of your children."

This was getting ridiculous. Tara sighed the same sigh she used to get her way with her husband. "There hasn't been a single incident involving other children."

"I'm aware of that. That's because they avoid Tom and—I mean, your kids. At recess, no one plays with them. During class, no one will pair up with them for art or science lab."

Tara glanced at her watch again, making no attempt to be furtive.

"Do you have ... pets in the house?" the teacher asked.

"We bought them a dog. A purebred German Shepherd that cost a small fortune. He ran away last summer."

Tara still had no idea how the beast got off its chain. It had been a bad dog, anyway. Always growling at the twins.

"Other pets?"

"We had a beautiful salt water aquarium in my husband's den, but the fish kept dying. They're very difficult to keep alive, you know. And a kitten, which accidentally drowned in the toilet."

There was also an iguana, but Tara had no intention of mentioning it. That was an honest mistake, born of curiosity. The twins had insisted they thought iguanas could fly. Why else would they throw it off the roof?

"Do they play with matches?" the teacher asked.

"Of course not! My husband spanked them both and took the matches away!"

Another serious look. "Harming animals and starting fires could be indicative of a bigger problem, Mrs., uh, Tara."

"Their grades are fine. We have absolutely no problems when they're at home."

Plus, they were both taking adult-strength doses of Ritalin. Something this stupid teacher didn't know about, because it was none of her business. But everyone knew it was impossible to misbehave on Ritalin.

"I'm only bringing all of this up out of concern," the teacher said.

"The only concern I have," Tara narrowed her eyes, "is the quality of the teaching staff at this school."

The teacher sat up straighter, as if someone had jammed a rod up her ass. She busied herself with organizing some papers on her desk.

"Well, thank you for coming in, Tara. I should inform you that if there is another incident, Principal Stephens will be sitting in on the meeting."

"I doubt there will be another incident. And I don't believe I'll be seeing you again."

Tara stood up, unaware of how prophetic her words were. Five nights later, while her husband was away on business, Tara died from third degree burns. The police report attributed it to smoking while removing her nail polish with acetone, a highly flammable solvent.

The twins corroborated that story, claiming that their mother had been sneaking cigarettes, even though she'd quit over three years earlier.

It was a closed casket funeral, but the twins somehow managed to get the lid open, leading to the casket tipping over.

Their grief counsellor said it was a normal, healthy reaction to such a terrible loss.

Their grief counsellor was wrong.

MONTHS AGO

SOMEWHERE

He opened his eyes to a world of pain. Everything hurt.
But being in pain meant being alive.
He was on his back. Immobile. Bandages covering his body.
He tried to move his arm.
Couldn't.
Not because of an injury. But because he was handcuffed to the bed.
"Nurse?" he called, his voice a painful rasp.
"No nurses. This isn't a hospital."
He turned, and saw a familiar but scarred face occupying the cot next to him, similarly handcuffed.
"Where are we?"
"I don't know yet," the man said. "But it's bad."
"How bad?"
The man frowned. "Bad enough that we're both going to wish we hadn't survived Mexico."

FORT MYERS, FLORIDA

JACK

For the first time in my life, I had a life.

I was in such a good mood that I didn't even mind getting a call from my ex-partner, Harry McGlade.

"Hiya, Jackie. How's things?"

"Wonderfully boring. I feel great, Harry. It's truly a joy not to be involved with anything dangerous."

"Good for you. I'm glad. Now I need your help with something dangerous."

I didn't hesitate. "No."

"You didn't even hear my pitch."

"I don't care, McGlade. I'm out. No more police work. No more detective work. My guns are in storage. The only cases I'm taking are cases of beer."

"You know I've got this blog, right?" he went on, undeterred.

"Yeah. I read it all the time," I lied.

"What do you know about human trafficking?"

"I know enough that I'm not helping you."

"Slavery is still a big business, Jack. Do you know that it's estimated that there are more than thirty million people enslaved today? And we're not just talking third world. It's happening right here, in the good old US of A."

"Tragic. Heartbreaking. Terrible. I mean that. And I'm not helping you with any cases."

"Remember Mexico?"

That hit a nerve. "Of course I remember Mexico." Some good people had died south of the border, helping me out. "Are you calling in a favor?"

"No. I'm *doing* you a favor."

"This doesn't sound like a favor."

"What if I told you," McGlade said, "that someone we thought was dead wasn't actually dead?"

I sat up in my chair so fast I spilled my coffee.

"What are you saying, Harry?"

"I'm on my way to your place right now," Harry said. "I'll tell you in person in about ten minutes."

Then he hung up, leaving me to wonder if Harry was talking about an old friend…

Or an old enemy.

SOMEWHERE IN NEBRASKA

YURI

The Cowboy wore a balaclava and a black leather Stetson with human teeth around the hatband.

The balaclava was a polyester microfiber that covered the neck, mouth, and nose, like a ski mask. Embroidered on the front was a realistic image of a human skull, making the Cowboy look like a skeleton with eyes.

The teeth on the hat were human, glued onto the band in an ever-widening mosaic. Some had fillings. Some were cracked, because there was a learning curve to the extraction process and it had taken a while for the Cowboy to get it right.

The Cowboy had many talents, but dentistry wasn't one of them.

The Cowboy always wore a black Outback duster jacket, a black button-down shirt, black jeans, and black crocodile boots with silver spurs. On a still desert night, when the LeTourneau was parked, you could hear the spurs jangle from fifty meters away.

Which was the point. Costume, theatrics, performance; all orchestrated to maximize fear in the prisoner.

The naked prisoner in the Punishment Room, his wrists bound to a ceiling chain with plastic riot cuff restraints, certainly appeared afraid.

When the Cowboy first began working for Yuri, there had been no costume. Just the unadorned Stetson. But Yuri had created the uniform based on one he knew well, from his days in Minsk, leading the death squad. When carrying out missions, they wore grotesque masks meant to terrify victims.

Fear was one of several currencies Yuri used. And it was highly effective.

Pain was another method of persuasion. But it only worked short term, while the pain was being applied. It was effective as punishment, and to break wills and crush resistance. Yuri knew this, from both ends of the cattle prod.

But pain compliance wasn't effective with slave labor. It was simple math. To constantly administer pain to thirty workers would require a full staff of slave drivers. Space was limited, and more men meant more living quarters, more necessary supplies, and less room for product. Burns and welts required healing time, which was time not spent harvesting. What was the point of having slaves if you weren't working them constantly?

So Yuri had to maximize the impact of limited enforcers, therefore maximizing worker output.

That required fear. The thought of pain, the dread of punishment, was a more effective motivator than the actual pain.

Unfortunately, in order to accomplish that, slaves had to occasionally be yanked from the harvest to get them to understand. And, sometimes, they had to be discarded, as a lesson to the others.

"Your output is unacceptable," Yuri told the chained man, speaking up so the GoPro video camera mounted to the wall captured every word. Yuri had been living in the US for over a decade, and his English was excellent, but he hadn't been able to shed all traces of his accent. He could mimic an American when required. But allowing his Belarusian roots to show seemed to be more frightening, for both the current subject, and those watching. That, coupled with his size—Yuri was a solid two hundred and eighty pounds, standing six foot six in his combat boots—was usually enough to scare anyone into compliance.

The prisoner didn't respond. He was probably too terrified to open his mouth. Not that he had any choice in the matter. An open mouth only required a simple tug.

"I'm out of patience. And you're out of teeth. You know the rules. Out of teeth, out of chances."

"Please," the man begged, showing his bare, red gums. "I didn't mean to pass out. If I only had more food."

Food, like sleep, was kept to a minimum. It was cheaper to buy new slaves than it was to feed them adequately. Besides, Yuri had seen men far more emaciated than this one do far better work.

"Too late. You've been replaced."

He nodded at the Cowboy, who drew the black revolver from the black gunslinger hip holster so fast that the naked eye couldn't even see it. In a fraction of a second the shot was fired and the gun was holstered again.

It never failed to make Yuri smirk. As a child, his only exposure to America had been bootlegged videotapes of old Hollywood Westerns. He'd always thought of the USA as a country full of armed sharpshooters and desperados who would kill you just as easy as looking at you.

And now he had his very own cowboy on payroll. Proof that the American dream was attainable by all. Even immigrants. Even former KGB.

The slave, missing the back of his head, hung limp by his wrists. His skull poured out brains like oatmeal from a bowl.

Yuri turned to the camera. "I hate having to remind you all of the consequences of insubordination. The rules are simple. You can eat and sleep if you make your quota. If you don't, the Cowboy takes a tooth. When your teeth are gone, the Cowboy takes your life." He waved a dismissive hand. "Break is over. Get back to work."

Yuri shut off the camera, his arm twitching in a spasm. He stilled his shaking hand by making a fist until the tremors stopped. Once it did, he consciously scratched at the scar tissue beneath his shirt, then silently cursed that *chertovski ublyudok*, Lukashenko, and spat on the floor of the train.

"*Skoro moy prezident. Skoro.*"

FT. MEYERS

JACK

Phineas Troutt stood in the kitchen, rinsing out a bowl. The house smelled heavenly. During his long recuperation, he'd taken up baking. In the past few months, Phin had made more than a hundred loaves of bread. I'd gained eight pounds, and we were the hit of the neighborhood because we gave away the surplus.

"Your mom?" Phin asked, glancing at the cell phone in my hand.

My mother was the only one who called on my cell. Because, other than McGlade, she was pretty much the only one who knew I was alive. Long story, but my younger husband and I were living in Florida under the names Gil and Jill Johnson. As far as the rest of the world knew, Jacqueline Daniels was dead.

"Yeah," I lied, handing him my empty coffee cup. "She said you need to get a job."

"That's sexist. I'm a homemaker. I take care of the baby while my spouse brings in the dough."

"You seem to be making a lot of dough lately," I said, eyeing the bread on the cooling rack.

"Sue-Ellen up the block says I should open a table at the farmer's market at St. Joseph's. They have one every Sunday."

I couldn't stifle my smirk. Phin narrowed his eyes.

"I thought you liked my bread."

"I love your bread, babe. It's just... when I met you, you were hooked on coke and beating people up for money. And now you're doing a bake sale. It's...quite the turnaround from being a bad ass."

Phin rinsed my cup, wiped his wet hands on the sink towel, and then came over. He had a slight limp, and he carried himself like a man overcoming injuries. Which, indeed, he was. He placed his hands on my hips and pulled me close.

"Are you saying that bad asses don't bake?" His face was serious.

I offered a mock protest. "I would never say such a thing."

"Because, if you want, I'll go out right now, get really high, and beat up a bunch of people."

"You'd do that for me?"

He smiled. "You know I'd do anything for you."

And he would. Which is why I'd lied to him about talking to McGlade. I had a feeling Harry's news would lead someplace dark.

My husband's dark days were over, by mutual decision. He still wasn't back to a hundred percent health.

He might never be back to a hundred percent.

I stretched up, kissed him. He tasted like rye. The bread, not the whiskey.

"You working tonight?"

I'd gotten a job at a local shooting range as an instructor. It wasn't as stimulating as solving cases or catching criminals, but it carried much smaller risks. There was still a chance I might get shot, but it wouldn't be by someone intentionally shooting at me.

"Night off. I'm heading to the store. Need anything?"

"More ant killer." Fire ants were one of many adjustments moving from Chicago to Tampa.

I gave him another quick peck, then pinched off a bite of rye bread, cooling on the kitchen countertop rack.

No bullshit. The man had mad baking skills.

"Taking Bud?" Phin asked.

Bud was our daughter. Her real name was Samantha Adams Daniels. But with the move, and our subsequent new identities, we jokingly referred to her as Bud. With Gil subbing for Phin and Jill subbing for Jack, Budweiser seemed like a suitable alias for Sam Adams.

We'd been drinking at the time, and the nickname stuck.

"Where is our love child?"

"Out back. Pouring ant killer on hills."

I pulled away from him. "Phin! That shit is poison!"

"She's wearing a mask. I checked."

"She's four!"

"It was her idea. You try to talk her out of it."

I checked out the clock. Still five minutes before Harry's announced arrival. So I went out the patio doors and onto our deck.

Sam was standing in the backyard. She wore a one-piece swimsuit, and had such a deep tan it made her blonde hair appear almost white. Next to her, ever loyal, was our hound dog, Duffy. As her father stated, Sam had a filter mask over her nose and mouth as she poured toxic powder onto an ant hill with razor-like focus.

Duffy saw me and woo-wooed, then came bounding over. I gave him a scratch between his floppy ears.

"Sammy, you need to let Daddy do that, sweetheart."

Sam looked up at me. "I like doing it."

"It's dangerous."

"Is it dangerous for Daddy?"

Smart kid. "Daddy is bigger."

"I don't like the ants. They bite."

Shortly after we'd moved here, Sam had stepped on a fire ant hill and been bitten a dozen times. They were called *fire ants* for a reason, and she'd cried for ten minutes straight. Now Sam always wore clogs in the back yard, and had made it her mission to eradicate the species.

"I know. Come in. Daddy made rye bread."

Sam seemed to weigh her anticide calling against the allure of fresh baked goods, and the baked goods won out. She left the bottle of poison on the lawn, and ran past me, her tiny, chubby legs a blur. Duffy bounded after her. As Sam and Phin discussed the pros and cons of various flavored cream cheeses in the kitchen, I walked around the property to catch McGlade before he arrived.

We'd moved here from a suburb of Chicago, but the neighborhoods couldn't have been more different. There we had more land, more trees, more privacy, and no one knew us. This was like Mayberry, but hotter. Our neighbors on either side were so close we could spit on their houses from our property, if so inclined, which we weren't because they were good people. Sam already had three friends her age on our block, and two others a few blocks away, that we'd met at the local playground. Phin—er, *Gil*, and I had been invited to three potluck dinners by local parents, we went to the beach every Thursday, and I'd become an honorary bartender at my mother's retirement home in the center of the city.

After a lifetime of chasing bad guys, and losing far too many loved ones, I'd somehow lucked into leading a normal life. And, best of all, I found it suited me. No pangs for adventure. No longings for danger. No thirst for justice.

I was retired from crime-fighting. And I was happy. Maybe for the first time ever. My life was all about teaching self-defense shooting and playing family board games and eating freshly baked bread and reading all those trashy books I missed when they came out and watching my child grow up. And I loved it. I loved it so much, I could sleep at night, for a full seven hours, without any pills.

So whatever McGlade was pitching, I wasn't buying. No way, no how.

I'd barely made it to the Valencia orange tree out front when I spotted the Crimebago Deux coming up the street. McGlade's 'crime lab on wheels', as he called it, was a bright red Winnebago motorhome that he'd customized after watching too many episodes of *Pimp My Ride* on MTV.

I flagged him down at the end of the driveway, and he rolled down his window and leered at me.

"Hiya, Jackie! Where should I park? I don't think I can fit this beast in the tiny driveway of your tiny house."

"Keep driving. We'll go around the corner."

"You're not inviting me in? Are you embarrassed because you buy your furniture from stores where you have to assemble it with a hex wrench?"

Because the universe is unfair, McGlade was rich. He liked to proclaim it as much as he liked to proclaim that you weren't. But, to be honest, he'd been equally obnoxious and offensive when his income was unremarkable. Harry was a jerk before he became a rich jerk. But he was also like a brother to me. Or a cousin. That weird cousin from the estranged side of the family that you only see on holidays and that's enough.

"I haven't told Phin you're here," I said.

"But Phin and I are bros. We've been on a few adventures. Remember that abduction thing up in Minnesota?"

"I remember. I was there."

"Right. Did I ever tell you the time we were kidnapped by his insane brother?"

I knew Hugo, and didn't need any reminders. "Phin is out of this particular loop."

"We may need him."

"Not this time. Open up."

Harry hit the unlock button and let me in the side door.

That's when the bear attacked me.

It wasn't an actual bear. And its attack amounted to rearing up on its hind legs, throwing its enormous front paws over my shoulders, and licking my face.

"Good to see you, too, Rosa."

Rosalina was a Neapolitan Mastiff. All one hundred and fifty pounds of her. She looked like an overgrown Chinese Shar-Pei, and had so many wrinkles that her surface area was equivalent to three other large dogs.

"Down, girl," McGlade ordered.

Rosa dropped down.

"Sit."

The dog sat. This wasn't due to McGlade's dog-whispering skills. Her former owner, a deceased friend of mine named Tequila, had done the training. McGlade inherited the dog after Tequila was killed in the same incident that injured my husband.

I closed the door, turned to McGlade and—

"Holy shit, Harry. What the hell happened?"

He rolled his eyes and put the RV into gear. "Go ahead. Get it all out."

I looked him up and down. He sported the same scraggly face, but it had ballooned in size. His suit, by some trendy designer, wasn't as wrinkled as usual because the fabric was stretched to bursting.

"You're...*huge*."

Harry had never been svelte, but he'd put on a whole lot of weight since I'd last seen him.

He shrugged. "Stress eating. After Baja, I gained a few pounds."

"A few? You look like someone stuck a tube up your ass and inflated you."

"That's my joke."

"It fits. How much do you weigh?"

"I haven't checked lately."

"You know you can stand on two scales and add the numbers."

"Funny. This is a temporary thing. I just need to hit the gym."

"It looks like you ate the gym." I didn't mind ball-busting Harry because A: He deserved it, and B: He used to pick on an obese friend of mine in this very same manner.

"Does this motorhome have a weight limit?" I asked.

"Nice. You're on a roll."

"I was on a roll, until you ate it. You ate the whole basket."

"I'll speak to my agent, see if Kimmel has a late-night slot for you."

"Tell me, what's your belt size? Equator?"

"Keep 'em coming. I can take it."

"I'm afraid if I get too close I'll catch diabetes."

He waggled a finger. "Ahh. You can't actually catch diabetes. I looked it up."

"Yes, you can. I think you're sweating maple syrup."

"I spilled that during breakfast. And it was low fat maple syrup."

"I don't think *low-fat* matters when you're eating seventy-five pancakes."

"You're not being very supportive, Jack."

"The only support you need is a sports bra for those man boobs."

"*Man Boobs* was my nickname in High School." He frowned. "I always thought it was because I was a man who liked boobs. Now you've got me feeling slightly insecure about my silver dollar-sized nipples."

"Is this why you didn't fly here? You don't fit on a jumbo jet?"

He gave me a look. "I drove here because I didn't want to leave Miss Rosalina in a kennel. And because we're going to need the Crimebago Deux where we're going."

I stopped my ribbing and got back on task. "Okay. Get to it. You mentioned white slavery and someone dead who wasn't dead."

McGlade pulled over to the side of the road and turned to me, the rolls in his neck creasing.

"So, you know about The Mansplainer."

I nodded. That was the name of Harry's blog. I'd never read it, because I always had better things to do, like anything other than reading his blog.

"There are Internet stories about a guy known as the Cowboy. Part Slenderman urban legend meme, part Green River Killer of the Great Plains. I think he's real."

"He's a serial killer?"

"Sort of. He—"

"I'm out."

I reached for the door handle. Harry kept his finger on the automatic lock so I couldn't open it.

"Jack, just listen…"

"I'm done with psychos, Harry. That's why I'm living in Florida under the name Jill."

"I know that. You think I drove this land barge all the way from Chicago unless this was important? Let me finish, for crissakes."

"There is nothing you can say to convince me to help you with this."

Harry's face became serious. "Have you gotten over Herb's death?"

The words knocked the fight out of me. Herb. Herb Benedict. My longtime partner when I worked Homicide for the Chicago Police Department.

My best friend.

I'd lost him the same place I'd lost Tequila.

"I'll never get over Herb's death," I said softly.

"His body was never recovered. Neither was Tequila's."

"I know." That must have been maddening for Herb's wife. To never have closure. To never be one hundred percent positive that he was dead.

But I was one hundred percent positive. I was there when he was killed.

"Just give me thirty seconds, Jack. Please."

I let out a slow breath. "Okay. Clock starts now."

"So, I wrote this blog about adding an Amendment to the Constitution that forbids men from making laws concerning women's reproductive rights."

Harry fancied himself a feminist. And, in a way, he was. He treated everyone equally bad, regardless of gender.

"Twenty seconds."

"It went viral. I did a lot of talk shows. Did you see me on Colbert?"

"No. Fifteen seconds."

"So I'm getting all this press, and during one of the interviews I mention that I recently lost a friend. Herb Benedict."

It was a stretch to call Herb and Harry friends. But I only had to put up with this for a few more seconds, so I didn't bother to argue. I wanted out of this bubble of violent possibilities and back into my normal, average, boring home with my normal, average, boring family. I wanted fresh baked bread, not chasing psychos.

"A week ago, on my blog, someone calling himself the Cowboy leaves me this comment."

McGlade handed me his cell phone, already queued up to his URL. Going against the little voice inside that warned me not to, I read the entry anyway.

> They call me the Cowboy. Search for me and my content on darknet. I collect teeth. I also collect people. Here's someone I recently picked up. I'm in Nebraska. Catch me if you can.

Then there was a link to Instagram. I followed the link and… My breath caught.

The picture was a little out of focus, but it was of a man in a bed, his body swaddled in bandages.

The man's eyes were closed. The bandages were bloody.

But it looked like Herb.

It looked *a lot* like Herb.

"Is this real?" I asked, my voice low.

"A friend who works CGI for Hollywood took a look. She said it didn't appear altered in any way. No Photoshop."

I squinted at the face. "Maybe it's just someone who looks like him."

"That was my first thought. Or maybe it is Herb, but he's dead. Doesn't make sense to put bandages on a dead guy, though. And keep looking. There's something else."

I continued to study the pic. This wasn't a hospital. The bed looked like a dirty cot. The man who might be Herb had beads of sweat on his forehead.

"Dead men don't perspire," I said.

"They don't need handcuffs, either."

I checked his hands, and there was indeed a cuff on his right wrist, linking him to someone else.

Someone not pictured, except for half of his hand.

A hand with a butterfly tattoo.

"Your buddy, Tequila," Harry said. "He has a butterfly tattoo."

"Yeah."

"Does that tattoo match?"

I nodded, my stomach clenching into a big, twisted fist.

"I've done some research. I can fill you in on the way to Nebraska. Drop the kid off with Mom, grab Phin, and we—"

"Phin isn't coming with," I interrupted. "He's still recuperating."

"Jack, I think this is more than just this Cowboy asshole. I've put some hours in on this. I think there are human traffickers, operating out of the Plains states. We're going to need help."

"We're in America, McGlade. When we find Herb and Tequila, we'll bring in the authorities."

"*We?* So you're in?"

I'd thought there was nothing that could force me back into the game. But this was the only thing that could.

Herb. Jesus. Baja was over half a year ago.

We'd left him there. We'd left him for dead, and all this time…

"Of course I'm in." I checked the time on Harry's phone. "I need about an hour to pack and make up some lie to tell my husband."

"Say you're leaving him for another woman. That would be hot."

McGlade, unhelpful as usual.

"He'll be suspicious if I bring my gun," I said, thinking out loud.

"I got plenty of guns. And if you don't like any of them, we can buy you a gun on the road." He grinned, his smile as wide as a zebra's ass. "As you said; we're in America."

SOMEWHERE, SOMETIME AGO

HERB

It was impossible for Herb Benedict to know how much time had passed since he awoke in captivity. His beard was as long as his index finger, and he was notoriously slow at growing facial hair. What did that mean? Three months? More?

The bullet wounds in his chest, still swollen and tender to the touch, had scarred over. Healing was a slow, painful process. His only medicine had been antibiotics, and he'd run a high fever for weeks. Infections, for sure. Also a gamut of other diseases, which spread easily and quickly in the underground jail that had served as his rehab facility.

Herb believed he was still in Mexico. His captors spoke Spanish. His meals were beans, rice, tortillas. The heat was smothering.

But this wasn't a hospital. And it wasn't a traditional prison. His requests for a lawyer were met with dead stares. He never saw any police. Never was taken to court.

Herb didn't know where he was, but he knew two things. First, keeping him here wasn't legal. Second, escape was impossible.

He was shackled to the cot by the ankle, and the cot was bolted to the floor. There were no windows. Just cinder block walls. A bucket for the bathroom. The only light, a few low watt bulbs hanging from the ceiling from a spiderweb of old extension cords.

The cuisine was about the same quality as the accommodations. Small portions of beans and rice, twice a day. Every so often an egg, or some gamey goat meat, or a few chilis. The water they were given to drink was tepid, brownish, and smelled like sulfur.

They kept eight men imprisoned in this hole, all injured, rotating them out as they healed. Sometimes the smell of body odor and bodily functions became so raw, it made Herb's eyes burn. More than once, Herb lost hope. Hope of recovery. Hope of release. The pain of his injuries and illnesses paled next to his longing for his wife.

Only one thing stopped him from letting despair consume him. Tequila.

Not the liquor. Booze was yet another indulgence absent in captivity. The Tequila that kept Herb rooted in reality was Tequila Abernathy, a former mob enforcer Herb had met many years ago. He'd been on the mission in Baja, and like Herb, he'd been left for dead and picked up by the same group that was nursing them back to health.

Herb's injuries were like a paper cut compared to Tequila's. That guy had more holes in him than a golf course. Internal injuries. Broken bones. Blind in one eye. For a while, it was touch and go, and Herb was sure his friend was a goner. But the diminutive, muscular man had pulled through.

"Traffickers," Tequila had said, weeks ago as they watched another man taken from his cell, never to return.

Herb was familiar with the sex slave trade. But they were old, broken men, and he didn't think they had much value.

"I was hoping we were being held for ransom." Kidnapping gringos was common south of the border.

Tequila shook his head. "It's been too long for that. I think this is a slave labor operation. They bring in the nearly dead, wait to see if they recover, then sell them."

"For what?"

Tequila shrugged. "Labor. If we're lucky."

"It's the twenty-first century."

"As long as there are human beings, there will be slave labor."

Terrible as that sounded, Herb almost wished it were true. Working a mine, or a farm, would be better than rotting in this dark hole.

"You said if we're lucky. What if we aren't lucky?"

"They could be holding us to compete in gladiator games, like in Baja. Or worse."

"What's worse than that?"

"Snuff films."

Herb shook his head. "Those are urban legends. Videos do exist where people die. Those ISIS beheading movies. Serial killers with video cameras. But there is no such thing as a retail market for snuff movies. You can't manufacture, distribute, and sell evidence of a murder, without it eventually getting back to you. If someone was producing snuff films for money, they'd be caught."

"Did you ever hear of Usher House?"

It had a slightly familiar ring, but Herb couldn't place it so he said no.

"How about Silk Road?"

Herb nodded. Tequila was referring to the illegal trade that occurred on the uncatalogued parts of the Internet, commonly known as darknet. "Feebies shut it down."

"You can't shut down an idea. One black market gets closed, another opens in its place. With VPN and bitcoin, you can buy and sell anything you want to, and no one knows who the buyers or sellers are. Especially when no physical object changes hands. You can exchange a cryptocurrency for an encrypted media file, and there is no way either party can be caught."

"And this is a thing?"

"Selling illegal goods has always been a thing. Darknet just made it easier."

"Just when I thought my opinion of human nature couldn't get any lower."

"You say this while chained to a cot."

"Good point. So you think we're being nursed back to health so a bunch of rich cybergeeks can pay to watch us die?"

Tequila offered a rare smile. "Fingers crossed for slave labor."

Herb didn't smile back.

PRESENT

JACK

My husband appeared dubious. And rightfully so.

"A one-week Alaskan cruise. With your mother."

I tried to look flustered. Which was pretty easy, because I was flustered. "Her date broke a hip. And it's too late to get a refund."

He folded his arms across his chest. "And you're leaving right now."

"I don't even have time to fully pack. I'll probably have to pick up some things on the ship."

"And, on this cruise, are you taking your gun?"

"What? No. Of course not. It's a cruise."

Sam came wandering into the bedroom. "What's wrong, Mommy? You look upset."

"Mommy is upset because she's telling Daddy a lie," Phin told our daughter.

My little angel tugged on my shirt and looked up at me. "Why are you lying to Daddy?"

"Because she's doing something that would make Daddy angry," Phin said. "Something with Uncle Harry."

"Uncle Harry smells like feet and cheese," Sam stated. And she was correct.

"You saw his RV?" I asked.

"He left a message for you on the machine. He's here? Now? Did he park up the street?"

"When Uncle Harry farts, it smells like salami," Sam said.

"He needs my help with a case. And it isn't a dangerous one. I was telling the truth about leaving my gun."

"The guns are in the safe," Sam said.

"Yes, they are, honey." I squatted to her level. "Why don't you see what Duffy is doing?"

"He's chasing Mr. Friskers. They're fighting, like you and Daddy."

"Daddy and I aren't fighting. Why don't you and Duffy play catch?"

Sam's face became heartbreakingly serious. "That's why they're fighting. Mr. Friskers took Duffy's tennis ball. That cat is a real asshole."

"You're right, sugar pop," Phin said, scooping Sam up. "Mommy and I are fighting. And Mr. Friskers is a real asshole." He looked at me when he said *asshole*. "Let's go see what they're up to."

Phin walked out of the bedroom. Which is what I wanted, for him to let me do my own thing. So I wasn't sure why it pissed me off.

"That's it?" I followed them into the hall. "You're walking away?"

"There's nothing more to say."

Duffy began to bark. It sounded like he was in the living room. Phin led the way.

"I lied to you," I reminded him. "And I'm not telling you where I'm going."

"Obviously it's important to you. And obviously you lied because you knew I'd disapprove."

Duffy had Mr. Friskers cornered, and the cat was hanging, upside-down, from the top of the window shade. All of his hair was standing on end. Like he'd stuck his little kitty tongue into a lightbulb socket.

"And you're okay with this?"

Phin shrugged. "You can't train a cat. They do whatever they want to. And they don't care whether you approve or not."

"I meant with us."

"Does it matter? Go and do whatever you need to do."

That was about the most hurtful thing he could have said. And I almost spilled the whole story, right there. But if I explained, he'd insist on coming along.

Phin wasn't healthy enough to come along.

Mr. Friskers dropped from his perch, landing directly on Duffy's back, which freaked the dog out, and delighted our daughter. Duffy began to buck like a bronco, and the cat rode him, cowboy style, as he galloped out of the room. Sam followed, squealing with laughter.

"Phin…"

"I know. Samantha needs at least one parent."

I didn't reply.

"This is stupid, Jack. If anything happens to you, you know that I'm going to go after whoever did it. Don't we have better odds doing this together?"

"You're making too much out of this."

"I went through this same process. When I went after Luther Kite. I lied to you, and you couldn't have stopped me even if you tried."

"This isn't like that." I attempted to sound soothing.

"I know," Phin said. "I went after Luther for you and Sam. So we wouldn't have to keep looking over our shoulders for the rest of our lives. But you're not doing this because of me and Sam. You're doing this *in spite* of me and Sam. I wanted to keep you out of danger, to make sure some whackjob from your past didn't come calling. You're actually *looking* for danger. Why not just hold up a target in front of your body and dare the bad guys to shoot you?"

"Phin…"

He folded his arms across his chest. "If you care about us, you'll stay. That's why we're in Florida, living this life. That's why you faked your own death. Remember? *Jill*?"

Ouch.

"I'll be back in a week." I'd already lost the argument. The only decent thing to do was make an exit before one of us said something unforgiveable.

"Sure you will."

We stared at each other. I broke the stare first, and walked away.

As I packed, I considered taking my gun. Phin already knew I was full of shit. It's not like I'd be fooling him.

But I didn't bring it along. He'd know it was missing. And he'd worry about me even more. At least, with it here, he might think there was some truth to me insisting this wasn't a dangerous case.

Sam toddled in, her eyes wide as she watched me shove jeans into a duffle bag.

"Where are you going, Mommy?"

"Uncle Harry needs my help."

"When will you be back?"

"Soon."

"Soon isn't a time, Mommy."

I'd mentioned that offhandedly a few weeks ago, and it had stuck. Be careful what you teach your kids, because they use it against you.

I squatted down to Sam-level and brushed bangs out of her eyes. "I should be back in a week. You and Daddy watch the dog and cat for me, okay?"

She nodded, then wrapped her little arms around my neck. My daughter smelled like Florida sunshine, peanut butter and jelly, and baby shampoo. I wished I could bottle the scent and keep it in my pocket.

Hell, I wished I could keep her in my pocket.

I hugged Sam, tight, until she got wiggly and pushed free.

"I have to go number two," she said.

"Need help?"

Sam made a face. "No. Do you need help when you go?"

I smiled. "Everyone needs help sometimes."

"So why won't you let Daddy help you and Uncle Harry?"

I gave her a tap on the nose. "You're too smart, you know that?"

Sam nodded. "Grandma says I'm a lot smarter than you were."

"She does?"

"And cuter. And better at drawing. But that you're a damn good shot. When will you teach me to shoot guns, Mommy?"

"When you're older."

"That's not a number."

"Grandma's right. You are smarter than I was."

Sam gave me a quick peck on the cheek, then ran off to the bathroom. She passed Phin in the doorway.

My smile disappeared and I went back to packing, making a show of ignoring him.

"I can't believe you're leaving her," he said.

"You think laying on guilt will work?"

"Not guilt. Reality."

I shook my head. "I don't expect you to understand. But I can't say no to this one."

"That's the thing, Jack. There will always be one you can't say no to."

I wanted to tell him, so badly. I was doing this for old friends who had done the same for me. But I couldn't say more because then Phin would come with. I couldn't stand losing him. And, if things went really bad, I couldn't allow Sam to grow up an orphan.

"I'm sorry, Phin. I really, really am."

"I'm sorry, too. I was wrong. To go after Kite. I was worried trouble would come looking for you. That was a goddamn waste of time." He clenched his teeth. "Because as soon as you get the chance, you go looking for trouble."

I closed my eyes. "We're going in circles. And I don't want to leave with us fighting."

"Then don't leave."

I thought of my family. Of what I was potentially giving up.

Then I thought of Herb. He was family, too.

We had some money saved. Maybe Harry and I didn't have to do this by ourselves. We could hire someone to search for Herb and Tequila.

"What if I just packed up and left with Harry," Phin said. "What would you do?"

"Be pissed. Follow you."

Phin turned up his palms and shrugged.

"If you follow me, I'll kick your ass."

"Really? You think threatening your spouse with physical violence is a sign of a healthy relationship?"

Why couldn't he just trust me on this?

"Phin, I know this is messed up. But I'm asking you, I'm *begging* you, to let me do this."

"And I'm begging you to tell me what's going on, and let me come along."

I made sure Sam wasn't around, and I walked up to Phin.

"Put your fists up," I said.

"Seriously?"

I held up my palms. "Block me and you can come with."

"That's what this is about? You think I'm not healed yet."

"I know you're not healed yet. Block me."

Phin raised his fists.

I slapped him, lightly, across the face.

"I wasn't ready," he said, adopting a fighting stance. "Again."

I tagged his chin, his left kidney, and pulled a punch that would have shot his balls up into his throat.

Phin was worse than I thought. He missed some easy blocks, and even more troubling, he flinched when I tapped him.

Flinching was the fear reflex taking over. Not only was his body still recovering, but he was showing classic PTSD symptoms. There was even sweat beading on his forehead.

And he knew it. And he knew that I knew. And the pain on his face made me feel like the worst human being to ever live.

"I don't need my fists to cover you," he said.

But this wasn't about letting him keep his dignity and feel like a man. This was about stopping him from following me. I went to my top drawer, and took out a laser pointer I used when teaching. I turned it on and shined the red dot at the far wall. In a quick, precise motion, I traced the outline of a painting hanging a few meters away. Straight lines. Ninety-degree corners. Quick and smooth and damn near perfect.

Next, I pointed it through the doorway, into the hall, at a framed modern masterpiece; a turkey Sam drew on construction paper by tracing the outline of her hand. I used the laser to follow the crayon lines of her small fingers, and did it precisely.

Then I handed the pointer to Phin.

His rectangle was jerky, his hands shaking, like he was tracing a jagged trapezoid rather than a painting.

He didn't even bother with Sam's turkey.

"So this is how you persuade me." he said softly, holding out the pointer. "Making me feel worthless."

"You're still healing."

"I can still watch your back."

"Role reversal. Would you let me come with you if I couldn't even block a face slap?"

Phin didn't answer. I went for the knockout blow, softening my voice, laying it on thick.

"Honey, how am I supposed to do my job if I'm worried about you?"

He seemed to deflate, the fight going out of his eyes. Phin despised pity. But he wasn't ready to quit yet. "This isn't your job."

"You have to believe me. It is."

"Don't go."

"I'll check in twice a day. Seven pm, seven am. I've got tracking on my cell. If you don't hear from me, come find me."

After a few seconds of silence, he nodded.

Looking at him, it felt like a cinder block had dropped on my chest.

"I love you," I said.

He nodded again. But he didn't return the sentiment. Instead, he walked out of the bedroom, leaving me to wonder if I was making the absolute biggest mistake of my life.

NEBRASKA

THE COWBOY

Without mask or black uniform, wearing a brown, felt cowboy hat and brown boots, the Cowboy parks the pick-up truck on dirt, in the middle of nowhere; an uncomplicated task because just about everywhere in Nebraska is the middle of nowhere.

Stepping out of the cab, the Cowboy straps on the black holster with the blued Ruger Bisley Vaquero nestled in its leather sheath. The revolver is chambered for .357, which means it can also shoot the lighter .38 rounds; perfect for target practice.

The air is cool and dry, a five mile an hour wind coming in from the west. Staring out over the vast plains, the world feels both enormous and tiny all at once.

Time to shoot some stuff.

Cinching on the belt, the Cowboy runs a finger over the hand cut notches along the top.

Thirty-five of them. For thirty-five lives, going all the way back to the Cowboy's youth.

Over half are executions. No sport in it. A blind, drunken child can't miss at point blank, and though the Cowboy dutifully marked them, there was no pride in those killings.

Pleasure, maybe. But not pride.

Nineteen of the thirty-five required skill. Eleven are for tracker jobs; hunting down strays. And eight notches are for fights against armed men.

Those eight are a source of tremendous pride. The true test of a gunfighter isn't the ability to shoot. It's the cool-headedness to shoot back. To use cover, talent, and guts to kill someone who is trying to kill you.

It's the reality version of Gunslinger Showdown.

Gunslinger Showdown, known as GS, is an underground contest that pits the best of the best single-action shooters in the country against one another. It's underground, rather than a sanctioned or sponsored competition like Cowboy Action Shooting, because GS could never get the necessary insurance or permits.

It's too dangerous, and potentially deadly.

GS involves three events. The Saloon Shootout, which requires bursting into a staged bar and nailing three desperados before they shoot you. You enter through the swinging doors with your gun drawn and have six wax bullets vs. their eighteen. Because your opponents have their pistols holstered, and are required to remain stationary, it's a pretty even fight.

The second event is Quickdraw, with target shooting from the hip timed in milliseconds. Judges use digital recorders to time the draw and fire. The Cowboy's best is .313 seconds.

But the coolest event is High Noon, which is a reenactment of the classic western gunfight. Walk ten paces, turn, and draw.

The Cowboy is undefeated at High Noon, and has the trophies to prove it.

But being the best requires constant practice.

In the flatbed of the pickup are targets. Plastic prescription bottles. A case of empty beer longnecks. Two fifths of whiskey, every drop drained.

The Cowboy understands chemical escapes, and partakes on occasion. Not as much as some, but to each their own vices.

For the Cowboy, the ultimate pleasure doesn't come in a bottle or pill. And no nudity is required.

Shooting doesn't require condoms. And killing never involves consent.

The Cowboy loves to shoot.

And loves to kill even more.

Making things bleed and hurt and die is a buzz unlike any other drug. Not quite sexual, not quite pharmaceutical. But better than either.

The Cowboy begins to set up targets. The smallest at five meters, going back to fifteen meters. After a few practice draws, the Cowboy sites the targets and memorizes their locations.

Eyes closed, the Cowboy pulls the Vaquero and shoots six times.

The gunshots sound like thunderclaps, and come so fast it's practically one continuous sound rather than six distinct bangs. Impressive by any standards. More impressive because the Vaquero is single action. Unlike a double action revolver, which automatically cocks the hammer with each trigger pull, single action requires the hammer to be manually pulled back after each shot.

That might seem like a disadvantage. And perhaps it is, for those who didn't know how to properly use single action. But someone with experience can fire single action faster than double action. Faster even than a semi-automatic.

In old western movies, gunslingers will fan a weapon; hold down the trigger while slapping the hammer with the outside palm of the opposite hand. It looks great on screen while using blanks. With live ammo, each slap knocks the gun off target, making it a very difficult skill to master.

The competition way is to hold the gun with both hands, keep the trigger pressed, and draw the hammer with the opposite thumb.

If the shooter is good, the shots will be fast and accurate.

The Cowboy is fast and accurate.

Eyes open, the Cowboy sees five of the six desired targets have been destroyed.

A display of marksmanship worthy of Buffalo Bill's Wild West Show. Even more impressive because of the handicap involved.

But the sixth target, still upright, mocks the Cowboy.

So the Cowboy empties the brass, reloads, and repeats the exercise.

Again.

And again.

And again.

And again.

Until all the targets are obliterated.

The brass gets picked up, to be reused.

The dead bottles are left where they've been shot.

The Cowboy heads back to the truck, and sees movement in the brush, forty meters away.

Brown. Small. Quick.

A prairie dog.

Quick draw is different than multi-target shooting. It requires a special holster, reinforced with steel, so the weapon can be cocked as it is drawn. Then the shot is fired, from the hip, as soon as the pistol clears the leather.

It's the fastest way to draw and shoot a weapon.

The Cowboy's holster is reinforced with steel.

Point four seconds later, the rodent is a shredded pelt.

Not a world record. But drawing, shooting, and killing a varmint in four-tenths of a second is pretty damn incredible.

The Cowboy smiles. Now comes the delicious anticipation of waiting. Prairie dogs are social animals, and it won't be long before one of its colony mates comes by to investigate.

And then another will come. And another.

With a little luck, the Cowboy can bag four or five. The Cowboy's personal record is eleven.

It's so much more fun than shooting pill bottles.

Pill bottles don't squeal and bleed and die.

There's a buzzing sound. The Cowboy's cell phone.

A text message.

NEED YOU.

The Cowboy frowns. Now isn't a good time.

90 MINS, the Cowboy texts back.

It is nice to be needed. But right now, the prairie dogs need me more.

Somewhere, a coyote howls.

The Cowboy howls back

SOMEWHERE, WEEKS AGO

HERB

After several months of confinement, Tequila asked Herb for a favor.

The worst favor ever.

"They set my leg wrong," Tequila had told him. "It's healing crooked."

Herb didn't want to ask what needed to be done, but he had no choice. During their long imprisonment, Herb's diminutive, reticent friend had helped Herb retain his sanity. Herb had shared more with Tequila than he had with his wife, Helen, or his old partner on the force, Jacqueline Daniels. Stories he'd never told anyone. The embarrassment of losing his virginity in under five seconds (he'd vastly improved his time since then). How he'd sobbed with fear on his wedding day. The previous times he'd been kidnapped by maniacs (sewed his eyes shut). The men he'd killed. The women he'd loved. The dream he had, of retiring and buying a house on a lake to fish through his autumn years while listening to the loons hoot at each other.

Tequila didn't talk much, but he also opened up about his past. His violent father. His disabled sister. His collection of Italian firearms.

They played word games. Reminisced about old television shows. Played checkers on the cement floor with shirt buttons taken from other prisoners who didn't survive their injuries. Herb was also pretty sure—not entirely sure—but reasonably certain that Tequila sang an old Beatles song to him when Herb had been delusional with malaria, or dengue, or Montezuma's Revenge.

It had probably been a fever dream, because Herb recalled hearing both harmony and melody.

But it hadn't been a dream that Tequila had been with him throughout the illness. Changing his soiled sheets. Forcing Herb to drink water. Putting cool rags on his forehead.

Herb respected the man. And liked the man. And owed the man.

So when Tequila mentioned his badly healing leg, Herb immediately asked, "What can I do?"

"I need you to break it again."

As it turned out, the actual act wasn't as bad as the request.

It was much, much worse.

"How?"

Tequila laid on the floor, his bare leg stretched up so his heel rested on the cot.

"See the scar?"

"Which one?" Tequila had six bullet wounds in that leg.

"The shin. Five centimeters below the kneecap."

Herb saw it. "What do I do?" he asked, not wanting to know.

"Put your heel on the wound, and apply your weight until it gives."

"That's...*awful*."

"I've already lost my depth perception." Tequila had knotted together an eyepatch out of old bandana shreds. "I don't want to limp for the rest of my life."

Feeling nauseous, Herb agreed to the task. He gingerly placed his bare foot on Tequila's leg.

"Won't this break your knee?"

"No. I'm flexing my muscle."

Even pockmarked with scars and bedridden for months, Tequila had legs thick as tree stumps.

"Fast or slow?"

"Slow. Too fast and the bone could break through the skin."

"That would be bad."

"Agreed. I could get an infection."

Herb was talking about the pain and overall awfulness of a compound fracture, not any resulting infection. But Tequila was a textbook stoic. Hell, he made all other stoics look like whiney little babies.

Even so, Herb didn't want to hurt his friend. And this was going to hurt. A lot.

"You ready?"

Tequila nodded.

Watching Tequila's face, Herb began to bear down on his foot.

"Harder."

Herb put more weight on it. Tequila winced, but didn't make a sound.

"I'm hurting you."

"Lean into it. I can feel where the bone is cracked."

Herb didn't want to hear that. But he pressed down harder, letting that foot take most of his weight.

Tequila's leg, and most of his body, were trembling. He'd clenched his jaw, and his fists, and his face became glossy with sweat.

"More," he grunted.

"I've got all my weight on it."

"Bounce."

In his more reflective moments, Herb would recollect the things he'd done in his life, and judge them according to his own moral code.

Bouncing on a wounded man's broken leg easily hit the Number 1 spot of *Worst Acts I've Ever Committed*.

With each bounce, Herb swore he heard a cracking sound.

"Is that the cot?" Herb asked.

"Bone," Tequila barked. "Ends grinding together."

Herb eased up, feeling the vomit rise up his esophagus and burn his throat.

"Keep going," Tequila ordered.

"I...I can't."

"Keep going,"

"Tequila, this is..."

"Just do it, you worthless son of a bitch!"

Tequila's insult did the trick. Shocked by the change in his friend's demeanor, Herb let his foot take all of his weight, momentarily bouncing up into the air—

—snapping Tequila's leg with the sound of molars on wet celery.

Herb lost his balance and fell over, landing hard, the pain from his own injuries prompting a howl that competed with—and triumphed over—the urge to throw up.

Then, after howling, he threw up.

"When you're finished," Tequila said through clenched teeth, "I need you to pull my leg to straighten it out."

Herb took a quick glance.

Tequila's leg was bent so severely, his toes were nearly touching his own thigh.

After the vomiting, and a bit of sobbing—

"Relax," Tequila soothed. "It's not like we're not getting married."

—Herb grabbed his friend's mangled appendage and tugged and twisted according to orders, until Tequila was satisfied the bones were properly aligned.

Tequila had saved his old splint under his filthy mattress, and Herb did his best to tie it on without looking.

"Nice work," Tequila mumbled.

Then, blessedly, he passed out.

Herb, unfortunately, did not.

And no matter how hard he tried, he couldn't forget the cracking/grinding sound of bone-on-bone.

PRESENT

JACK

The side door opened, and I climbed into the Crimebago Deux and some creepy-looking dude with greasy long hair stuck a video camera in my face.

I relieved him of the camera with a move I'd practiced a thousand times, except I always expected to use it to disarm a weapon-wielding assailant, not a tech nerd.

"Whoa, easy there, karate chick," the camera guy said.

"Yeah, karate chick, easy there."

To his left was another creepy-looking dude with long greasy hair, holding a microphone on a stick. They had to be twins.

"Don't beat them up, J-Dawg. They're with me."

I shot a look at Harry, while trying to keep a lid on anger that was very close to boiling over, and saw he had on some sort of headgear with a mini camera pointing at himself.

"What the hell, McGlade?"

"I might have forgot to mention, this is my new YouTube show. *Private Dick Live and Streaming In Your Face.*"

I made a fist. "Are you streaming live right now?"

"No," said one of the greasy twins. "We're just getting some footage for the title credits. Can I have my camera back?"

I didn't give him his camera back. "Outside, McGlade. Now."

Outside must have been a word Rosalina knew, because the dog began to howl.

"Give me a second, guys." Harry took off his head harness, told Rosalina to shush, and then followed me out the side door.

I fiddled with the camera until I knew it was off, then said, "What the hell do you think you're doing?"

"This is the latest thing. These streaming shows rake in the cash."

"Why didn't you tell me?"

"Because you'd get all bitchy. Like you're doing right now."

I'd known Harry a long time, but I still didn't know if he was willfully ignorant, naturally stupid, or just played dumb to take advantage. "Did you forget that I'm supposed to be dead?"

"Of course I didn't forget, Jackie. That's why I called you J-Dawg. You'll be completely anonymous."

"People will recognize my face, you fat moron."

"First, words hurt, Second, the guys are gonna do that pixelated thing. You know, like when mob informers are on TV. They scramble up your face, make you sound like lispy Darth Vader, and no one will know it's you."

I folded my arms over my chest. "Not happening. People can still guess it's me."

"Let them guess. They don't know your new name. They don't know you moved to Florida. It will all be speculation and conspiracy theory, which advertisers love because it gets more views."

"This is my life, McGlade. I'm not risking it."

"Makes sense. But what if I asked pretty please?"

"No way in hell."

He sighed, and his face got all droopy. "Look," he said, lowering his voice, "it hasn't been announced yet, but my TV show—*Fatal Autonomy*—it isn't going to be renewed."

"Sorry to hear that. But not my problem."

Harry studied his shoes and scratched the back of his neck. "Well, you see, I was kinda counting on another season, because I'm sort of low on funds."

"I thought you were rich."

"Yeah, I've made a lot of money. But I haven't been what you'd exactly call *fiscally responsible*."

"No shit," I answered, eyeing the bright red Crimebago.

"In fairness, a lot of my money went to charity. You know how I've staunchly supported various causes."

"Name one."

"Unwed mothers."

"Buying cars for the strippers you're dating isn't a charitable donation."

"Don't tell that to Uncle Sam. I also helped organize that *Free The Nipple* walk in downtown Chicago. It's pure sexism and discrimination and an appalling double standard that women aren't allowed to be topless in public. You ladies should be able to take your shirts off whenever you want to. In fact, I'd be fine if you did so right now."

"I'm touched by your third wave feminism. And how much did that bit of philanthropy cost?"

"I don't know. I don't keep track of these things. Fiscally irresponsible, remember? I thought the gravy train would keep drowning me with enough greenbacks to pay taxes, but then those network assholes cancelled my cash cow, so I'm short. I need to make some money, fast."

"I'm not being part of your streaming show. Either you kick those twins out, or I will."

McGlade didn't answer. But he actually looked hurt. Not fake-acting hurt.

Real hurt.

"I owe two million dollars to the IRS."

I blinked. "You're kidding."

He dug into his back pocket and pulled out a letter. The actual total was one million nine hundred and eighty-six thousand.

I let the disbelief, and the accompanying disappointment, come out in my voice. "How does something like this happen?"

"I would have been fine if I hadn't been cancelled."

"Don't you have anything saved?"

"I did some investing. Nothing has panned out."

"Stocks? Gold?"

"When I first started making money, I had a financial advisor who told me collectibles were the way to go."

I could guess where this was going. "Don't tell me you invested in Pokémon cards."

"I wish. They've held their value. I've got a cool mil in Beanie Babies."

That made me blink. "You spent a million dollars on bean-stuffed animals."

"A little over a million. Back in 2005, Princess Bear and Garcia Bear were selling for thousands of dollars each. I was told that if I cornered the market on rare Beanies, I could drive the price up."

"And how much are they worth now?"

"A hundred."

"A hundred grand isn't too bad."

"Not a hundred grand. A hundred dollars. Talk about the bottom falling out."

I studied McGlade's eyes, and saw the self-loathing there. I had no idea what I'd do if he started to cry. Would I have to hug him?

I didn't want to have to hug him.

"I hope your financial advisor is in prison," was the best bit of commiseration I could come up with.

"He's dead."

I gave him a look.

"Not me. He overdosed on cocaine in a ten-grand-per-night suite in the Bahamas while having sex with four hookers on top of a pile of my money. Which is how I've always wanted to die. So he not only screwed me, he stole my suicide plan." Harry's eyes got even glassier. "Look, Jack, I'm not going to bring up all the times I've helped you out to try to convince you to do this. And there have been a lot. I know this because I've made a list of them. Want to see it?"

"No."

"All those times I selflessly saved your ass..."

"We're not doing this, McGlade."

"I can promise we won't show your face, and I'll tell Heckle and Jeckle to keep your screen time to a minimum. Please. Do me this small favor. It would mean a lot to me."

I felt myself start to give in, and folded my arms over my chest and kept my mouth closed.

"C'mon, Jack. Be a friend. The IRS is threatening jail time. I'm too pretty for prison, Jack. The lifers would pass me around like a jar of salsa. Everyone with a corn chip would dig in."

As amusing as that image was, I stayed strong.

"If you won't do it for me, do it for Herb. He needs us, Jack. *I* need us."

"You need an accountant and someone to slap you whenever you do anything stupid."

"True. But I can't afford either unless I do this live stream."

McGlade would continue to try and manipulate me until I gave in, or walked away. The thing to do, the best thing for me and my family, was to walk.

But it would be easier and quicker to find Herb with Harry than without him. McGlade had resources that I didn't have.

Don't try to justify this, Jack. Stay firm. Don't crack. Do. Not. Crack.

A tear rolled down his cheek.

I cracked.

"I don't want to be shown live. Even pixilated."

"We should be able to keep your screen time to a minimum."

"I want...what's it called when the director is allowed to release the version she wants to?"

"Final cut."

"I want final cut. Nothing goes on YouTube without my approval."

"We can do that. No problem."

Wincing, knowing I'd regret it later, I mumbled, "Okay."

Harry beamed. "Great!" He reached into his pocket and tugged out paper and a pen. "I need you to sign this release form."

There were only three paragraphs, and Harry had already written he wouldn't show my face or reveal my name. He also stated my IMDB.com credit would be listed as B. Chalda Thyme.

Bitch all the time.

I didn't do that, did I?

I'd signed enough releases for McGlade to know this one was fairly standard, scribbled on the bottom in a scrawl that couldn't be recognized as my actual name, and handed the papers back, already regretting the action.

McGlade, for his part, had gone from weepy and desperate to looking pleased pretty damn quick.

"Don't look so gloom and doom, J-Dawg. It won't be as bad as you think. We'll probably find Herb fast, no one will get hurt, and you'll be back to your mundane, anonymous life in short order."

Knowing McGlade, he'd be wrong about everything.

YEARS AGO

TOM AND JERRY

"I think of MotherBitch a lot," Tom said to Jerry. "Do you?"

"Truedoo," Jerry answered. One of their made-up words. It meant *yes*. "Miss her?"

"Notno."

"You remember her burning. Burnhurt and screamloud and begging for help."

A nod.

"I wish we could have seen it."

The twins had fled from the room and barricaded the door immediately after pouring the nail polish remover on her bed and throwing the match. Often they talked of what it must have looked like. How amazing it must have been to watch MotherBitch burn.

"You know what I want?" Tom said.

Jerry knew. He wanted the same thing. "You want to try it with someone else."

"Truedoo. Mega funfun. But who should we funfun?"

"FatherAss," Jerry said.

They despised their father as much, if not more, than they hated their mother.

"We can't. Not yet."

"Truedoo. We don't want to go into foster care. We have to wait until we're old enough."

Tom nodded. "Winheritance. We have to be eighteenadult to get the moneycash."

"Sadface. I'd love to watch the old fuckerfucker burn."

"Sadface times a million. But we can try funfun with someone else."

"A peopleperson?"

"Sure. More funfun than doggos and catnips."

"Whodoo?" He considered their choices. "Our assmates would draw attention."

"Truedoo. No one in our assclass. Or our cruelschool. Gotta be a peopleperson with no connections to us."

"Strangerdanger," Jerry said.

"Yeah. Strangerdanger. Remember when we drove past the bus station in FatherAss's limocar? He pointed the strangersdangers out. Said they had no homes. Called them worthless."

"Homeworthless," Jerry said. "No one will miss the homeworthless. The bus station is next to the library."

"Wedoo funfun?" Tom asked.

"Wedoo funfun."

"Heart cross?"

"Heart cross."

The twins bumped their left fists, then crossed their hearts. Then they went to ask FatherAss for a ride to the library.

Naturally, FatherAss said no. He was wussycrying about MotherBitch being all burnhurt. But he called for the limocar.

Driveyday, driveyday, off to mega funfun.

Jerry put a squirt bottle of lighter fluid in his bookbag.

Tom brought the matches.

They discussed taking photopics, and decided not to. They learned their lesson from Fluffy. Don't leave evidence. If there was no evidence, then it didn't happen.

The driver waited in the limocar, and Tom and Jerry went into the library and straight out the back entrance. After an arguefight about which direction the bus station was, they realized they could follow the street signs and ten minutes later were standing in front of a homeworthless man propped up alongside the brick wall of the depot. He wore a stained shirt, ripped pants, had a scraggly facebeard and smelled like pisspee.

"You... you kids got any money? I want to get some food."

His voice was warbly, like MotherBitch when she was pilldrunk.

The twins didn't respond.

Jerry squirted him with the lighter fluid.

Tom lit the match.

They had to back up, because the homeworthless man started thrashing and kicking and rolling around, but they took turns squirting him and stayed and watched until he stopped moving.

Murderdead.

Megamega funfun.

The twins threw the matches, and the empty can, onto the burning body, and then walked away, holding hands when they crossed the street, like they'd been told to do.

After all, FatherAss often repeatsaid; the world was a dangerous place.

SOMEWHERE, ONE WEEK AGO

HERB

Tequila's leg was still healing when the guards came for Herb.

Herb awoke with two men standing over his bed. Thick, middle aged, mestizo, dressed in beige fatigues. He pegged them as mercs, former military, and hadn't ever seen them before.

Neither carried a sidearm, squashing Herb's first instinct to reach for their guns. But they did wield weapons. The shorter of the two carried an asp, and the taller a cattle prod with a forked electrode on the end.

While the man with the prod hovered it over Herb's face, the other quickly unlocked his ankle shackle.

Relief temporarily overrode all fear. He was being taken out of that hellhole. Maybe to a worse hellhole, but Herb had nearly given up hope of ever seeing the outside again. Even if they were taking him out to shoot him, at least he'd be out.

"Que tal mi amigo?" Herb asked, indicating Tequila.

They yanked Herb to his feet, placed a wire loop around his neck, and began to lead him away.

"Llévame también," Tequila said. He was sitting up.

"Mala pierna, pendejo." The taller merc said, pointing the prod at Tequila's leg.

Tequila pounded a fist against his chest. "Soy fuerte."

The man touched Tequila with the prod, and there was a flash and a zapping sound. Herb had no idea how much it must have hurt, but it couldn't have been pleasant.

Tequila didn't even flinch.

"Estas loco!" the merc said, giggling and apparently delighted. But he walked past Tequila and instead went to the cot directly behind him. A young, skinny Mexican kid, who'd been brought in a few weeks ago. They uncuffed him, put a wire loop around his head, and led him past Tequila.

Tequila kicked out his good leg, fast as a snake—

—and snapped the boy's knee in a direction it wasn't supposed to go.

The teenager fell, screaming.

The merc reached out to zap Tequila with the prod again, and Tequila grabbed it by the electrodes, taking the shock.

"Llévame," Tequila grunted in his throat, teeth clenched and arm shaking. "Take me."

The man pulled away his cattle prod, then had a rapid-fire discussion with the guy holding Herb's noose, speaking too quickly to understand. They reached some sort of decision, dragged the kid back to his bed, then slipped the wire noose around Tequila's neck.

Herb offered Tequila a small grin. "If I didn't know better, I'd say you had a crush on me."

Then the cattle prod was thrust into Herb's belly, and he doubled over with a pain that was otherworldly. Herb dropped to his knees, tears squeezing out of his eyes, and then he was dragged out of the hospital/dungeon, up a flight of crumbling stone steps, and outside into the night.

The stars were bright enough to blind him.

The air was fresher than he'd ever smelled.

The desert seemed to stretch on forever in all directions.

The sand under his feet felt like walking on clouds.

Herb's tears of pain were hijacked by tears of joy. He wasn't free, and at the same time he'd never felt freer.

Then he was roughly shoved into the back of a windowless cargo van. Tequila was pushed in on top of him, and the door slammed to darkness.

"You okay?" Herb asked his friend.

"Gotta say, I'm not a fan of cattle prods."

"That little thing? It was like being tickled."

"Do you always cry like a baby when you're tickled?"

"Absolutely."

The vehicle started up, and when it lurched into gear Herb was jostled against the side of the van.

"Might as well check out our new accommodations," Herb said.

As his eyes adjusted to the darkness, he began to feel around. The floor and panels of the van were lined with sheet metal. The rear doors had no handle.

"I found a jug," Tequila said. "Water."

"I found a bucket." Herb took a tentative sniff. "It's our new commode."

Tequila grunted. "We may be in here a while."

"At least we aren't chained up. Hey, when we were outside, wasn't it the most beautiful thing you've ever seen?"

"I can't recognize beauty."

Herb knew Tequila was somewhere on the autism spectrum, so he didn't pursue it. He took a deep breath, hoping to smell the outdoors again. All he could detect was the stench of his own body odor, and the toilet bucket.

Herb stretched out, his head against the metal floor.

"For whatever it's worth," Herb said, "thanks for coming along."

"I couldn't let you go alone. Who would help if I needed my leg broken again?"

For some reason, Herb found that hysterical, and he began to laugh.

Tequila didn't join in. That spectrum thing again.

"They said I had a bad leg," Tequila mused. "That's why they didn't want to take me."

"They wanted two healthy men."

"So it would seem."

"For what? Something we already discussed? Slave labor? Snuff movies? Gladiator games?"

"They might want us healthy because we're being sold as boy toys to rich female celebrities to be used for sex."

"You think?"

"No," Tequila said. "My money is still on snuff films."

Herb frowned in the darkness.

NEBRASKA, PRESENT

THE COWBOY

As the Tor browser loads through the virtual private network, the Cowboy plugs the memory stick into the USB slot of the laptop and uses a different window to check current bitcoin exchange rates. After a quick and anonymous search on Tor, the Cowboy logs onto https://w9sioi30982ls9089dpv2p.onion and checks the number of preview hits.

Six thousand nine hundred and thirty-five. Of those, two hundred and sixty-one people downloaded the full video, for a total of 1.189 bitcoin.

Which is about eight thousand dollars in the Cowboy's wallet. Cha-ching.

But this isn't about the money.

It has never been about the money.

Darknet and the Wild West have much in common. Each is a lawless, untamed land, where the strong survive and profit off the weak, and the legends are equally revered and feared.

The Cowboy is among the most popular uploaders on Snuff-X, a hidden service that was one of the premiere dark websites.

Thank you, Uncle Sam.

Tor—an acronym of *The Onion Router*—was invented by US military to communicate anonymously. Normal browsers can't open Darknet domains. They're created using random characters by an Onion server, which uses so many nodes that it is impossible to trace the data.

Or something like that. The Cowboy didn't really understand how it worked. Only that you can buy and sell anything, especially things that are illegal. Stolen merchandise, user and system passwords, credit card numbers, firearms, drugs…

People.

The slave trade is alive and well on darknet. You can bid on humans, much like eBay. It's where Yuri gets many of his volunteers. Children, and attractive women, command the most money. The Belarusian always bids low on damaged or defective people, or buys them outright without bidding, and constantly rotates his workforce as they die out.

The Cowboy understands Yuri's ambition. He needs to make enough money to launch, and that singular obsession drives the man like a Russian Ahab. But Yuri is missing the forest for the trees. Making thirty million dollars selling shit, just to get into orbit, is a limited mindset. Even if the ultimate goal is mass murder. Say what you will about vision, or scope, or changing the course of history, life is about more than simple revenge.

It has to be. Lest you be consumed by it.

That's why the Cowboy had goals that were diversified. There is beauty in nuance. Value in hobbies. Being the best of the best, the most popular, is a pleasure more fulfilling than overthrowing a country.

It's not like Yuri can become king once he executes his plan. After he's extracted his pound of flesh, the man will no longer have a purpose.

Such a shame. Purpose is essential.

The Cowboy intimately knows the allure of revenge. Knows how it consumes. And also knows how it disappoints.

There needs to be more than that.

Yuri holds the power of life and death over his slaves. But it holds no appeal for him. It's a means to justify the ends.

Life isn't about reaching your destination. It's about enjoying the journey.

Brute force, wars, political and military bullshit; it's all so 1990s.

Power in 2017 has morphed into something else. These days, it's about followers. About likes and retweets and upvotes and rank. The world is more than the insignificant ten million people living in Belarus. It's about the three billion people online.

That's why the Cowboy uploads videos of his teeth extractions, his fish-hooks, his tortures, his kills, to darknet.

Once Yuri reaches his quota, he'll sell the Cowboy the LeTourneau. And the Cowboy won't fill it with poppies.

The Cowboy will fill it with something a lot more interesting.

JACK

Heckle and Jeckle busied themselves on their laptops. Occasionally they would nudge each other, glance at me, then smirk. I guessed they were either texting one another, or communicating telepathically.

I had a bad feeling about these guys.

I'm no psychologist, and it has been my experience that those who spend a lot of time trying to figure out human nature are usually doing it in an attempt to understand themselves. Putting people into groups, labeling them, and deciding that some traits are normal and some aren't, always felt like a way to intellectualize bigotry.

I've met a lot of criminals in my line of work, and many had things in common. Being able to spot those things gave me an edge when it came to solving crimes and trying to predict the behavior of those who would harm others. But most aren't that easy to categorize, and stereotyping leads to cops shooting innocent civilians.

I'm not interested in law and order to the point where people get charged with thought crimes. So I try to reserve judgement for actual criminal behavior, rather than hunches that someone is up to no good.

Some of the biggest sociopaths I'd ever met—I'm talking about those who lack the ability to empathize with other people and instead learn to mimic social cues and behavior—weren't killers. The majority of them were leaders of some sort. CEOs of companies. Politicians. Managers. Coaches. Ministers.

I'm not saying that every mayor or priest is a sociopath. I'm also not saying that sociopathology is even a negative trait. Some kid who steals a bike might grow up to be a reputable stockbroker or a banker, instead of a bank robber. Along with genetics, it depends on their environment and circumstance.

So as I watched the twins Harry had hired, I gleaned a lot about them, but it didn't offer me any more insight into their future actions than the color of their eyes, their height, or their muscle mass.

All of that aside, a little voice in my head told me these two were bad news, and worth keeping an eye on.

My first hint was their utter lack of interest in anything other than their computer screens and each other. It was behavior that teens could get away with, but these guys were in their thirties. They pretty much ignored me, except when they were snickering. They ignored Rosalina, even when she made attempts to play. They sat so close together, their legs were touching, even though the Crimebago had ample room to stretch out. And when they laughed, it wasn't nice laughter. It was the secret, cruel laugh of bullies and assholes.

Their appearance was also unusual. Long hair, greasy and knotted. But their sideburns were razor straight, meaning recent shaves. Shirts looked like they came from a thrift shop, with stains and holes, but their loafers were Ferragamo, at least five hundred bucks a pair. They had body odor, strong enough for me to consider saying something about it, but they also had recent manicures.

Spoiled rich kids trying to portray a hipster image? But who were they dressing up for? Themselves? Each other?

Something was wrong with these guys.

"Do you have a lot of video experience?" I asked.

They looked at one another again and laughed their mean boy laugh.

"Heckle and I worked on a lot of docs," Jeckle said. "Some underground horror grinds. Some adult stuff."

"Anything I can look up on IMDb?"

Another shared glance, another chuckle. "IMDb is wacky-packs," said Jeckle.

Heckle nodded. "Total lamestream."

"Got a YouTube channel?" I asked.

"Most of our work is password protected, if you catch our wave."

"I don't catch your wave."

Jeckle grinned in a way I didn't like. His teeth were white and perfect, but there was something black stuck in his gums. "You know crush? Soft crush? Hard crush?"

"Never heard of it."

They traded another telepathic look, and then Heckle turned his laptop screen toward me.

There was a movie playing. A woman's legs, from the knee down, wearing stockings and a pair of strappy heels, walking across a carpeted floor. It had that cheap look of digital video, rather than the grittiness of film.

I waited for something to happen, to see where the actor was heading, but when she reached the end of the room she simply turned around and walked back. After returning to her starting spot, she sat down, took off a shoe, and rubbed her foot.

Then she put her shoe back on and walked the same route.

We never saw her face, or anything above her hips.

There didn't seem to be any plot at all.

I was about to ask what the point was, and then I realized what I was seeing.

It was one of those fetish videos. For people who were turned on by feet and shoes. There was no plot because walking around *was* the plot.

I didn't judge. Whatever got people off, as long as there was legal consent. But the name was odd. *Crush?* Why did they call this—

Then the woman walked over to a kitten, sleeping on the carpet.

I glanced up at Heckle and Jeckle, who were eyeing me like scientists studying a particularly fascinating petri dish.

I turned back to the screen.

As I'd feared, the woman had her heel poised over the kitten, ready to stomp on it.

"Squeamish, Lieutenant?" said Jeckle.

"You've seen a lot worse than this," said Heckle.

For the moment, I ignored the fact that they knew who I was. Instead I concentrated on not showing any emotion at all.

I watched.

I didn't wince.

They were right. I'd seen a lot worse.

But the terrible things I'd seen didn't make watching some faceless woman stomp a kitty to death any more pleasant.

Rather than react, I tried to glean what I could from the production. The mewing sounds. The squirting blood. The quick cuts.

Hmm. Quick cuts.

"Is this real?" I asked.

They exchanged a glance, then Heckle reached into his pocket and took out something small and white and furry and wiggling.

A mouse.

A moment later, he had the mouse next to his mouth.

Heckle smiled big—

—and bit it in half.

I stared as blood pumped out of the mouse's lower half, arterial sprays that almost reached the roof of the Crimebago Deux.

I gave them blasé. "So this is your thing? Pretending to kill little furry animals?"

"Pretending?" said Jeckle.

I waited.

They waited.

The blood continued to pump, staining Harry's rug.

I sighed. "The blood tube is up your sleeve, running to your other pocket. What's in there? A squeeze bulb?"

"A syringe," said Heckle, taking it out and showing me. If I'd spoiled his trick, he didn't seem upset about it. "How did you know?"

"That's about fifty times more blood than a mouse has in its body. Its little heart couldn't spray it that far. And when an artery is severed, it jets out in spurts, not a steady stream. Plus, you bit off the top half. The part with the heart in it. The bottom half wouldn't be squirting anything."

"How about the movie?" asked Jeckle.

"The effect was good. But there were edits. Why have edits? If the actor is stepping on a cat, why not show it all in one take? Prove it's the real thing? There were different takes, and you substituted a real cat for a fake one."

"Did it look realistic?" asked Heckle.

I had zero inclination to praise their weird kink. "People actually buy this stuff?"

They didn't answer.

"What's the difference between soft crush and hard crush?" I asked.

"Soft crush is invertebrates," said Heckle. "Worms, spiders, roaches. Hard crush is animals with bones."

"Bones make noise," said Jeckle.

"And there's an actual market for that?"

Heckle answered, "You should know the depths of human depravity better than we do, Lieutenant. You tell us."

I did know something about depravity. I also knew I was supposed to be anonymous on this little expedition.

"Did Harry tell you who I was?"

They shook their heads.

"Serial killers are our hobby," said Jeckle.

"Serial killers, and those who hunt them," said Heckle.

"Serial killers, and those who hunt them," repeated Jeckle.

They leaned forward, in unison.

"We know all about you, Lieutenant Jacqueline Daniels," said Heckle.

Again, I kept my face neutral. But inside I was cursing McGlade for bringing these idiots along and blowing my incognito, and cursing Phin for being right about me inviting trouble back into my life.

"What is it you know?" I asked, keeping it light. Conversation, not interrogation.

"We read all the books," said Jeckle.

"The Korks," said Heckle. "Brother and sister, both psychopathic serial killers. They worked separately, and as a duo. How often does that happen? Crazy scary."

"Scary crazy. We dig this stuff. That's how we got this gig," said Jeckle. "Private Dick McDude did a Craigslist, and we knew him because he was married to one of them."

"Crazy scary," said Heckle.

"Scary crazy," said Jeckle.

"We're also fans of the other killers you chased," said Heckle. "Fuller. Mr. K. Donaldson. Kite. Schimmel."

"Though, technically, Schimmel was more of a mass murderer," said Jeckle. "Wouldn't you say?"

"I'd say," said Heckle. "But our personal favorite is the Gingerbread Man."

"Whatever happened to those viddies he sent you?" said Jeckle.

They were going back and forth so quickly it was like watching a tennis match on a very small court.

"They were destroyed," I lied.

"We'd really like to viddywell those viddies," said Heckle.

"Did you make any personal copies?" said Jeckle.

"We'd be very interested in seeing them," said Heckle.

My creep radar was beeping, and I chose to deescalate.

"Let's set a few ground rules," I told them. "I'm just here to help some friends. I don't want to discuss my old job. In fact, I don't want to be a part of this movie at all."

"It's a live webstream."

"Whatever it is. I'd appreciate it if you don't point the camera at me."

"Private Dick McDude said we can pixilate your face and alter your voice."

I almost said, *Private Dick McDude won't break your camera over your head and make you eat the pieces.* But if you want to make nice with a stray dog, you talk soothing and offer it a bone. You don't scream at it and throw rocks.

"I may know someone who has a copy of those Kork VHS tapes," I said. "If you guys keep my identity secret, I may be able to get you a screening."

They looked at each other.

"Deal," they said at the same time, both of them offering their hands.

Jeckle's hand was like grabbing a cold, dead fish. Heckle's was warm, moist, and wiggly, reminding me of the kitten in their crush video.

Ugh.

I considered my first impression, and how I'd gotten a bad vibe from the duo.

The vibe I currently had was a whole lot worse.

DAYS AGO

HERB

"We're slowing down."

It was Herb talking. Tequila hadn't said more than a few words since they'd been thrown into the van. He'd always been a man of few words, but he'd been especially quiet for the hours (days?) they'd been in transit.

In the darkness, drifting in and out of sleep, Herb had been in a kind of twilight consciousness, sometimes dreaming, sometimes hallucinating. The heat added to the disorientation. So did the thirst.

Tequila tapped Herb's leg, acknowledging he'd heard him speak, and confirming he was still alive. Smart to stay silent. Herb's throat was as raw and dry as a dead armadillo baking on Arizona asphalt, and talking felt like swallowing hot coals.

He was pretty sure they'd stopped at least twice. For gas, he guessed. But no one had opened the door, regardless of their banging on the side panels. They'd long ago finished their plastic jug of water, and the toilet bucket was nearly full.

The van stopping gave Herb a smidge of hope that the rear doors would open. But it was a false hope, like a dog watching his abusive owner eat pizza, knowing there wouldn't be any for him.

Hope was a terrible thing. It didn't keep you going, like you'd guess. In fact, it did the opposite.

Each poisoned hope made the concept of death a little bit sweeter.

Herb thought about prison. He'd been thinking about it a lot lately. Confinement changed a person. And not for the better. The hustle and bustle of a busy work week—the job and bills and trying to keep a marriage going while dealing with the worst of society—had taken its toll on Herb's mind and body. Overeating, high blood pressure, heart disease, ulcers, pre-diabetes; stress had been killing him. Herb's favorite part of the day had been his morning toilet ritual. For five minutes, he was all alone, and all the stress was gone.

Herb used to envy the many criminals he'd put away. Three square meals a day, no work, no responsibility. Even solitary confinement didn't seem like real punishment. Herb would have paid good money to be thrown in a dark cell without any contact with the outside world.

Well... like most fantasies, the reality was different. Since his imprisonment, all of Herb's physical ailments had reversed. No more angina or heartburn. No more stomach pains. Skin hung on him where fat used to be. Herb would bet his cholesterol had never been better.

But being locked up was far more brutal than the stress of everyday life. The loneliness. The hopelessness. The boredom. The longing. It was turning his brain to mush, and scrambling his emotions to near-insanity. Herb would laugh for no reason. He'd cry so hard he had to bite his fist to stop. Months ago, he'd plucked out every hair on his chest, making some kind of crazy game out of it.

But these last few dozen hours, locked in a hundred-plus-degree van in complete darkness, was a type of torture worse than the times Herb had actually been tortured.

He'd had a few fleeting suicidal thoughts during his captivity. But being in the van made him long for death. It was a never-ending, hellacious fever-dream of heat and dehydration and crazy ideas.

At one point, Herb thought he heard his mother. She'd died decades before, but had returned as a disembodied voice to tell him to wear his mittens.

Another time, he swore he saw his friend, Jack Daniels, glowing pale green and hovering above him, staring. The image was so real Herb slapped himself—a useless movie trope that turned out to be ineffective at separating fantasy from reality.

Herb held out hope that Jack, and the others, had escaped. But the hope had dimmed as the months passed. If Jack had survived, she would have come for him by now. No other possibility could exist.

Jack. Indestructible, formidable, unstoppable Jack...was dead. And the world was darker for it.

Yet, somehow, Jack floated a few feet above him, almost close enough to touch. She didn't say anything. Just stared at him, a sad expression on her face. Something like pity. Or disappointment.

Herb and Jack's relationship was hard to explain to anyone. Bernice, Herb's wife, had some jealousy issues when Jack had first been assigned as Herb's junior partner. But there hadn't ever been anything sexual between Jack and Herb. They didn't have that kind of chemistry. It was more like some combination of brother and sister, work friends, and soldiers in the same platoon. They liked each other, tolerated each other, forgave each other, and counted on each other when the heavy shit went down.

Herb had never seen Jack naked. Never even thought about it. But she knew things about him that Bernice didn't even know. They'd saved each other's lives. Risked their lives for each other. And had developed a trust that was somewhere beyond work or friendship or intimacy or even love.

Herb felt the same way, maybe even more so, about Tequila. Something about fighting in the foxhole together took human relationships to a whole new level.

Was the bond Herb had with Jack the reason she was floating above him?

Was the afterlife real, and Jack's ghost had come to escort him away?

"I'm ready," he rasped at the apparition.

But then Jack was gone. And she didn't bring him along.

The van came to a halt. Another gas stop? Previously, they'd pounded on the walls and yelled for help, but none came, and the drivers seemed unconcerned. Either the van was soundproof, or they were nowhere near civilization.

Maybe they were being driven to the moon. Or Mars.

Mars wouldn't be a bad place to die.

The rear doors abruptly opened, and the outside spilled in with cool air and shocking silence and a clear, sunny sky that was so bright it stabbed Herb's brain through his pupils.

Tequila launched himself at the merc standing there, and was met with a blow to the side of the head. He fell to the ground on all fours, and the man raised his club again.

"Enough," said a voice. A low, soft voice, and Herb couldn't distinguish if it came from a man or a woman. As Herb squinted in the blinding sun, a figure seemed to materialize out of the glare, and he saw…

A cowboy. All in black. Black hat. Black boots. Black duster jacket. With a scarf covering the nose and mouth, in a pattern that looked like a skull.

Behind the figure, stretched out immobile against the infinite grassy plains, was—

A truck?

No, it's far too big. And at least two hundred meters long.

A train of some sort?

What kind of train has giant wheels?

The wheels are twice as tall as me…

Herb was mesmerized by the vehicle, which was painted brown like the plains around them, and consisted of thirteen, no, *fourteen* enormous, linked cars.

Then he heard a musical jangle.

Spurs. The silver spurs on the cowboy's black boots.

"We won't pay for damaged goods," the cowboy said to the merc, in an emotionless, sexless monotone.

The merc lowered the club. Tequila lashed out a hand at the man's ankle, quick as a rattlesnake strike, and then the world exploded.

Herb recoiled from the gunfire, from the searing muzzle flashes and thunderous cracks of the shots, the ground in front of Tequila coughing up dirt as the bullets struck.

The cowboy had drawn and fired so fast, Herb hadn't even seen it. As Herb's eyes adjusted to the gun currently pointed at Tequila, he noted it was a single action revolver.

Single action meant the hammer had to be cocked after every shot.

So the cowboy had not only fired fast as a machinegun, but had done it manually.

The merc backed away. Tequila raised his hands over his head.

The gun zeroed in on Herb.

"You. Out of the van."

Herb had no idea if science could calculate the speed of thought, but in just the briefest of moments, a whole fantasy played out in his mind.

I can lunge, reach for the cowboy's gun.
The cowboy, acting on instinct, will shoot.
Chances are good I'll be killed.
No more hope.
No more pain.
Just nothingness.
Beautiful, blessed nothingness.
It sounds so lovely.

Being shot was horrible, Herb knew from experience. But whatever was happening now was probably worse.

Herb had been contemplating death for many months. Courting it like a lover flirts. Bullet wounds were agonizing. But being held captive was a suffering Herb could no longer endure.

Death is inevitable.
Misery doesn't have to be.
All I have to do is lunge. A bullet to the head will end it all.

The idea was more than just seductive. Herb craved it. A pang for death, overriding all other emotions.

Lunge. Die. Stop the pain.

And Herb was ready to do it. The impulse took over, and his muscles tensed, coiled and ready to spring—

—and then he heard Tequila say his name.

"Herb."

He didn't say it as a warning. He didn't say it as a question. Tequila's voice was calm, quiet, soothing.

And Herb knew what Tequila was saying. Tequila knew Herb's intentions.

Tequila was telling him goodbye.

Herb went limp. His infatuation with a sudden death was strong, but he couldn't leave his friend alone, to face whatever new nightmare they'd entered.

Herb got out of the van, slowly, kneeling in the dirt next to Tequila.

"I'm the Cowboy," said the black clad figure. "You work for me now. Whatever life you used to have, that's over."

The accent was American. This was the first gringo they'd seen for as long as they'd been prisoners. Could they actually be in the United States? Herb hadn't ever been to the Great Plains west of Illinois, but he'd seen pictures. Were they in one of the Dakotas? Missouri? Nebraska? Wyoming? Oklahoma?

Am I actually back in my homeland?

"I'm a cop," Herb rasped, buoyed by the possibility. "My name is Sergeant Herb Benedict, I'm from Chicago. There are people looking for me."

The Cowboy's eyes were as dead as any corpse Herb had ever seen. "You don't have a name. You don't have a past. No one is looking for you, because you no longer exist."

Herb should have ended it there, but that son of a bitch named hope kept his lips flapping.

"Listen," he implored, "I have money, and I'm sure we could make some sort of deal and—"

The Cowboy drew the pistol, whacked Herb across the side of the head, and holstered it before Herb hit the dirt, face-first.

The pain came fast and hard. Herb reached up, felt blood on his temple.

"I already made a deal." The Cowboy's voice was flat, devoid of humanity, but oddly soothing in Herb's ringing ears. "I bought you for three thousand dollars. You're my property, to do with as I please. If I want to hurt you—"

The Cowboy kicked Herb in the crotch.

"—I'll hurt you. And if I want to kill you…"

The Cowboy drew, superfast, pointing the gun at Tequila's head.

"Don't," Herb groaned through clenched teeth. Both hands were cupped around his groin, and he'd curled up into the fetal position. His head and balls were having a contest for which throbbed more, and the balls were taking the lead.

"Don't?" the Cowboy asked. "Livestock doesn't give orders. A cow doesn't say *don't*. It stays compliant, until it's slaughtered."

Tequila stared, unflinching, at the Cowboy. "Go ahead and kill me. Throw your money away."

"True. I need you to work. But you can work with only one knee."

The gun went from Tequila's head to his leg. His bad leg.

"Please," Herb groaned.

"Begging is useless. I demand obedience."

Herb stole a glance at Tequila's leg, remembering how horrible it had been to break it. "We'll obey."

"Of course you'll obey."

"I don't have a name," Herb quickly said. "I don't have a past. I no longer exist. I'm your property."

"That's not obedience. That's just repeating what I said."

"Whatever you want us to do," Herb continued, "we'll do."

The skull face bandana made reading the Cowboy's expression impossible. But it seemed like the Cowboy was going to shoot, just to prove a point.

"Whatever I want," the Cowboy said.

Herb nodded. "Yes."

The Cowboy looked to Herb. "Break his nose."

"Break his nose?"

"Punch him in the face and break his nose, or I'll blow off his kneecap."

Herb looked at Tequila.

"I've played this game," Tequila told him. "I've followed orders, and I've hurt people. You can't change the outcome of things. Whatever is going to happen, will happen. But you don't want to be the one who makes it happen. You have a choice."

"What are you saying?" Herb said.

"Don't do it. I'll take the bullet."

"You have five seconds," the Cowboy said.

"That's insane," Herb argued with his friend. "A broken nose isn't as bad as a shattered knee."

"This asshole is going to hurt us. Making us hurt each other is worse."

"Two seconds."

Herb looked at the Cowboy—

—then punched Tequila in the face, hard as he could.

His nose burst like a ripe tomato being thrown to the ground.

Tequila took the hit, and didn't make a sound, even as the blood poured down over his chin.

But he looked sadder than Herb had ever seen him.

"Good," the Cowboy said. "Here's what is going to happen next. I'm going to put you on the land train, and you're going to be put in a cultivation car. After some quick training, you'll be required to harvest a daily quota of sap. If you fail to meet the quota, I'll pull out one of your teeth. If you show any insubordination, I'll pull out one of your teeth. You can't escape. You're going to die here. But how many days that takes depends on how hard you're willing to work. Do you understand?"

"Yes," Herb said.

Tequila said nothing.

The Cowboy squatted down to Tequila's level. "You're a hard man. I can see it. I've dealt with hard men before. The last one, I heated up some metal-working pincers, heated them until they glowed orange, and stripped off all the skin on his chest. He lived for two more days, begging me to kill him the whole time."

"And begging is useless," Tequila said.

The Cowboy nodded. "The question isn't if you obey or not. The question is how much suffering are you willing to endure before you obey."

"Stay alert," Tequila said. "Because the moment you lose concentration, the moment you zone out for even one second, I'm going to take that Ruger Bisley Vaquero out of your cute little leather holster and show you what real sharpshooting is."

Herb braced himself for the violence.

But instead of lashing out, the Cowboy asked, "You think you can shoot?"

"I could shoot your balls off at two hundred meters," Tequila said. "But someone seems to have beaten me to it."

The Cowboy stared. Just stared, without moving or talking. Herb knew Tequila was going to get himself shot and he couldn't bear it because, dammit, he had his own chance to die a moment ago and threw it away and now he was going to be all alone in whatever fresh hellhole this was.

"I'm a good shot," Herb said, thinking quickly. "My former partner was a great shot. Won trophies." He pointed at Tequila. "But in the truck, he told me he was the best of all time. Better than you? I dunno. You seem to have skills. I guess there's no way to prove who's superior..."

The appeal to vanity was a long shot. But Herb didn't think the Cowboy was here for the money. There was some other motivator at work. Sadism, obviously. But maybe ego was also a trigger.

Herb had known his share of psychopaths. Some of them couldn't handle being shamed. They'd take any dare, no matter the risk, to prove their superiority.

Hopefully, the Cowboy fell into that group.

"Have you fired a derringer?" the Cowboy asked Tequila.

Tequila answered with his eyes.

"My back-up pistol is a two shot Bond Arms Cowboy Defender. Know it?"

"It has a rebounding hammer that allows it to half-cock, so it won't fire if you drop it."

"Exactly."

The Cowboy kept the Vaquero on Tequila and lifted a leg, reaching into a boot. Out came a tiny, silver gun with no trigger guard. The Cowboy reared back and hefted it into the plains, at least fifteen meters away. It landed with a plume of dust.

"Go fetch," the Cowboy said to Tequila.

"You have six shots," Tequila said.

"I never need more than six. But, for you, I promise to only use two."

Tequila seemed to consider it. Then he nodded.

"The moment you pick up the gun, I'll draw."

Tequila stood, then began to limp over to the thrown firearm.

"Which knee should I shoot," the Cowboy asked Herb. "Left or right? I'll let you choose."

Herb stayed silent.

"Pick one, or I'll shoot them both."

Herb already felt sick for punching his friend in the face. He didn't want to choose which knee. But if he didn't, he knew the Cowboy would make good on the threat.

"I just met the guy," Herb said. "He means nothing to me."

Tequila was almost there. But as good a shot as the man was, Herb had no hope that he'd prevail. The derringer had a two-and-a-half-inch barrel, compared to the Vaquero's five-and-a-half inches. Even if Tequila had been in perfect health on a windless firing range, and was able to take his time aiming and firing, hitting anything beyond seven meters with a gun that small was blind luck. At this distance? Quick draw? In his condition? Injured and dehydrated and exhausted? Tequila might as well have been unarmed.

"Fine," the Cowboy said. "I'll shoot both knees."

Herb felt like throwing up.

"The left one," Herb said.

He figured that leg was already injured. Why harm the healthy one?

The Cowboy took ten paces away from Herb, then holstered the revolver.

Tequila stopped and stood over the derringer. He glanced at it, then stared at the Cowboy.

"Whenever you're ready," the Cowboy called. "Or maybe you're too scared to—"

In one fast motion, Tequila dropped to his good knee and snatched up the gun, falling to his left as he brought it to bear with his right hand.

The Cowboy, caught off-guard, drew the Vaquero and fired at the same time as Tequila.

It all happened so quickly that Herb couldn't be sure how many shots rang out. If he had to guess, it was two from Tequila and four from the Cowboy.

Tequila continued to pitch sideways, then sprawled out onto the ground. Herb couldn't tell if he'd been hit.

The Cowboy remained standing, no trace of injury.

"No!" Herb yelled. He moved to get up, to rush to his friend, but the Cowboy pointed the revolver at him, dissuading Herb from the notion.

"I still have two in the cylinder."

Herb stayed still.

So did Tequila.

"Get up, or I'll shoot your friend," the Cowboy called.

Please don't let him be dead.

Please don't let him be dead.

Please oh please oh please oh—

"You winged my hip," Tequila shouted.

"I told you to get up."

Tequila awkwardly got to his feet, his hands over his head. Herb saw his pants leg was soaked with blood.

"I want my derringer back," the Cowboy said. "Toss it over here."

Tequila chucked a furious line drive directly at the Cowboy, who had to duck to avoid getting beaned in the head.

"You still haven't learned who's in charge." The Cowboy stood up straight. "This will teach you."

The Cowboy aimed at Tequila.

Herb closed his eyes so he didn't have to watch.

The gunshot was the loudest thing he'd ever heard.

PRESENT

YURI

For the Belarusian, the nightmare was always the same.

He was in the palace dungeon. Naked. Manacled. Immobile. Helpless.

His own men, men he fought with and spilled blood with, stood around him. Hard men, with hard eyes, but Yuri saw the fear in them.

Fear that they, too, might end up like Yuri.

"You are lying," the President said.

"No, my president. I would not dare."

"You are from Polotsk. The heart of White Russia. From a noble family. A warrior family. And yet, you betray me."

"I would never. My loyalty is with you."

"We shall see. You are a big man, Yuri. But big men can be broken."

Then the torture began.

They said the brain had no memory for pain. It was the reason women had more than one child, because if they could truly recall the agony of their first, they would never repeat it.

But in the nightmare, Yuri relived every kiss of the whip. Every caress of the cattle prod.

It went on and on, until he broke, willing to confess to anything.

But still it continued. Continued until Yuri couldn't remember his own lies, which made the torture even worse.

Eventually, mercifully, Yuri woke up. He didn't wake up screaming, because his whole body, including his jaw, was cramped, teeth clenched to the cracking point.

His bed was always soaked. Sweat. Urine, still stained with blood this many years later, from the internal injuries he continued to suffer.

For a moment, Yuri just laid there, willing his muscles to relax, letting the memory of the pain subside. Then he changed the sheets on the air mattress—an indignity not befitting a warrior such as himself—while thinking of all the things he'd do if he had the President at his mercy.

Thoughts of vengeance were the only thoughts that keep him sane.

The blood and piss soaked sheets were thrown out the window, lest his men discover them. The whole train reeked of bodily fluids, but Yuri used Lysol to mask his own.

A huge man, he felt an equally huge amount of shame.

Then he looked out the window. Looked up to the pinpricks of light in the black sky.

Most were stars. But there were manmade objects there, too. More than two thousand satellites circle the earth.

"Soon," he whispered to the night.

He had whispered that to the night many hundreds of times. But his nightly promise was close to coming true.

So very, very close.

Yuri then reached for his glass pipe, lit it, and the sickly-sweet opium filled his lungs.

It helped.

But the memory of the pain won't fully go away.

JACK

Traveling in the Crimebago Deux was sort of like being in a five-star restaurant that served food you hated. The seats were plush and comfortable. The toilet had a heated seat and one of those Japanese built-in bidets. The motorhome had Direct TV, and a computer with Wi-Fi, and was well-stocked with a high-end variety of booze and snacks.

At the same time, I'd rather be anywhere else.

I was having a hard time focusing. Not because of the ample distractions; I ignored those. I needed to be thinking about Herb, about finding him, but instead I was beating myself up over my fight with Phin, and wrestling with my cop-sense that told me something was very wrong with Heckle and Jeckle and I needed to follow-up on that hunch.

The vehicle came to a stop—probably for gas, because this beast got half a mile to the gallon—and I heard a knocking sound, coming from my right. I ignored it, thinking it was just some random RV noise, but then I heard it again, and noted it was coming from the refrigerator.

Heckle and Jeckle, sitting on the sofa across from me, looked at each other and snickered.

Rosalina whined, and nudged the refrigerator door with her nose.

"What's in the fridge?" I asked.

"See for yourself," the twins said in unison.

I took a few steps over to the fridge, grabbed the handle—

—and hesitated.

"McGlade," I called. "There's something in your refrigerator."

"That's Waddlebutt," he said from the driver's seat. "Probably hears you talking, wants to say hello."

That made about as much sense as anything else since I'd climbed aboard, so I opened the fridge, and found myself staring at a bird.

A black and white bird, about twenty inches tall and maybe seven pounds in weight, with black flippers for wings, a black beak, and little yellow eyes.

It chirped at me, an abrasive sound not unlike rubbing a wet finger across a water balloon.

Harry walked up and squatted next to the animal.

"J-Dawg, meet Waddlebutt. He's dressed like a butler, but don't let that fool you. He's a penguin."

Waddlebutt was standing on the bottom shelf of the fridge, in the center of a pile of small, round stones. The upper shelves had been removed.

"Harry," I said, using my patient Mom voice, like the time Sam flushed a Costco five-pound bag of Goldfish crackers down the toilet to set them free. "You can't keep a penguin in the fridge."

"He likes it in there. It reminds him of winter in the Arctic, where there's no sun. And no air."

"You're being an idiot again."

"How? There's no air in the Arctic. It's a proven fact."

"Penguins live in the Antarctic, not the Arctic. And they have air there."

"Have you been to the Antarctic, Miss Know Everything World Traveler? No, you haven't. Everyone knows you can't go there without oxygen."

"You're thinking of Mount Everest," I said. "Or scuba diving."

"You have no idea what I'm thinking. My mind is an enigma. What am I thinking about right now?"

"Porn," I said.

"Okay, you got one right." Harry made a face. "So, should I punch some air holes in the fridge?"

Waddlebutt chirped, or quacked, or whatever you called it. While it wasn't exactly cute, I couldn't stop staring. It was like one of Sam's stuffed animals, come to life.

"Why is he sitting on a pile of rocks?" I asked.

"Don't touch them!" McGlade slapped my hand just as I was reaching for one.

Waddlebutt squawked, then pecked me in the foot.

"Chinstrap penguins make nests out of stones, and steal them from one another. So he's really protective."

I rubbed my toe. "So…this is the latest in your stupid pet collection."

Over the years Harry had owned a parrot, a monkey, a pig, a mudskipper, a miniature pony, and a few more inappropriate creatures I'd intentionally forgotten.

"Waddlebutt isn't stupid. He's a social animal. Just don't take his stones. Or try to pet him. Or look him directly in the eye. Or make any sudden movements."

"Yeah. Real social."

"We should probably just back away slowly."

"Where the hell did you get a penguin, anyway?"

"I got a guy. Hey, did you know that penguins are one of the only animals that have no inherent fear of man?"

"Fascinating," I said. I wasn't actually fascinated.

"You want to feed him?"

"No."

"There's some shrimp in the crisper."

"I don't want to feed him."

"You guys need to bond. The best way to bond is to share a shrimp cocktail. Works on the ladies, and also works on penguins."

"No, thanks."

Harry nudged me. "Stop being a baby, Jack, and just give the poor waterfowl some shrimp."

I sighed. What the hell.

I reached for the crisper drawer, and Waddlebutt pecked my hand.

"Go slow. He thinks you're trying to steal his rocks."

"He drew blood," I said, squinting at my fingers. That's when the smell hit; rotten fish and ammonia and dirty diaper.

Harry picked up a bottle of Febreze, and began spraying it everywhere.

I began to gag. "Jesus, McGlade. He smells like a spoiled ass sandwich."

"He just needs a bath," Harry said. "Rosalina! Bath time!"

Rosalina padded over. Waddlebutt chirped at her, and the dog swallowed him in one bite.

I glanced at Heckle and Jeckle, wondering if this happened all the time and maybe they knew what to do. But they just sat there, expressionless, two sacks of suspicious potatoes.

"Shouldn't we stop this?" I asked McGlade.

"It's okay. They're friends."

Waddlebutt's little bird head poked out of Rosalina's gigantic, floppy jowls, and the dog trotted over to the rear of the Crimebago and spat the penguin out into a bucket of water.

Waddlebutt screeched, splashing around, flapping his flippers.

"He can't get into his bucket by himself because he's short and flightless," McGlade said. "Isn't this the cutest thing you've ever seen?"

Waddlebutt stuck his butt out of the water, lifted his tail, and squirted a stream of yellow feces three feet across the room, onto Harry's carpet.

I lowered my face into my hand and rubbed my eyes.

McGlade frowned. "He's not potty trained yet. We bought him kitty litter, but all he does is defend it like he defends his rocks."

"You've become a parody of yourself, Harry."

"Nature is miraculous, J-Dawg. You've lost your childlike fascination with the world. That's why you've got so many more wrinkles than I do."

"You don't have wrinkles because you're too fat for wrinkles."

"So we're back to body shaming?" he gave me a sidelong glance. "I can't help but notice that muffin top spilling over your pants. And are grey roots in fashion this season? If they are, you're ready for the cover of Vogue."

"You really want to do this?" I said. "You're a squatting fat guy."

"What's wrong with squatting fat guys?"

I held up my index finger, paused for dramatic effect, and then poked Harry in the shoulder and gave him the tiniest push. Gravity took over, and he toppled, rolling into the mess of bird poop.

"Squatting fat guys have poor balance," I answered.

McGlade flopped around, like a fat man who had been pushed over.

"Aw, c'mon! Dammit, Jackie, this is my only blazer that fits."

"Maybe you should consider dieting."

He tried to sit up using his stomach muscles, failed, and then rocked himself forward and back until he got onto his butt.

"FYI, I am dieting. I'm currently on the all carb diet."

"Which diet?"

"All carb. For breakfast I had a potato sandwich. Nothing but bread and boiled taters, topped with spaghetti."

"That sounds amazingly unhealthy."

"Impossible. The spaghetti was plain. I didn't put any sugar on it, like last time."

"It's called a *no carb* diet, McGlade. Not an *all carb* diet. Carbs are what make you fat."

He tried crossing his arms, couldn't because of his weight, and then scratched his elbow, trying to make it look like that was his original intent. "Don't be stupid, Jackie. Everyone knows it's sugar that makes you fat."

"Sugar is a carbohydrate."

"I know. That's why I've reduced my sugar intake to only two Snickers Bars per day."

I saw no need to argue with him. It was like talking to your television, expecting it to respond.

McGlade grunted, trying to look over his own shoulder, unable to. "Is my jacket stained?" he asked, showing me his back.

It looked like he'd rolled around in penguin shit.

"Can barely notice," I told him.

Heckle and Jeckle began to cackle. I saw they were recording this.

"My face better be blurred out," I said.

"This is B reel," said Heckle.

"Not streaming," said Jeckle.

"We'll alter it before posting," said Heckle.

"You got that lens filter on?" asked McGlade. "The one that makes me look thinner?"

"Of course, Private Dick McDude," said Jeckle.

"They've got a lens filter that makes me look thinner," McGlade told me, as if I hadn't just heard the whole exchange.

"No such thing." I took out my cell. "They're trolling you."

"Is there a such thing?" McGlade demanded of his videographers.

They chuckled.

"How about that lens that makes my dick look bigger?"

"That one is real," I said. "It's called a zoom lens."

Heckle and Jeckle cackled.

Waddlebutt squawked.

Rosalina barked.

I checked the GPS map on my phone.

We weren't even out of Florida yet.

This was going to be a really long trip.

DAYS AGO

THE COWBOY

The hunch had been correct. The man in the picture *had* been Herb Benedict.

Small world.

So small that some things aren't even coincidence. They're eventualities.

Herb Benedict falling into the Cowboy's world wasn't luck. It was inevitable.

While hackers and coders maintain the darknet, it's surprisingly primitive and low tech from a visual standpoint. It took geniuses to figure out Tor and VPNs and encryption, but they made it easy for luddites to surf and explore. Because of the unsophisticated criminal element that took to the deep web like bees to pollen, many destinations look like AOL websites circa 1998. But the black market doesn't require bells and whistles. When the Cowboy logged into the slavery store to check what was available to buy, and saw Herb's blurry, low-res picture, it was a galvanizing moment.

But there was no way to be sure it was actually Herb without putting him into the shopping cart and buying with bitcoin.

Even at delivery, the Cowboy hadn't been entirely certain. Herb looked ten years older than recent social media pictures, had lost a whole lot of weight, and was all scarred up. He also had the *dead look*; what Cowboy called it when slaves gave up on living and were just waiting to die. So it was hard to tell if this was the right man.

But the idiot cop had come right out and identified himself. That's fate.

Using CyberGhost to anonymously log into the net on a cell phone, the Cowboy visits Harry McGlade's blog, The Mansplainer, and posts to the latest comments.

> They call me the Cowboy. Search for me and my content on darknet. I collect teeth. I also collect people. Here's someone I recently picked up. I'm in Nebraska. Catch me if you can.

Then the Cowboy adds a picture hosting URL, with the blurry photo of Herb.

Perhaps this is too soon. It's still more than a week before the final delivery. The smarter move is to wait until the Cowboy owns the land train, and gets the project rolling.

But the Cowboy hasn't felt this excited since childhood, and literally can't wait.

More than a decade ago, Harry McGlade had taken something away from the Cowboy. Not long after, his friend and Herb Benedict's old partner, Lieutenant Jack Daniels, had taken something even more valuable from the Cowboy.

These debts need to be paid.

If only I'd acted sooner.

The Cowboy spent years training for a showdown that would never happen. The deceased Lieutenant had been an excellent shot, and the Cowboy had ached to gun her down. The same way Jack had gunned down…

Stop it. Thinking about it just makes me angry.

But after all the practice, all the Gunslinger Showdowns, and all the fantasizing, Jack Daniels had been killed by someone else in Baja.

Lesson learned; don't put off until tomorrow what you should do today.

The Cowboy almost went after McGlade right then. But instead, got seduced by the dream of darknet stardom. To own a streaming website to compete with Snuff-X. Live torture and death, twenty-four hours a day.

And it wouldn't befall the same fate as Usher House.

Usher House was a clandestine, underground abattoir where the rich and deviant could indulge in all manner of pain and suffering without having to travel to some underdeveloped, third world country. Sure, you could visit the Philippines and take a child sex tour, or if you knew the right people in Romania and had the cash you could spend some quality time playing real-life Torquemada, torturing kidnapped victims to death. But Usher House had been on American soil, not in some shitty, third-world hellhole. You could also hunt humans for sport, shop for transplant organs, make your own snuff films with state-of-the-art video equipment and a professional crew, and indulge in the finest cannibal cuisine on the planet.

For the record, people didn't actually taste like chicken. They tasted like stringy pork.

Unfortunately, having a death factory in a single location was just begging for the authorities to bust you. And all the deviant types that gathered there didn't always play well with each other. On top of all that, it was also expensive, and exclusionary.

Usher House, majestic as it was, fell like its Poe namesake. And that was probably just as well, because with new technology came a paradigm shift.

America had gone from being a nation of doers, to a nation of voyeurs.

Birthrates were dropping because couples were bingeing on Netflix rather than making love. Amazon paid almost a billion dollars for Twitch.tv, a live streaming video platform where a hundred million visitors a month watch other people play videogames. YouTube has become the most popular site on the Internet.

Why do something when it's so much easier to watch other people do things?

Charging some rich sheik fifty thousand dollars to hunt and eat a little boy was trivial compared to charging a hundred thousand viewers fifty dollars each to see the live stream of the same event.

With the anonymity of the deep web, and the lessened risk, you could attract many more visitors than Usher House ever could, and be much more reasonable in your pricing.

Even so, illegal websites got raided all the time. The world police were pretty good at finding criminals online and locating them in real life. Ask the poor bastards at The Pirate Bay, forced to shut down and move every few months.

But what if the servers were mobile?

Enter the LeTourneau Overland Train.

One of the largest vehicles ever built, commissioned by the US military in the 1950s for hauling equipment across Alaska, it consisted of fourteen massive cars on sixty gigantic wheels, each with its own electric motor and independent steering, capable of carrying over a hundred and fifty tons of cargo. Built to traverse rough terrain and handle all weather conditions, it was perfect for Yuri's mobile poppy farm. The Belarusian had pimped it out with modern tech, including electronic camouflage, hybrid energy, and radar.

It was perfect for growing opium without being discovered by the Feds, and just as perfect for the Cowboy's planned, movable reboot of Usher House.

So the Cowboy continues playing lapdog to the megalomaniac Russki, pulling teeth and keeping order, until Yuri no longer needs the land train.

Then the Cowboy plans to make McGlade the first honored guest of Usher House 2.0, streaming that asshole's death to a bitcoin-paying group of worldwide degenerates.

It's a solid plan. Worth the wait.

But seeing Jack's former partner, Herb Benedict, for sale on a slave darknet site, was too irresistible to pass up. It was also the perfect lure for McGlade.

It shouldn't complicate the Cowboy's plans. McGlade is an idiot. By the time the Cowboy allows him to get close, Yuri will already be out of the picture.

It's all coming together in such a lovely way.

The Cowboy powers down the cell phone, then takes off the duster jacket, opens up a few shirt buttons, and examines the Level IIIA carbon nanotube body armor underneath.

The two .22lr slugs hit the Cowboy in the breastbone and stomach, and the impact spots are sore. There will be bruises.

It shocks the hell out of the Cowboy. To be hit—twice—at that distance, with a short-barreled derringer, should have been impossible.

But Herb's diminutive companion had either gotten ridiculously lucky, or was one of the best marksmen the Cowboy has ever seen.

If the Cowboy knew how good a shot that man was, there would have been no playing around. If the guy had aimed higher, or the Cowboy hadn't replaced the standard Bond Arms stock .45LC barrel with the much smaller .22lr, there could have been serious injury, or even death.

The Cowboy never underestimated someone to that degree before.

It won't happen again.

But the Cowboy needs to learn more about this man, and how he acquired these skills. After putting the coat back on and adjusting the balaclava, the Cowboy heads for the Punishment Room in #12. Unlike a commuter rail train, the land train has no traversable connections between cars. Each car is as big as a semi-truck trailer, completely enclosed, connected by massive hinges longer than eight meters in length. The only way to get from one section to the next is to exit the car and walk on the ground, only possible when the land train is parked.

Yuri parks as often as he can. Moving the beast requires a ridiculous amount of energy, and the batteries deplete fast but take comparatively long to charge. Happily, the Great Plains stretch out over 1.3 million square kilometers, and there are plenty of spots to hide. It's the most uninhabited part of the United States. Fewer than 400,000 people live here. Rural flight has left thousands of towns abandoned, making for plenty of places to hide from the authorities.

Or satellites.

Every so often, drunk on vodka or high on something stronger, Yuri will brag about how cheap the entire operation is to run, between the green energy and the miniscule payoffs to local law enforcement to look the other way. In Belarus, a poppy farm would have cost millions in bribes alone. The LeTourneau subsists on a fraction of that.

And it will soon be the Cowboy's.

After climbing down the ladder to reach the ground, the Cowboy walks across the plains, dusty earth and rocks crunching under booted feet, and then ascends to Car #12.

The Punishment Room is only a small compartment in the pantry, no wider than a large closet. It smells like human piss and shit and puke and blood.

The smell of uncontrollable fear.

Herb's short companion is naked, wrists bound in two pairs of plastic riot cuffs because one didn't seem like it would be strong enough. Riot cuffs are a double loop of zip ties, used by law enforcement because they can quickly and easily be applied with just one hand. For the Cowboy, this is essential, because the other hand is always occupied with the Vaquero.

The cuffs are connected to a sturdy chain attached to the ceiling, and the Cowboy takes a moment to study this man. His skin is a roadmap of bruises, wounds, and scars, including two that are still bleeding. The graze on the man's hip, from the High Noon outside, and the side of the man's head where part of his ear used to be.

The Cowboy comes close to killing this man. But there are questions. Taking an ear is punishment enough.

For now.

The Cowboy switches on the wall camera, waits for the blinking light to make sure it's on, and then faces the man.

"Who are you?"

The man stares, but doesn't answer. There is no fear in his face. In fact, there is no expression at all.

The Cowboy has gazed into eyes like that before. Emotionless, but alert.

"You've killed before," The Cowboy says. It isn't a question. "Are you military?"

No answer.

"Who trained you?"

The man continues to stare.

The Cowboy places a gloved hand on his broad chest. Trails it down the man's hard stomach, going lower, and lower, watching his eyes.

Nothing there. Just two holes.

Even when the Cowboy cups his balls.

Even when the Cowboy squeezes.

The man grunts. His body tenses up.

But the eyes show no fear.

The Cowboy admires that. Envies it, even.

"Talk to me, and I'll stop hurting you. I promise."

Silence.

"Let's start with something easy," the Cowboy says. "What's your name?"

Again, no answer.

This might take some time.

After one more hard squeeze, the Cowboy releases the man. The man untenses, hanging limp by his wrists.

It's a common acceptance that everyone breaks. The reason torture is so unreliable as a way to gather information is because captives reach a point where they will say anything to make it stop. The truth, yes. But lies as well.

The Cowboy is sure he can get something out of this man. But there's the issue of time. Yuri demands that the harvest quota must be met in just a few days. And the Cowboy has work to do.

"Your lips are dry," the Cowboy says. "You're thirsty."

There are water bottles on a nearby shelf. The Cowboy opens one, tilts it up to the man's lips.

The man drinks in large, greedy gulps. Some of the water spills down his chin, his chest.

"So wounded. So beaten. I bet you were quite impressive, in your prime."

When the water is empty, the Cowboy walks over to the wall of tools, and removes the pneumatic piercer from the peg.

"Have you ever had a piercing?" The Cowboy asks, expecting no answer.

Expectations are met.

"This is a nail gun. It's been modified to fire piano wire instead of nails. Right now, you're in the middle of nowhere. No people for hundreds of miles. But some volunteers still try to run, even when there isn't any place to run to. For a while, we tried an old standard. A ball and chain. But, incredibly, volunteers were willing to break their own feet and heels to get out of the shackle. So I came up with a modern take on an old classic."

The Cowboy places the barrel of the piercer under the man's lower lip, pointing downward.

"I'm going to shoot a length of 3mm steel wire through your chin, and attach the other end to a large weight. I call it *fishhooking*. This is a ball and chain you won't escape from. Unless, perhaps, you break off your own jaw. I don't recommend that, by the way. This part of the body is just packed with sensitive nerves."

The Cowboy gets in close, to watch his eyes.

"Hold still. This will only hurt... for the rest of your life."

The man's eyes remain steadfast. Even when the Cowboy pulls the trigger.

There is minimal bleeding, but the Cowboy knows from first-hand accounts that the pain is considerable. Screams and tears are common. Begging and whining almost universal.

This man doesn't make a sound. His pain tolerance is exceptional.

There is no time to test that tolerance now. But maybe, after Yuri hits his quota…

It would be an interesting way to kick-off the 24/7 live feed of Usher House 2.0.

With a quick motion, the Cowboy pulls half a meter of wire through the man's flesh and bone, and makes a loop under his chin. There's already a steel sleeve on the long end, and the Cowboy threads the short end through it, then uses a large pair of specialty pliers to crimp them together.

"Does it hurt?" the Cowboy asks.

Rather than wait for a response that won't ever come, the Cowboy pulls down on the wire, making the man's mouth open like a ventriloquist dummy.

"Yes, Cowboy, it hurts a lot," the Cowboy says in a lower voice, matching his words to the jaw movements.

Amusing as it is, the man doesn't smile.

The Cowboy returns to the tool wall and selects the tin snips, cutting the wire after measuring out four meters. The long end gets clamped to the handle of a thirty-six pound cast iron kettlebell.

"I've hunted down over a dozen men who've tried to escape. This weight might not seem like a lot, but after a mile it might as well weigh a million pounds. You're strong. But no one is strong enough to get away."

The Cowboy gives the leash a firm tug.

The man doesn't make a sound.

It's kind of exciting.

So exciting, that the Cowboy switches off the cameras. For some privacy.

Vibration in the front pocket, and the Cowboy checks a message.

COMING HOME TONIGHT?

The Cowboy eyes the half-naked man and texts back, *NO*.

After the reply, the Cowboy turns off the phone and tucks it away.

There will be no further disruptions.

"You don't fear pain," the Cowboy says to the man. "Do you fear intimacy?"

No reply. Just hollow eyes.

The Cowboy removes a glove, and again touches the man's chest.

Goes lower.

And lower.

"Remember what I told you? You're my property, to do with as I please."

Then the Cowboy begins to stroke.

PRESENT

JACK

I was out of the camera frame, Harry had cleaned up his jacket, and the twins were fussing with their laptops.

"We're running the opening in ten, and then live in twenty," said Heckle.

They'd set up a laptop teleprompt monitor for Harry, and I watched as the opening title sequence played out.

First it was a shot of McGlade, at a desk, looking constipated and pretending to type on a keyboard.

Cut to McGlade on a beach, surrounded by women in bikinis.

Cut to McGlade on a firing range, shooting his .44 Magnum.

Cut to a stock footage explosion.

Cut to some guy in a ski mask, breaking into a house.

Cut to McGlade, with an AR-15 rifle.

Cut to the Crimebago Deux, with a crash zoom.

Cut to me, from earlier that day, squatting next to Waddlebutt. As promised, my face was pixelated. Crash zoom on the penguin.

Cut to black and white security footage of a robbery in progress at a convenience store.

Cut to McGlade, fake-punching someone in the face.

Cut to two people having sex on infrared video.

Cut to a stock footage explosion. The same explosion as before.

Cut to title, PRIVATE DICK LIVE AND STREAMING IN YOUR FACE.

Cut to a tight shot on McGlade, looking serious. Then silly string shoots up into frame from below his waist, and he winks.

"Subtle," I said.

"Shh," said Heckle, "we're live in three, two…"

He pointed to Harry, who began to read his lines.

"Greetings, Tubers. As you probably know, I'm Harry McGlade, rich media celebrity and real-life private detective, and I'm ready to stream all over your face."

I rubbed my eyes and tried to pinpoint all the life mistakes I'd made to lead me to this moment. There were too many to count.

"This week on Private Dick Live and Streaming In Your Face, I'm taking you along for a ride in my fabulous crime lab on wheels, the Crimebago Deux, as we hunt an American modern slavery ring and the notorious serial killer known only as the Cowboy."

The monitor cut to a recording of an older guy who had uncombed Einstein hair and a face shaped like an egg. He was sitting at a desk, and there were books on a shelf behind him. The graphic at the bottom of the screen read, *Dr. Cornell Holden, Columbus College, Chicago.*

"Isn't Columbus a joke college where the only admission requirements are a check and a pulse?" I asked.

"Shush," McGlade shushed me.

"Slavery is a thirty-billion-dollar industry," Dr. Holden said. "To put that in perspective, Starbucks has seventeen thousand shops worldwide and made ten billion last year."

Cut to a prerecorded McGlade, sitting across from Dr. Holden, looking serious. "So you're saying that human trafficking is three times more popular than coffee?"

Cut to Holden. "That's what I'm saying."

Cut to McGlade. "Does that include all of the non-coffee items that Starbucks sells? Like scones?"

Cut to Holden. "I would assume so, yes."

Cut to McGlade. "Scones make me unhappy. Are they bread? Are they dessert? Make up your damn mind already. So… this modern slavery problem, this certainly doesn't happen in the US." He leaned closer and raised an eyebrow. "Or does it?"

Cut to Holden. "It does. The majority of people sold are women and children, for the sex trade, but adult males are commonly sold for slave labor. It's estimated that over three hundred thousand Americans are victims of human trafficking every year. That's the population of Orlando, Florida."

Cut to McGlade. "So Orlando is where all the slavery is happening?"

Cut to Holden. "No. I just used that as a comparison."

Cut to McGlade. "Is Disney a part of this?"

Cut to Holden. "I don't think so."

Cut to McGlade. "Are you sure? What kind of person would wear a Donald Duck costume in hundred-degree heat? I'll say it if you're too scared; a person with no choice. Tell me, Dr. Holden, how slavery can hide in plain sight in this country. Surely not all slaves are dressed up like lovable cartoon characters."

Cut to me, unable to comprehend the stupidity playing out before my eyes.

Cut to Holden. "Chances are you've run into a sex slave and didn't even know it. Forced marriage, prostitution, even adopted children, could be human trafficking victims. With labor slaves, you may have seen them on farms, or in factories, forced to work. Some slaves are domestic, like live-in maids or nannies."

Cut to McGlade. "So a man could have a wife, children, and a maid, all living with him, and they could all be slaves."

Cut to Holden. "Correct."

Cut to McGlade. "Like some sick, twisted, modern day slavery Brady Bunch."

Cut to Holden. "I suppose."

Cut to McGlade. "But even worse, because Alice isn't allowed to date Sam the butcher."

Harry, sitting near me, said, "Heh. Good line. How many views we got?"

"Two hundred sixty thousand, and going up fast," Heckle said.

Color me incredulous. "You're kidding."

"How much ad revenue is that?" Harry asked.

"Figure eight dollars per thousand views, that's about two grand."

Harry nodded. "Not bad for the first two minutes."

I was obviously in the wrong profession. "You really just made two thousand bucks?"

"Gross, not net. YouTube takes forty-five percent. Uncle Sam takes a chunk, as you know. But if we hit two million views a day, like I'm hoping, I can clear about a quarter mil per month."

"Private Dick McDude, you're live in three, two…"

Heckle pointed. Harry read off the monitor and spoke into the camera.

"So according to Dr. Holden, human trafficking is a huge problem. And so are serial killers. As many of you are aware, I know psychos. I was even married to one, ha ha ha. My dear friend and former partner, the late, deceased, no longer alive Jacqueline Daniels, and I have managed to catch or kill more than a dozen of these assholes over the last few decades. And while Jack is very much gone, may she rest in peacepants, I am continuing the good fight and once again will risk my life and limb to chase yet another fine specimen of human garbage. This time, I'm after a real whacked-out pinhead who calls himself the Cowboy."

The monitor cut back to pre-recorded video, ominous organ music playing over a sketch of a crazy-looking man dressed up as a Cowboy.

Dr. Holden's voiceover: "The FBI estimates there are between one hundred and three hundred serial killers currently active in the United States. They're responsible for three percent of all murders, which accounts for roughly five hundred victims per year. But what's worse than a serial killer? How about the *ghost* of a serial killer?"

"What did he just say?" I asked, as a very bad Flash animation ensued of the Cowboy picture starting to shimmer and float.

"Paranormal shit gets more hits," Harry said. "We found that out in the market study. Focus group ate it up."

I shook my head. "This is ridiculous."

"Heckle, hit count?"

"Three hundred twenty thou."

"Who's ridiculous?" Harry asked me.

"Dressed in black," Holden continued as the scene changed to a landscape shot, "always wearing a mask, the Cowboy's identity is unknown. What is known is his trail of victims, by some estimates more than sixty, strewn across the Great Plains, tied together by the specter's unmistakable signature; a bullet in the head. But prior to that fatal coup de grace, a gristly commonality... most, or all, of the victims' teeth... have been removed."

Cut to a skull animation, the teeth disappearing one by one.

"Could the Cowboy be the disembodied spirit of Charles Kork, infamously known as the Gingerbread Man?" Holden asked. "Roaming the countryside, seeking vengeance against the man who killed him?"

Cut to a newspaper headline and picture, featuring Harry, from the Gingerbread Man case.

"On in three, McDude. Three, two..."

Jeckle pointed. McGlade read off the prompter.

"We know very little about the Cowboy," Harry spoke into the camera, "but besides the bodies of the deceased, we do have eyewitness statements. Rumors of a ghostly ghost train that silently roams the Midwest, searching for victims. Stories of modern day slaves being hunted and killed for sport. We also have an actual survivor. Someone who escaped the Cowboy, and lived to tell the tale. Watch the countdown clock and tune in again for our next episode of Private Dick Live and Streaming In Your Face. I'm Harry McGlade. Keep your lights on and your doors locked."

Cut to end credits, which lasted only a few seconds, and then Heckle said, "We're off."

"That's it?" I asked.

Jeckle nodded. "We're keeping the episodes under four minutes. Studies have shown that's when viewers' attention starts to wane."

I noted the clock on the monitor was counting down from one hundred and eighty minutes.

"And you're going live again in three hours?"

"That'll give us enough time for ep one to go viral on social media," said Heckle.

"We should have triple the audience for ep two," said Jeckle.

Harry turned to me. "What did you think, J-Dawg?"

"I weep for humanity's future."

"Did you like Dr. Holden? He's head of the Urban Legends Department at Columbus."

"You just made that department up."

"I didn't. But its existence is shrouded in doubt and speculation."

"What does Dr. Holden have a doctorate in?" I asked. "Chupacabras?"

"I dunno. Horticulture, I think."

"He's a tree doctor? Seriously?"

"No. It was something else with an *h*. Uh…" Harry snapped the fingers on his good hand. "Human Resources."

"He's got a PhD in HR," I stated, letting it sink in. That seemed even more ridiculous than horticulture.

"Jackie, J-Dawg, you're missing the bigger picture here. We got—how many views, Heckle?"

"Just passed half a mil."

"Half a million hits. And that episode will continue to get hits, forever, without putting any more work into it. With TV, you get paid when it first airs, but the residuals for reruns and Blu Ray releases are miniscule and eventually taper out. By the time it gets on Netflix, the only one making money is the studio. But this web series will still be lucrative when Harry Junior is my age. It's like a stock that keeps paying dividends. And as more eps are produced, the dividends are going to go up."

"So it doesn't matter that it's awful?"

"Do you live in this world, Jack? Everything is awful. That's not the point. This show will get me back on the A-list. Lucrative endorsement deals. Hollywood parties. Dates with beautiful women that I don't have to pay by the hour. Maybe the show is a bit sensationalistic and caters to the lowest common denominator, but there's no downside here."

I frowned. If I'd learned anything from my five decades of life, it was that there is always a downside.

And it would probably come from out of nowhere and blindside us.

THE MAN

The man follows Harry McGlade on social media. He's been following him for quite some time.

He sits in front of his laptop and begins to watch Episode One of *Private Dick Live and Streaming In Your Face* for the second time. He pauses during the opening credits. Pauses on the brief shot of the woman, squatting next to the penguin.

Her face is blurred out, but the man knows who she is.

Jack Daniels.

He knows all about Jack.

Harry McGlade says that Jack is dead, but that's not the truth.

She's very much alive.

The man goes to the gun safe.

Chooses a rifle.

Ready or not, Jack. Here I come.

PRESENT

HERB

Car #4 was hot and humid, smelled like body odor and piss, and every breath was labored. It felt like there was a truck parked on Herb's chest, his head seemed to pound with his heartbeat, the metal cable looped through his jaw felt like a non-stop toothache, and he was so tired and hungry that he was practically sleeping on his feet, even though the overhead UV grow-lights were brighter than an operating theater.

But, paradoxically, he was neck-deep in beauty.

Hundreds—thousands?—of long, green pods, some almost as tall as he was, surrounded him, growing out of the dirt on the floor.

Their bright flowers, pink and white and purple, waving on long stems.

And when Herb leaned in close enough, the stench of enslaved men was masked by a scent of cherry blossoms, vanilla, a hint of citrus.

It was a heavenly garden, located in the darkest pit of hell.

Herb wasn't sure how long he and Tequila had been working on the poppy farm. Probably no more than a few days, judging by scab formation. But it seemed so much longer.

This place made the Mexican rehab prison look like an all-inclusive luxury resort.

Clutched in Herb's hand was a curved metal spatula, made of cheap, bendable tin and roughly the size of a cake server. On the back end of the wooden handle was a tiny fork with three prongs, each only a millimeter long.

The routine was simple.

Score the poppy pod with the fork. The pods ranged in size from golf-ball to plum, and the prongs made them weep a milky white fluid out of the three parallel cuts. This was called *making the poppies cry*.

The next day, use the spatula to scrape off the gum that had oozed out, which had dried into a dark brown, sticky resin. That resin was raw opium.

Scrape the opium into a small, wooden measuring cup.

This was called *drying their tears*.

Repeat the cycle of crying and drying until your cup was full.

Working quickly, it took between five to seven hours to fill the cup. If you didn't fill a cup every eight hours, three cups every day, the Cowboy yanked out one of your teeth.

Herb and Tequila had been working in shifts, taking alternating sleeping breaks in the dirt, filling each other's cups as needed. But they'd been barely making the quota. The stale tortillas they were fed once every day didn't have enough calories to nourish. The lack of sleep didn't replenish energy.

They were disposable, meant to be used up and discarded. And it didn't take long for that to happen.

Any day now, one or both of them was going to lose a tooth.

There was no guard in the car with them. Only cameras mounted on the ceiling. They were shoeless and shirtless, which the Cowboy said was a deterrent to discourage trying to escape. Not that they could. The door leading outside was reinforced steel, and locked tight. Their single cellmate was a man named Juan. Talking was rare, because it hurt to move your jaw, and energy was best reserved for farming. But through minimal communication Herb found out that Juan had been there between three weeks and a month. He was stooped, wrinkled, pale, with sagging eyes, bony limbs, and hair that appeared to be patchy with mange. Juan's face had the sunken, skull-like appearance of POWs.

Juan looked to be about eighty years old.

He was actually thirty-three.

Juan's performance, and appearance, weren't helped by the fact that every so often he would dip into his own cup and swallow small amounts of raw opium. Herb couldn't really blame the guy. But the higher he got, the less productive he became, which was going to hasten his eventual demise.

After being fish-hooked, Herb had eaten a pea-sized amount of opium to help with the pain, but the revolting bitter taste and gagging nausea it caused was almost worse than the injury he'd sustained. Tequila recommended he rub some on the chin wound, because it had antibiotic as well as analgesic effects, and that worked to some extent. But Herb couldn't imagine swallowing any more, unless it was to intentionally overdose.

Which, every few hours, did cross his mind.

Herb glanced at the clock. Ten minutes to the next cup check. He was almost full, as was Tequila.

Juan still had half a cup to go.

Their Mexican cellmate wasn't going to make it.

Time to have the discussion again.

Herb stepped away from the poppy plant he'd finished harvesting, one with over thirty pods, pods as scarred and used-up as he was. He pissed in the dirt on the plant stem—which was encouraged because apparently urea and feces acted as a fertilizer—and then gripped his metal rope and tugged his weight to the far wall of the train car, over to the water tank. Herb drank from the spout until it felt like his stomach was about to burst, then spit some on his hand and gingerly cleaned his chin wounds. The holes were hot and tender to the touch. Infection. Herb dabbed a finger into his cup, and smeared a tiny bit of opium around both piercings.

As he applied the resin, he said to Tequila, "You got a headache."

"Yeah." Tequila pointed at a vent in the ceiling.. "Carbon dioxide generator. Feeds the plants."

"Won't we suffocate?"

"If we're lucky."

Herb glanced at Juan. "We need to help him."

Tequila didn't answer.

"He's only got a few teeth left."

Tequila gave his head a shake.

"We have to."

"We can barely help ourselves. We can't save him, too."

Herb understood Tequila's reasoning. The reality was brutal, but true. And, Herb admitted, there was something strangely seductive about Tequila's black-and-white attitude.

But Herb wasn't built like that.

"If you put a bunch of crabs in a bucket," Herb said, "they climb on top of one another to try to escape. But because they're all out for themselves, none of them can get away. They all die."

"Not true. The weak die. The ones who saved their strength can climb the bodies of the dead."

"You know what I'm saying."

Tequila faced him. "We're batteries, Herb. And we're running low. We can save our energy for ourselves, or we can waste it on someone who is already doomed, which means we get depleted sooner. That's stupid."

"That's human."

"You're a fool."

"I'd rather be a fool than lose my humanity."

Tequila adjusted the wire in his chin, and Herb was hit by a wave of nausea.

"When I broke that kid's leg back in Mexico, so I could come here with you, how did you feel?"

"Relieved," Herb admitted.

"Would you feel relieved if I went up to Juan and snapped his neck?"

Juan was watching them talk, but his face registered nothing.

"Of course not," Herb said.

"If it's you or Juan, I'm choosing you."

"And what if it comes down to me and you?" Herb asked. "Am I going to be one of the corpses you climb over?"

Tequila stopped working and stared at Herb. "You're really asking me that?"

"If you had a chance to escape, without me, would you take it?"

Tequila didn't answer. It hurt Herb more than he thought it would.

"We've been through a lot," Herb said. "You're like my brother. You'd actually leave me behind?"

"Self-preservation is a powerful motivator. You never know how you'll act until the situation arises."

Herb knew that answer to be true, but he didn't want it to be. Instead of replying, he dragged his kettlebell over to Juan, and traded his full cup for the man's half-empty one.

Tequila said nothing. And the instant Herb finished, the moral superiority he was feeling vanished, replaced by pants-wetting fear.

Herb stared at Juan, but the younger man seemed oblivious to the gift he'd just received. His eyes were empty. His face was slack. He looked more zombie than human.

Herb's fear was overtaken by anger.

"I'm going to lose a tooth for you," he snarled. "At least say *thank you*."

Juan continued to absent-mindedly scrape poppy pods, even though his cup was already full.

"The guy is gone," Tequila said. "Take your cup back."

Herb reached for it—

—then stopped himself.

"Herb," Tequila said, "we still have a chance. But the weaker we get, the more injuries we sustain, the odds get worse."

"I don't know how long I've got left, brother," Herb said. "But however long it is, I have to be able to live with myself."

"Martyrs die, Herb. They're no good to anyone."

"Isn't it better to die a martyr than live a coward?"

"No. Trust me on this."

The overhead LED clock showed a minute until weigh-in. Herb felt the land train come to a stop.

"I've got thirty-two teeth," Herb said. "I can save a man with just one of them."

"You're not saving him. Juan isn't going to make it. Prolonging the inevitable is cruel."

"Everything is cruel," Herb said. "But that doesn't mean I have to be."

"You want to do this now? This could be a stop where they open the door."

Seemingly at random, the land train would let prisoners out of the farming cars to spend a few minutes outdoors. It happened twice so far, and Herb had learned quite a bit about their situation during those stops.

First, there were thirty prisoners, three in each of the ten farming cars.

Second, they were in the middle of nowhere. Nothing but sky and land, far as you could see.

Third, if you didn't meet the quota, the Cowboy marched you to the Punishment Room and you lost the outside time.

And the outside time was... glorious.

Tequila lowered his voice to a whisper. "We can make a run for it."

"We won't get far with forty-pound weights attached to our jaws."

"Watch how far we get."

Herb considered it. Just stepping outside for a few minutes was a high better than any drug he'd ever tried.

What would freedom feel like?

Herb was a crusty shell of his former self. Exhausted and malnourished and beaten and broken and even with ten years of convalescence and rehab, he'd never be back to his old self again. But Herb knew that the mere thought of being free would give him the strength to run a barefoot marathon over broken glass.

After letting the fantasy play out in his head for a few tantalizing seconds, he glanced at Juan. The man was staring at his full cup as if noticing it for the first time. He had tears in his eyes.

"Go without me," Herb said.

Tequila didn't answer.

"You're stronger. Always have been. Get away. Bring back help."

The side door opened, and the Cowboy came in the car.

"Line up for weigh in," the Cowboy said, setting a digital scale down on the table. "Keep your kettlebells on the floor, keep your movements slow and easy. If you disobey, I'll shoot you in the kneecap."

After repeating it in Spanish, Juan trudged over to the scale. He set down his cup, and the Cowboy checked the weight, had Juan scoop it out into a plastic bag, and then threw a tortilla on the ground and pointed at Tequila.

Tequila approached, dragging his weight, and the Cowboy took a step back, a hand on the butt of the Ruger Vaquero. After Tequila proved he made quota, the Cowboy ordered him to scrape the resin into the bag, and then step back.

"Good boy," the Cowboy said. "Here's your treat."

A tortilla was tossed, frisbee-style, into the poppy plants. Tequila made no move to retrieve it.

"Now you."

Herb felt his stomach twist. He shot a look at Juan, who was munching on his tortilla, oblivious to the reprieve he'd been given.

Rather than feel pride from his selfless deed, Herb was paralyzed with fear.

"Move it."

Forcing his legs to work, feeling light-headed, Herb approached the Cowboy, eyes lowered, and placed the half-empty cup on the scale.

"I saw what you did," the Cowboy said. "You traded with this worthless idiot here. You're willing to take the punishment for a man you don't even know. You think you're a hero?"

"I'm obeying," Herb said. His voice sounded tiny. "I'm just helping others out."

"There are no heroes here."

Then there was a blur, a shot that made Herb's ears cry, and Juan slumped to the ground, a chunk missing from the side of his head that resembled a large bite in a peach.

Herb squeezed his eyes shut, turning away, and then a terrific jolt of pain came as Herb's chin was yanked forward by the metal wire leash.

"Pick up your weight."

The Cowboy jerked the wire and Herb went down to his knees, an obedient dog. With the other hand, the Cowboy pointed the Ruger at Tequila.

"I know you want a second date," the Cowboy told him, "but it isn't your turn. We'll get together later."

Herb picked up his kettlebell, then he was pulled to his feet and led out of the train car.

JACK

We stopped in Macon, Georgia for gas and cleaning supplies; Waddlebutt shot a stream of feces on the couch and McGlade had gone through two rolls of paper towels trying to sop it all up. He'd only succeeded in smearing guano into every nook and crack.

The joys of pet ownership.

While Harry pumped sixty gallons and stockpiled Lysol wipes, I was left alone with Heckle and Jeckle. My opinion of them had steadily declined since our first meeting, and the detective in my DNA had begun a casual interrogation.

"So, you knew Harry?"

"We follow Private Dick McDude on Twitter. He posted on Craigslist looking for viddies," said Heckle.

"Viddies?"

They looked at each other and did their mean kid snicker.

"Vid techs," said Jeckle. "We viddy-well."

"You viddy-well?"

"Nadsat," said Jeckle. "Don't you know *A Clockwork Orange*?"

I knew it, and didn't care for a film where the hero was a glorified rapist and murderer who gets away with it. "Does Harry pay well?" I asked, assuming he must.

"No pay," said Heckle. "We're doing this free."

"Free?" Cop 101. Just repeat the last word the suspect said and let them keep running their mouth.

"We don't need the cheddar," said Jeckle.

"We're independently wealthy," said Heckle.

"Made our fortune the old-fashioned way," said Jeckle.

"We inherited it," said Heckle.

They bumped fists, grinning.

"You guys seem pretty close," I said. "I bet you got into a lot of trouble when you were younger."

Another sidelong glance. More like lovers than brothers. I wondered if they fooled around with each other, and wouldn't have been surprised if they had. I remember McGlade once saying that he wished he had a twin, because it would be like masturbation, only with more positions.

"Trouble is where you find it," said Jeckle.

"Or where you make it," said Heckle.

"What kind of trouble?" I asked.

They didn't answer.

I tried a different tack. "Why do you follow McGlade on Twitter?"

"There are two ways to get famous," said Jeckle.

"You can do it on your own," said Heckle.

"Or you can entangle yourself with someone who already has fame," said Jeckle.

They began reciting names back and forth.

"Godse."

"Chapman."

"Booth."

"Oswald."

"Ruby."

"Hinkley."

"Ray."

They bumped fists again, looking equally smug.

"Those are all assassins," I said.

They didn't respond.

I kept my voice neutral and asked, "Is that how you want to get famous?"

"You mean kill Private Dick McDude?" said Heckle.

They giggled.

"No way," said Jeckle.

"No way," said Heckle. "We just want to be there to film it when he gets popped."

Rosalina whined. She was sitting next to the side door, waiting to be walked. I would have been up for the task, but I knew that the moment I left the RV, Heckle and Jeckle would be pawing through my suitcase. Or stomping on Waddlebutt, who was building a second nest on the floor out of dog biscuits. This put a strain on the friendship the penguin had with the Neo Mastiff, because whenever Rosa began to sniff near the treats, Waddlebutt squawked and flapped his little featherless wings. It was the penguin equivalent of flipping someone off in traffic.

Harry eventually poked his head in through the side door, and asked if any of us wanted moon pies.

"They have both flavors," he said. "Brown and yellow."

We all declined, and McGlade let Rosa outside without a leash.

Waddlebutt pecked at the empty dog biscuit bag, and then stared at me like I should do something about it.

"I got nothing," I told the bird.

He gave me a *go to hell* expression.

Pets. It's so lovely how they enrich your life.

I stared out the window, watching Rosalina run circles around Harry. Thought about calling Phin, but it wasn't seven yet.

"On McGlade's blog," I said, thinking out loud, "the Cowboy mentioned darknet. Do you guys know it?"

"Onionland," said Heckle.

"Darknet is part of the deep web," said Jeckle.

"Which is?" I asked.

"The deep web is all the parts of the Internet that search engines don't index," said Heckle. "Paywalled sites, password protected sites, private networks, archives, scripted and unlinked content… Google and the rest can't find these places. No way for their engines to crawl them. They can only be accessed if you know the specific URL and the proper authorization."

"Darknet is a privacy network that can only be accessed, peer-to-peer, with special software that has layers of encryption, so both parties are anonymous," said Jeckle.

I could see how that would be useful. On the side of good, whistleblowers and watchdog groups couldn't be identified or targeted. On the side of bad, you could sell illegal stuff without getting caught.

But something didn't make sense to me. "The Cowboy said to search for him and his content on darknet. How is that possible if search engines can't access it?"

In unison, Heckle and Jeckle said, "Uncensored Hidden Wiki."

"And that is…?"

"Like it sounds," said Jeckle. "It's like Wikipedia, but anything goes."

"We can search for the Cowboy there?" I asked.

They glanced at each other, and I made the connection.

"You've already searched for the Cowboy."

When they didn't respond, I knew I was correct.

"What did you guys find out?"

Heckle shrugged. "We're revealing that on the next web stream."

"How about you reveal it to me right now?"

Jeckle said, "Private Dick McDude—"

"Won't mind," I said. "We're partners, remember? What Harry knows, I need to know."

"Then maybe you should ask him," said Heckle.

I considered my options. When I still had a badge, I could make the appropriate threats, and they had some gravitas. But I didn't think threats would work on these guys. They seemed to delight in their antiestablishment attitude, and playing authority figure probably wouldn't get me anywhere.

Instead of using the stick, I weighed my carrot options. I'd already alluded that I could show them a screening of the Kork tapes, in return for keeping my face hidden, but I didn't intend on following through on that unless forced to. Offering these creeps serial killer trophies would be like giving matches to a pyro.

Back in my younger days, I used to be able to get perps to open up by being a little flirty. But, truth told, I'd forgotten how to flirt. I'd been with Phin for too long, hadn't felt attractive lately, and wasn't sure I was emotionally equipped to handle the rejection if my feminine wiles were rebuffed. Plus, these guys were downright repulsive, and I wasn't that good of an actor.

Which left me without recourse. At least, with these weirdo twins.

Fortunately, I had friends in the know.

I seated myself in front of Harry's laptop and whipped out my cell phone. She picked up on the third ring.

"Hey, Val. It's… Jill." I'd almost said *Jack*.

Val Ryker was a former colleague who now resided in Wisconsin, doing consulting work for the Sheriff's Department in Baraboo.

"Jill, how's things?"

"Peachy."

"Really? That good?"

"That good. You?"

"Peachy."

Nice. Apparently both of our lives sucked.

"I'd love to catch up, but had a work question. Tell me everything you know about darknet."

"Easy. I know nothing."

"Great. Gotta go."

"Good catching up."

I disconnected, then stared at my phone, trying to think if I had any other friends. I knew some actual spies who no doubt had darknet experience, but I had no way to get in touch with them. And if I did, I'd probably shoot one of them on sight. Her name was Chandler, and she was the reason we'd left Herb and Tequila behind in Baja.

Just before I began loathing myself for having shitty interpersonal skills that left me friendless, I remembered Tom. I found his number.

"Tom, it's... Jill."

"Hey, *Jill*. Been a while."

Tom Mankowski once worked under me on the CPD. Last I checked, he was still recuperating from a serious injury.

"How's the rehab?"

"Slow. But it isn't boring, because of all the pain."

"Nice."

"Am I slurring? Because I've got a Duragesic patch on each leg. Pro tip; you never think you'll miss jogging, until you can't jog."

I had only visited Tom once since the shooting, and I sensed both the pain and the painkillers in his voice. One more regret for the regret-pile.

"Tom, what do you know about darknet?"

"You were never one for small talk, Loot."

Loot was short for Lieutenant, my old job. Tom was smart enough to not call me by my first name on the off chance anyone was listening, but apparently that savvy didn't extend to his nickname for me.

"Small talk is great for cocktail parties and strangers on a plane ride. I need help."

"I know my way around darknet. What do you need?"

"Can you guide me through an Uncensored Hidden Wiki search?"

"Are you in front of a computer?"

"Yeah."

Tom directed me to download the Tor browser, but I didn't need to because it was already on Harry's laptop screen. After opening up the application, I saw that Tor wasn't much different than Google, Bing, or Safari. I typed "uncensored hidden wiki" into the text box, and a search engine called DuckDuckGo gave me several pages of hits.

"You're looking for a URL that's a bunch of random letters and numbers and ends in *dot onion*," Tom told me.

"There are a few of them."

"Okay, first thing to know is that about seventy-five percent of darknet is broken or bullshit. Scams and garbage and links that don't work. About twenty percent is legit markets. Well, legit in that they aren't rip-offs, but they are illegal. Stolen credit card numbers, fake passports, counterfeit currency, drugs, and H/P/A/W/V/C services."

"Which is?"

"Hackers, phreaks, anarchy, warez, virus, cracks. You can hire guys to do DDoS attacks, spam and harass people, hack passwords, phish, spread trojans; upstanding stuff like that."

"Nice."

"Now the last five percent of darknet, that's where the really bad stuff happens. All the illegal pornography, human trafficking, rape and assassination services, sex tours, firearms and munitions—and we're talking big shit like rocket launchers and land mines."

I spent a good portion of my life looking for bad people hiding among the good. Now it seemed they had a whole section of the Internet to themselves, where they didn't even need to hide.

"Lovely."

"Thank the US government. They wanted a way to do all of their covert, nasty shit without being traced, and then they got pissy when civilians used the same technology to do covert, nasty shit without being traced."

"Where would I find a serial killer who calls himself the Cowboy? He mentioned darknet."

"A serial killer? I thought you were...uh...*retired*."

I bridled, just a little. "Are *you* retired?"

"I'm on a medical leave of absence."

"So, when you're ready for duty again, are you going back to the Job?"

"Joan and I have talked a lot about this. I... I'm going to pursue a different career path."

"That's good," I said, honestly. "I wish I'd gotten out sooner. But can you say, for sure, that nothing would ever get you to take a case again?"

"I don't want to get into a war of ideologies, Loot, but retired is supposed to mean retired."

"And what if something from the past, something like an old case, came back? Would you run and hide? Or would you face it?"

After a pause, Tom said, "I see what you mean."

I found the uncensored wiki page, and it came up on a random page, showing part of an article called "Seducing the Reluctant Nine-Year-Old."

I winced. "This wiki site is disgusting."

"Try searching for your guy."

There was a cowboy link. But it was for a sex position that involved more than one species.

"Nothing. Where else can I try to find him?"

"You can try Torbook. It's a deep web social media site."

"Got a URL?"

"Hidden Wiki should have a link."

"Okay. Can you hang on while I check?"

"Sure. I'm waiting for my Honeybeast Slayer to regenerate her licorice tail."

I blinked, not understanding. "Is that code for something?"

"No. It's *Zombie Sugar Jackers 2: SmackPack SnackPack*. It's a social media game. My life has been reduced to opioids and phone apps."

"I read about that game. Supposed to be more addictive than cocaine, and drives people to bankruptcy."

Tom didn't answer.

"Tom? You there?"

"Sorry, I got attacked by the Butter Scortcher and had to buy a Gumdrop Torpedo upgrade."

"Of course you did."

"Something about cocaine?"

"I said I read an article that the game you're playing—"

"Hold on," Tom interrupted. "Rival clan attacking my Caramel Crop. Gotta buy a Cotton Candy Shield."

I rubbed my eyes. "Do they also sell a Pavlov bell?"

Tom didn't reply, but in the background the jovial beeping continued.

Losing my friend to Zombie Sugar Jackers 2, I navigated the treacherous and ugly waters of the hidden wiki on my own and managed to find Torbook. The homepage demanded I create an account before proceeding.

"Tom?"

"Mmmm."

"It wants me to put in an email and password."

"Mmm-hmmm."

"Is that safe?"

"Mmmm."

"Tom?"

"Shit! The FrucTortise ate my ChocoStalk harvest."

"Tragic," I deadpanned. "What am I supposed to do on Torbook?"

"The harvest takes three days to replenish unless I boost it with Vanilla Brownie Fertilizer. But I'd have to use my last Kiss-A-Lanche. You know how much a Kiss-A-Lanche costs? It's not like I'm made of Gummy Gold."

"Are you listening to yourself talk?"

"Blame the morphine. I think I'm addicted."

"You sure you aren't addicted to something else?"

"I have crutches. Don't judge."

"Torbook log in?"

"Just make up an email address. That's what everyone does. Ah, shit, the goddamn FrucTortise is in my Sugar Silo."

I typed something made-up into the text boxes, and was rewarded by being able to access the main site. It looked a lot like Facebook, to the point where it must have been stealing the design code. There were a few ads; buying marijuana, buying stolen credit cards, trading bitcoin. I did a quick search for *Cowboy* and got over a thousand hits.

Remembering the Cowboy's comment on Harry's blog, I searched for *Cowboy+teeth*.

That gave me just one hit. And I immediately knew it was the one I wanted, because the avatar picture was of a black Stetson hat with human teeth glued on the hatband.

It didn't look fake. It looked real.

Staring at it, I *knew* it was real.

Part of me didn't want to view the profile. I'd carefully—and finally—structured my life so I wouldn't have to deal with psychos like this. As Tom had said, I was supposed to be retired. No more chasing predators. I should have been hiding from them, not seeking out the latest.

But if there was even the slightest chance Herb and Tequila were still alive...

I moused over the hat and was ready to—

"Dammit!" Tom's yell was so loud I flinched. "I need to go up a level before I can upgrade my Smiley-Smiley Spell Factory."

"I think I can take it from here, Tom. Thanks for your help."

"Sure. Anytime, Loot. Hey, if you want to join my Sugar Clan, I can send you an invite."

"Thanks, but I pass."

"We can both get double Gummy Gold once you spend your first fifty dollars."

"Goodbye, Tom."

"Goddamn it! The goddamn FrucTortise is back!"

He hung up.

I clicked.

The Cowboy only had one message posted on his wall. An unnamed Onion link.

There were three pictures in his photo album.

The first two were of corpses, parts of their heads missing. Gunshot wounds.

The last was of a half-naked man, his wrists bound over his head.

My breath caught.

"Tequila," I whispered.

I managed to keep my rage below the simmering point and didn't punch the screen, but I was so upset my whole body shook. Fighting against anger for top of the emotional dung heap was bone-piercing guilt, and an overwhelming sense of helplessness.

Tequila is alive.

All these months.

And I've been doing nothing.

"Do you know him?"

Heckle and Jeckle had snuck up behind me, peering over my shoulders.

I didn't reply. Instead I clicked on the onion link that the Cowboy had provided. The page took forever to load, and then a crude homepage appeared, red font on a black background.

"Snuff-X," I read. "You guys know it?"

"No," they said in unison.

I clicked on the ENTER button, and then the page filled with rows and rows of small pictures. Pictures of...

"What the hell is wrong with people?" I whispered.

Every thumbnail was of a human being. And each human being was either bleeding, screaming, or dead.

"Whoa," said Heckle.

"Whoa," said Jeckle.

I spent thirty seconds trying to recognize Tequila or Herb in the terrible images, didn't find them, and then checked out the sidebar which had sign-in boxes. As I'd done with Torbook, I made up a user name, password, and fake email address, and then I logged in.

Jesus. If hell had a website, it was Snuff-X.

Whoever ran the site was kind enough to make it easy to search for whatever deviant behavior your sick little heart desired. Want to watch children get raped? There were eight different channels. Dogs and cats being dismembered? Five channels. Torture? Pick your favorite type. There were subsections devoted to branding, whipping, electrocution, beating, and waterboarding.

Just to see what happened, I clicked on an image of a man with a towel over his face, having water poured on him, because a blinking icon next to it said LIVE.

Rather than show me the stream, a pop-up obscured the picture. It was asking for BTC.

"Bitcoin," said Heckle.

"It's a cryptocurrency," said Jeckle. "Decentralized, peer-to-peer, anonymous."

I'd heard of it. "You're supposed to mine bitcoins, right?"

"You can mine them by verifying the blockchain using the SHA-256 hashing algo," said Heckle.

"You can also buy bitcoin," said Jeckle. "There are brokers."

I didn't want to pay to watch some poor bastard get waterboarded. I closed the pop-up, and found a search box. I typed in COWBOY.

The first hit was The Cowboy Channel. The image was the same black hat, banded with human teeth. The description was as follows:

I'm a slaver, and the slaves need constant punishment. This includes fish-hooking through their chins with wire, and pulling out their teeth when they disobey. If they lose too many teeth, it's execution time.

Keywords included *tooth extraction, torture, piercing, execution, hunting humans.*

The Cowboy had 14,261 followers.

"He's got a live feed," said Heckle.

Nearing my vomit threshold, my eyes sought out the blinking word LIVE, and there, grimacing in a still shot—

"Oh...Jesus..."

Herb.

My best friend, Herb Benedict.

Emaciated. Bearded. A wire jabbed through his chin. Strung up by his wrists.

I'd never seen anything more horrible.

To witness someone so dear to me, being abused, was worse than if I'd traded places with him.

That it was happening, right now, and I couldn't do anything, was maddening.

I was the one who left him for dead. I was the cause of his agony over the last few months...

I've had a long-standing idea on how to stop war. Every time a soldier died, everyone up the chain of command got a half-dollar-sized brand on their chest. How eager would the President be to send young people into battle knowing that he'd get an agonizing, permanent scar for every single one who didn't come home?

Looking at Herb's picture, that's what I felt. Like I deserved to have a branding iron, held to my flesh, once a day for every day he'd been missing.

"Bitcoin again," said Jeckle.

"0.002742," said Heckle. "About twenty bucks to watch live."

"How do I pay?" My voice came out somewhere between a whimper and a croak.

"Got your wallet?" asked Jeckle.

I reached for my purse, fumbled for my wallet, and Heckle and Jeckle barked their mean little laugh.

"Your bitcoin wallet," said Heckle. "It's an app."

"I...I don't have that."

They exchanged a look, then Heckle took out his cell. Over my shoulder, he did something with the computer involving his phone camera and QR codes.

"Done," he said.

Nothing happened on the monitor.

"Now what?" I asked.

"It can take a little while to verify in the blockchain."

I stared at Herb's frame-captured picture. "How long?"

"A few seconds. A few minutes."

"Litecoin is faster," said Jeckle. "But this site doesn't accept Litecoin."

I wanted to hit something. I wanted to cry. I wanted to scream. I wanted to puke. I wanted to be drugged up, knocked out, put under, so I wouldn't have to face this horrifying situation.

Then the screen flickered, and Herb's picture became a live movie.

Standing next to Herb was a figure in black. Black pants. Black shirt and vest. Black boots.

A black Stetson, human teeth mosaiced around the hatband.

The Cowboy.

I couldn't see his face. He was wearing one of those bandana masks that covered up his nose and mouth. There was a design printed on it, making him look like he was a zombie.

"We've got an audience," the Cowboy said. His tone was odd. Devoid of emotion, and something else.

Gender. The voice was completely neutral, not traditionally male or female.

"Smile for the people watching."

Then the Cowboy yanked the wire connected to Herb's chin, opening up my friend's mouth.

I whimpered.

After securing the wire to a clamp in the floor, the Cowboy went to a wall of tools.

I couldn't watch.

I had to watch.

Behind me, I was vaguely aware that Jeckle was recording the screen with his camera.

The Cowboy selected a pair of pliers.

Keeping my eyes open was torture.

But it wasn't nearly as bad as what poor Herb endured.

YURI

After the train stopped, the driver—an old comrade from Belarus named Dimitri—called on the intercom. Yuri reached across his desk and pressed the button to answer.

"Da?" He winced. "Yes?"

The intercom transmitted a weak radio signal, and there weren't any towns within fifty square miles. But you never know who might be listening in. Yuri tried to avoid speaking Russian and Belarusian since coming to America. But in moments of fatigue, or stress, he sometimes lapsed.

"We have problem."

Unlike Yuri, Dimitri couldn't shed his accent, and often omitted words when speaking English.

"What kind of problem?"

"Bank 6 not charging to capacity."

"Is Bank 6 connected to solar or the turbines?"

"Turbines. Wind good, blades spinning. It battery."

"How long?"

"Ten minutes. Ten hours. Maybe bad wire, or cooling fluid. Maybe leak. I need look."

Yuri eyed the CO_2 monitor on his office wall. Fifty thousand parts per million. Getting close to toxic levels. It was a tightrope walk between worker productivity and plant health, but lethargy, and death, delayed crop yield.

"Anything on radar?" he asked Dimitri.

"We're alone out here. Like Siberia."

Yuri was pleased it wasn't Siberia. That hadn't been a pleasant experience for him.

"Has the Cowboy arrived?"

"Hour ago. Currently with one of the volunteers."

Dimitri chuckled. He thought calling them *volunteers* was amusing. His driver was also amused by torture, rape, and murder.

That was one of the problems with being a criminal. Your best friends tended to be the worst kind of scum.

Yuri hit the button for the Punishment Room. "Cowboy, air out the workers."

He switched to the monitor view of the sleeping car. Chained by his wrists to the ceiling was an older man. White. Bearded. Flabby, like he'd quickly lost a lot of weight. An American, who'd run into some trouble in Mexico.

Yuri usually passed up buying US citizens, because too often they had people searching for them. But that drawback made them half the price of Mexicans. And Yuri, who'd grown up under the auspices of communism, had a hard time passing up bargains. This business was all about the margins, and if Yuri could save a few bucks here and there, he could reach his goal that much sooner.

So he bought some forgotten, old, broken gringos, and the Cowboy was applying some fear compliance.

Yuri checked the CO_2 levels again, then pressed the intercom.

"Cowboy, you can finish with the volunteer after the stop."

The Cowboy stared up at the camera and raised a finger, indicating one more minute. Yuri scowled, unhappy with being disobeyed. But the Cowboy was someone that Yuri didn't want to unduly annoy. Yuri had met many ruthless people throughout his career. Killers and torturers, sadists without a shred of emotion, some gripped by uncontrollable psychoses. But the Cowboy was one of the scariest. There was something so efficient, so commanding, about the Cowboy, that it bordered on supernatural. Even though Yuri was almost a foot taller, and over a hundred pounds heavier, he didn't want to push it too hard.

"Fine," he said. "Be quick."

Yuri left the speaker on, watching and listening to the bound American scream as the tooth was yanked from his mouth.

THE COWBOY

The Cowboy holds the tooth—a molar—in front of Herb's face as blood soaks into his beard, tinging the gray a soft pink.

The former cop looks suitably terrified and agonized. But there is something else in his eyes.

Defiance.

"Something tells me you haven't learned your lesson," the Cowboy says. "Do I need to take another?"

The Cowboy pokes the pliers into Herb's open mouth, tapping the metal tips over the man's incisors. Herb tries, comically, to push away the pliers with feeble jabs of his tongue. The Cowboy considers pinching the tongue, yanking it out. But that's much more serious than it seems. The last man the Cowboy tried it on choked to death on his own blood, and Yuri wasn't pleased. Plus, without proper cauterization, infection would set in. They were so close to reaching their quota, it would be counterproductive to weaken the workforce.

But one more tooth won't hurt anything.

Well, other than Herb...

The Cowboy grips a front tooth with a beautiful *CLINK* sound, and begins to squeeze.

"The workers!" the intercom booms.

Yuri is pissed. He doesn't like to repeat himself.

"Saved by the bell," the Cowboy says.

The Cowboy puts the tooth extractor pliers back on the wall of tools, selects a pair of small but sharp wire cutters, and walks behind Herb, pressing the Vaquero into the man's back.

"Stay still, or I'll shoot your spine. You can still harvest opium while paralyzed. But trust me, you won't enjoy it as much."

The Cowboy stretches up overhead, then snips the plastic band, freeing Herb's hands. The man staggers forward, then drops to his knees.

"Now take your wire out of the floor clamp," the Cowboy says, tucking the snips into a vest pocket and walking around to Herb's front.

The ex-cop fumbles with the wire, unable to open the mechanism.

"Just squeeze the sides. It opens like a clothespin."

More fumbling. This man is incompetent. The Cowboy wonders how Jack Daniels put up with him for all those years.

"Hands above your head, you idiot. Now."

Herb raises his hands, and the Cowboy presses the gun to his temple and leans down, feeling for the clamp while locking eyes.

Herb's eyelids flutter—

—and then the weakling tilts sideways, feebly pawing at the Cowboy's chest before passing out flat on his face.

The Cowboy unclamps the wire just as Herb begins to sob.

"You're inhuman!" Herb wails.

This amuses the Cowboy. "I'm completely human. Depravity is a wholly human trait."

"I can't...I can't take any more."

The Cowboy faces the wall of tools. "Stop being a baby."

"I CAN'T!" Herb screeches, pounding on the floor of the train car.

Then there's screaming. Screaming that cuts right into the Cowboy's head, threatening to squat there and cause a migraine.

"Shut up," the Cowboy warns.

Herb doesn't shut up. It's so loud it makes the Cowboy's eyes ache.

"Shut up!"

The Cowboy considers kicking the hell out of him, but Yuri is probably watching, getting angrier and angrier that the volunteers haven't been aired out yet. So instead of an ass whupping, the Cowboy grabs Herb's wire in a gloved hand and yanks it, hard, practically jerking the cop to his feet. Herb struggles to heft up his kettlebell and the Cowboy drags the cop out of the Punishment Room.

"Wait until this train is mine," the Cowboy says. "The first thing I'm going to do is fill your mouth with razor blades and then sew your lips closed."

The threat seemed to work, because Herb instantly shut up.

YEARS AGO

TOM AND JERRY

Not long after MotherBitch got murderdead, FatherAss took the twins to a grief counselor. This counselor, a humorless moron named Dr. Bartholomew, believed in expressive therapy. That is, he insisted the siblings use artistic expression to come to grips with their feelings. This involved drawing, painting, writing, sculpting, and, ultimately, making videos.

Tom and Jerry knew that Dorkter Barfolopew was major lametime, but they did have a lot of fun with the video camera. They'd sneak into FatherAss's room as he slept, and make movies of them taking turns pissing on his legs. This was incredibly difficult to do without busting up laughing. Equally hard was staying straight-faced the next morning at breakfast, searching their father's eyes for incontinence shame.

They never showed those movies to Dorkter Barfolopew. But they did show him elaborately staged reenactments of MotherBitch's fiery demise, using red and orange crepe paper streamers as the flames, taking turns flailing about and screaming while a Halloween smoke machine filled the room with glycerin clouds.

The dorkter thought it was cathartic.

The twins thought it was hysterical.

They also reenacted the death of their schoolmate, Travis Hitchen, who drowned in a pond by the park. Jerry flailed around in FatherAss's pool, spitting water and screeching for help, as Tom taped the theatrics. When Jerry as Travis eventually succumbed to the water, they applied blue make-up to his face and had him float on his back, staring blankly into space.

It required several takes, because Jerry kept blinking, complaining that the chlorine hurt. But eventually, the twins got the shot.

Dorkter Barfolopew was neither offended, nor worried, about the production, which the twins titled *Tragic Swimming Accident Part 2*. Nor was the idiot psychotherapist inclined to ask about Part 1, which was more proof that the hack was simply cashing Father-Ass's checks without any true concern for the twins' mental health.

While Tom and Jerry were particularly proud of *Tragic Swimming Accident Part 2*, especially the quick cuts and Dutch angles used to emphasize the drama and horror, they both preferred Tragic Swimming Accident Part 1, where they tied a barbell around Travis Hitchen's legs and pushed him into the pond.

The pond was murkydark and muckydeep, but they were able to record some blurry underwater flailing and a lot of air bubbles that, when they broke the surface, sounded like faint screams.

It was all over very fast; much faster than the elaborately acted Part 2, and Tom lost at rock-paper-scissors which meant diving into the murkydark and cutting poor Travis's legs free so the death appeared to be an accident.

Jerry got that part on video as well, and Tom really hammed it up, pretending to try and rescue Travis, pulling the boy ashore and even trying mouth-to-mouth for real. Jerry got some great shots of Travis's chest going up and down while Tom blew into it, and then stopped the production because Tom was doing such a good job that he feared Travis might actually come back to life.

So Tom pulled Travis back into the pond, face-first to make sure he was fully murderdead, and the twins sneaksnuck back to their house without being seen. After a shower, they buried Tom's muckydeep clothes in a bag, in the woods, at their special place.

Dorkter Barfolopew never saw Part 1.

Some months later, the Dorkter suffered a personal tragedy while driving when an unknown assailant dropped a cinderblock from an overpass onto his windshield.

In their video reenactment, Jerry rode his bike under the same overpass while Tom simultaneously filmed it while dropping a fake foam rock they'd bought at a Halloween store. They had to do five takes before the lightweight rock actually hit Jerry, because the wind kept blowing it off course. But when it did hit, Jerry did a dramatic scream and fell off his bike onto the grassy embankment. Then they got close-ups of Jerry writhing around, covered in ketchup and ice melt salt to simulate the blood and broken glass.

The twins loved their sequel, but agreed it wasn't nearly as much fun as *Dorkter Barfolopew Has A Crushing Defeat Part 1*.

Pretending was hellahella funfun.

But nothing beat murderdeath for real.

PRESENT

JACK

Something jabbed me in the side, and I swung my head around and noticed Waddlebutt, standing next to me in the bathroom. On my knees, he was about even with my waist.

I spat, put my hand on the pedal to flush the toilet, and as my vomit swirled away the penguin pecked me again.

"What?" I gave the bird my full attention. "You trying to cheer me up?"

He pecked again, this time grabbing my sweater button in his beak.

It wasn't sympathy. It was robbery.

Waddlebutt managed to yank the button free, then waddled away to add it to his nest. I placed my hands on the toilet to stand up, hit a button, and got squirted in the face.

Harry's bidet.

The thought was gross, but my stomach had emptied two dry heaves ago. I managed to make it to my feet, turned on the sink faucet, and splashed some water on my face.

I avoided the mirror. I didn't want to see my face, because I'd just want to punch it.

"Herb... I'm sorry. I'm so, so sorry. I'm going to find you. I swear it. I will find you."

My vow sounded as hollow as I felt.

We were on the road again, having just blown through Nashville. I checked my phone GPS and saw we were nearing the

Kentucky border. It was about ten to seven, but I needed to hear my husband's voice, so I called Phin earlier than promised.

"Hey," I said.

"Hey."

I couldn't glean anything from his tone. Was he still angry? Did he hate me?

Of course he hates you. You're the worst person to ever live.

"How's Bud? Can I talk to her?"

"She's sleeping."

I closed my eyes. I wanted so much for Phin to be there, holding me tight as I sobbed into his shoulder. That was impossible. It was also stupid. Look what happened to Herb because of me. I needed to keep Phin as far away as possible.

Instead, I would have settled for a kind word. Anything. A half-hearted *I love you*. A mumble that he understood.

But I didn't deserve even that.

So I did what any deservedly self-loathing jerk would do. I picked a fight.

"If you can't trust me enough to support me, Phin, then maybe we shouldn't be together."

"Is that how you feel?"

"I should be able to tell you I'm doing something, and have you back me up."

"I can't back you up, Jack, because I don't know where you are or what you're doing."

His tone was even and neutral, so I knew I was getting to him.

"You don't trust me."

"You're baiting me. What's wrong?"

What's wrong? I was just watching my best friend, the one I left for dead, get tortured live on darknet. And I can't tell you about it because your body and mind are still damaged from the last time you went all white knight and tried to save me.

So instead I told him, "The problem is you don't respect me."

"Of course I respect you. And I love you."

Crap. Giving me what I needed was fighting dirty. I changed tactics.

"Maybe it's an age thing," I said.

"What is?"

"I'm ten years older. Wiser. Know things you don't know. Maybe you'll never know them. Maybe waiting for you to catch up to my emotional level is a fool's game."

"Are you even listening to yourself?"

I was not. But my words made me feel worse, so I knew I was onto something.

"If I asked you to do something for me, no questions asked, would you do it?"

"Of course," Phin said.

"Then let this one go. Pretend I'm on vacation. Stop questioning me, stop judging me, just let me work this out."

Phin didn't answer. I braced for him to yell, because I was being a completely hypocritical, unfair, psychotic bitch.

"Fine," he said.

Fine? Since when did my drug abusing, criminal, hard ass husband get so pussy whipped?

And how was I supposed to keep the fight going when he was giving me what I said I wanted?

"I'll call you tomorrow," I said, feeling like I'd flushed my entire will to live down the toilet with my vomit.

"Jack... I love—"

I hung up on him.

Then I sobbed into my clenched fist and tried to find strength in the fact that I was a worse person than I thought.

HERB

He couldn't remember a time when he'd seen so many stars.

Growing up in Chicago, stars were in short supply. The city's own illumination, coupled with pollution, meant that astronomy was a hobby for those with telescopes. But kneeling outside on the ground, somewhere in the Great Plains, Herb could see millions of stars. They were so bright that Tequila's eyes shone like they had an internal light.

It was startling. And beautiful.

And the wrong time to run.

Herb was used to the bone-gnawing cold of Midwestern winters. The kind that got inside your jacket and tore at your bare skin underneath, had become so commonplace that Herb often forgot to wear a hat, even when the wind-chill was ten below.

Outside the land train, without a shirt or shoes, it felt ridiculously cold, even though it was probably no cooler than fifty-five degrees. Herb had gotten used to slowly broiling in the furnace of Mexico, and being half-naked, emaciated, exhausted, and in pain, made the cold all the worse. The winds cut like knives. The teeth that Herb was grateful to still have chattered together.

It was the wrong time to run.

There would be other chances.

When it was darker.

When it was warmer.

When they were closer to civilization, because as far as Herb could see, in all directions, there were no lights from towns or houses or even cars.

Wrong time to run.

"Fuck that," Herb said. "Let's do it."

Using the hand snippers he'd swiped from the Cowboy's vest and shoved down his pants during his Oscar-worthy screaming performance, Herb cut the wire on Tequila's chin, and then cut is own.

Pulling out the wire felt terrible, and at the same time felt amazing.

"Gimme the pliers," Tequila said.

Herb complied, and his friend picked up his kettlebell and walked over to the nearest slave. Herb heard him whisper, "Free yourself and pass it on," before handing the man the snips.

When Tequila returned, Herb wiped away a tear with a shaking hand. "I don't know what's wrong with me. I was so anxious to get away, I didn't think to help any of the others."

"Neither did I," said Tequila. "But the more people escaping, the harder it will be to catch us."

Good point.

Herb squinted at the plains around him. The ground was cold and hard, lots of rocks, not the best terrain for bare feet. Not much cover, either. Some bushes, and mountains in the far distance, but a whole lot of flat everywhere he looked.

"Where's the Cowboy?" Herb asked.

"In Car #4. There are still four cars to air out. Two minutes per car, we've got about an eight minute head start."

"Can you run?"

"Watch me."

Tequila hobbled ahead of Herb, into the cold, cold night, and Herb followed.

JACK

It was a little after three in the morning, and I was embracing insomnia like a long-lost love. Heckle and Jeckle were on pullout bunk beds in the living area. Or maybe they were sharing the same bunk bed. The privacy curtain was drawn, and I had no desire to check.

I was in Harry's bedroom, lying on top of the sheets because McGlade had joked about having quote *super herpes* once too often for it to be funny. We were still chugging along, because he'd taken a bunch of trucker stimulants that he'd picked up at a roadside gas station. Something in an obnoxious neon green bottle called *No Sleep 4-Ever!!!*

Yeah, it actually had three exclamation points. And a warning label longer than a chapter in a James Patterson novel. So while McGlade kept the hammer down, cruising at our top speed of 53mph, I stared out the window into the night, thinking about Herb and Tequila, and about the apology I owed my husband.

By the time four am crawled up on me slow as a frightened caterpillar, my eyes hurt so much from crying they felt like peach pits. I gave Rosalina a pat on her enormous head—she was sprawled across most of the bed like a lumpy, snoring bearskin rug—then got up in search of Visine.

Nothing in the bathroom medicine cabinet but stolen little bottles of hotel shampoo, so many condoms I wondered if Harry had stock in the company, and more trucker pills, these in an obnoxious bright orange bottle with the label WOKE AS FUCK!!! Three explanation points again. Maybe that was a thing.

I braved going through the curtain, expecting to see the twins spooning, but they were awake and on the Internet.

Snuff-X.

They looked at me like their mother just caught them with a Playboy mag, and I brushed off the mixture of shock and disgust and asked them if they'd seen any more of my friends.

"There was one viddy of that short guy," said Heckle.

"Tequila," said Jeckle.

I didn't want to know what was on the video. Which was why I asked.

"Cowboy dude has some sort of gun, shoots wires through their chins."

"Your buddy didn't even flinch. Tough mofo."

I clenched my jaw, nodded, considered asking them for Visine, decided not to because taking any sort of drug from those two seemed stupid as hell, and walked past them.

McGlade called the cab of the Crimebago Deux the *cockpit*, because he's a pig, and there was a door separating it from the rest of the RV. I didn't want to walk in on something gross, so I knocked first.

"If that's Waddlebutt, I'm out of pebbles," Harry said.

"It's me."

"Where's the penguin?"

I glanced back at Heckle and Jeckle, and they pointed to the fridge.

"He's cooling off. Do you have any eye drops?"

"Jackie, I'm on a cross country road trip. I've got enough eye drops to lubricate a giant squid."

I didn't get it.

"I don't get it," I said.

"They have eyes the size of dinner plates."

"Can I borrow the eye drops?"

"Biggest eyes in the animal kingdom. I thought everyone knew that."

I'd run out of patience for Harry back in Murfreesboro. "McGlade..."

"Yeah, you can have some. Give me a second to put my pants back on."

I waited.

"I was kidding, Jackie. Yeah, come in."

I opened the door and came in. There was an... odor. And to make things even more disturbing, Harry was driving in his underwear. His boxer shorts had Spider-man on them.

"You said you were kidding."

"I was. About putting my pants back on. If I try that while driving, it could kill us all."

"Eye drops?"

"Glove compartment."

I sat in the passenger seat and opened up a glove compartment the size of my kitchen closet.

"Put your seatbelt on when riding shotgun," McGlade said.

Rather than argue I was only going to be a few minutes, I clicked it on. That's when I noticed the jug of liquid on the floor next to Harry.

Pale, yellowish liquid.

"Don't tell me that's urine," I said.

"Fair enough. I won't."

"You're disgusting."

"Kidding. It's iced tea. Want some?"

"Pass."

I continued to hunt for eye drops. I found a large first aid kit, some reflective Mylar emergency blankets, a flashlight, some baby powder—

"Gimme the baby powder," Harry said.

—an expired energy bar, more condoms, a stick of deodorant, a pair of socks—

"And the socks," Harry said. "My tootsies are freezing."

—and some warranty papers. No Visine.

I handed over the socks and baby powder.

"I thought you said there were eye drops in the glove compartment."

"Nope. I just said *glove compartment*."

"Where are the eye drops?"

He pointed to the dashboard, at the bottle of eye drops. I wouldn't say it was giant squid-sized, but it was a pretty large bottle.

I squirted some in each eye, and after a few seconds of stinging I felt better.

"So here we are," Harry said. "Once again."

I didn't reply.

"Harry and Jack, off on another adventure."

I closed my eyes, staying silent.

"On the road. Confronting evil. Saving the world. Just like old times."

I thought about Phin. Thought about what a jerk I was. Wondered if four in the morning was too early to call and apologize.

"You still going to be in this self-loathing funk when the heavy shit comes down?" Harry asked.

That got me to respond. "What heavy shit? When we find them, we'll call the police."

"That's the plan. Sure. But how often do plans go our way?"

"This one *will* go our way."

"Right. That's why you brought Phin with. Because there will be absolutely no danger at all."

"We're going to let the police handle this, McGlade."

"Of course we are. But that doesn't mean there won't be any risk. There's always risk. Don't you get that? After doing this shit for three-fifths of your life? Admit it, Jack. There's risk."

"What do you want me to say, McGlade? That I'm some kind of thrill seeker, getting off on chasing psychopaths?"

"No. I want you to say that we've chosen professions where a lot of things can go wrong. And do go wrong. Right?"

"Sure. Whatever."

"I know it. You know it. And you know who else knows it?" Harry glanced at me. "Herb and Tequila."

I felt my eyes start to burn again.

"It isn't your fault, Jackie. They chose this profession. Same as us."

"It's not the same. They did it for me."

"They knew the risks. Stop blaming yourself."

"I left them there."

"*We* left them there. For dead. Because we thought they were dead. And we had to get out of there before we were dead, too. And if circumstances had been different, they would have left us there. But now that we know better, we're going to make it right. Except we can't make it right if you're being a drama queen, focusing on your feelings instead of the task at hand."

I didn't reply. Mostly because I hated it when Harry was right. Happily, it didn't happen very often.

"I need more caffeine," he said, reaching for his bright yellow bottle. "Can you get me a water from the pantry?"

"How about your iced tea?"

I picked up the bottle, and noted how warm it was just as Harry gave me a look that said *of course that isn't iced tea don't be an idiot.*

I dropped the bottle. "Yuck, McGlade."

"Don't judge."

"What am I supposed to do? Be proud of you? You want an *atta boy* for pissing in a bottle?"

McGlade turned unusually solemn. "Before my last livestream, while you were walking Rosalina, Heckle and Jeckle showed me the footage. Of Herb. I'm not stopping for anything until we get him. Including stopping to take a piss."

He looked as serious as McGlade was able to look.

"That's... actually a pretty good reason."

"I thought so. Until I did it." He shrugged. "Big mistake."

"Not the urinary experience you were hoping for?"

"It was awful. Why do you think I'm in my underwear?"

"Because you're a weirdo pervert."

"True. But pissing in a bottle with one good hand while driving isn't easy. Jack…" Harry's wince made him look like a gargoyle. "…it got everywhere. My pants. The steering wheel. The dashboard. The windshield. And the trucker pills didn't help any. It was like a dropped firehose, spraying out of control."

That was an image I didn't need in my head.

"That's an image I don't need in my head."

"And I didn't need it all over my pants. See how much is in that bottle? That's not even a third of it."

There was a whole lot of pee in that bottle.

While this was a perfect time to heap on the criticism, I felt an unusual streak of empathy for the man.

"Want me to drive for a bit, while you clean up?"

"Thanks, Jackie. I really appreciate it."

"No problem."

"Grab a towel. My seat is still soaked."

"Pass," I said.

"Can you pull off my damp socks?"

"No." I stood up.

"Help me put some baby powder on?"

"Sure, Harry. That's what friends are for."

"Really?"

"No, not really. Even you're not that stupid."

"My thighs are chafing," he whined. "I think I gave myself diaper rash."

"See you later, Harry."

"At least bring me my water."

I didn't bring his water.

After passing the browsing Brothers McCreepy, I climbed back onto the bed, laid on my back, and spent a full minute staring at my cell phone.

"Screw it," I whispered. "I'm telling him that I love him and I'm sorry."

I dialed Phin.

Phin didn't pick up.

THE COWBOY

They're gone.

Over a dozen volunteers that Yuri insisted on airing out are no longer standing next to the LeTourneau.

As the Cowboy stares out over the dark, vast plains, the immediate reaction is surprise. There have been many escape attempts in the past, and one mass escape, but they'd been quickly resolved. A man can't get far lugging a thirty-five pound weight, especially barefoot over rocky terrain. The tracking and rounding up had been simple, even somewhat enjoyable. But the pulling teeth had been like...well...pulling teeth. Even sharing some of the workload with their crazy driver, Dmitri, it had taken over five hours to properly discipline the workers. The Cowboy's shooting arm had been sore for days.

So after the momentary shock, the Cowboy descends into full-blown annoyance. They'll have to organize teams, break out the GPS equipment, unload the all-terrain vehicles—

"Oh...shit."

The tactical flashlight the Cowboy is using focuses on a kettlebell, resting in the dirt, the wire cut.

Then another.

And another.

The realization comes like a slap.

The GPS trackers are in the kettlebells.

The anger envelops the Cowboy like an old cartoon, a red thermometer line rising from toes to head until it feels like steam is about to come whistling out of the ears. The Cowboy's hand goes for the gun on reflex, draws, and almost shoots into the night when something more powerful than rage takes over.

Doubt.

Yuri is going to be furious.

The Cowboy isn't afraid of the Belarusian. With proper planning, and the element of surprise, killing everyone on the LeTourneau, Yuri included, would be as easy as winning the Saloon Shootout in Gunslinger Showdown. It might even be fun.

But there would be consequences. Yuri has mob ties. Former KGB. Bratva. The Cowboy needs to acquire the land train free and clear, not through devious means, or else spend the next decade worrying about being hunted down by some very scary folks.

Making the white Russian happy is the key to Usher House 2.0. That means no shooting into the plains. That would scare the volunteers, make them run faster, make them harder to catch. Or it might even kill one, and with Yuri so close to his deadline, the loss of a slave would delay things even more.

The Cowboy holsters the Ruger, then hurries to Car #1 to inform Dmitri of the escape.

This is just a minor setback.

It has to be.

As good as the Cowboy is, taking on the Russian mob would be one of the ugliest forms of suicide imaginable.

And the Cowboy needs to live for a long, long time.

HERB

He had no idea how many days had passed since that fateful shootout in Baja. It seemed like a lifetime ago. A lifetime filled with pain, fear, suffering, despair, and painful, debilitating hope.

But running through the cold desert, the wind chilling him like an ice bath, the stones and twigs underfoot pinching and stabbing, the days and weeks and months of injury and sickness and malnutrition, Herb had never felt more alive.

Herb's grandfather, a child of the Great Depression, had often told Herb that to fully understand the value of a bowl of soup, go a week without any food.

Herb had grown up in the US of A. Home of the free.

But he hadn't truly understood the value of freedom until that very moment.

It was a high like no other.

Herb turned, to check on Tequila, who was laboring a few steps behind. He waited for his friend to catch up, and strained to see the land train lights behind them.

How far had they gone? A kilometer? Two?

The mountains were still impossibly far away. The plains stretched out forever in all directions. No roads. No fences. No farms. No woods. Just dirt and rocks, grass and scrub brush, the trees so few and far between that they would provide zero cover come daylight.

Tequila caught up, and Herb clapped his bare shoulder, surprised by how cold his skin was.

"You okay?"

Tequila was shivering. "Going to need shelter soon. Exposure. Can't keep my core temp up."

"What can we do?"

"I'll build a shelter out of rocks and grass. We can rest and warm up, and it will hide us."

"You can do that?"

Tequila made a strange coughing sound. It took a few seconds for Herb to realize his friend was laughing.

"Sure, start gathering pebbles while I weave us a roof."

"Funny. Real funny."

"Sorry. Delirious. Not thinking straight."

"Want me to... hug you?" Herb asked.

"You want to bond? Now?"

"I saw it in a movie. Skin-to-skin contact could warm you up."

"You're just as cold as I am. That would be like putting ice on ice."

Herb looked out over the plains. "So what do we do?"

"We run until we find shelter," Tequila said. "Or until we drop."

It was as good an idea as any.

They ran another forty paces.

And then Tequila dropped.

THE MAN

Logging on, he checks Jack's phone.
She's stopped. In Nebraska.
If he drives fast, he can be in Omaha in under ten hours.
He wonders if he should wait. Watch to see if she keeps moving west.
After a few seconds of pondering, he grabs his bag, his guns, and heads for the car.
Waiting was never his strong suit.
In the car, he smiles, thinking of Jack's reaction when he shows up.
She'll be very surprised.
And she's not going to like it.

YURI

Dmitri came on over the intercom. "There has been an escape."

"Is the Cowboy handling it?" Yuri replied.

"He needs help."

"Help to catch a single runaway?"

"There was more than one."

"How many?"

Dmitri paused, then said, "Fifteen."

The words were like daggers piercing Yuri's temples, twisting in his brain.

"Fifteen," he repeated, keeping tenuous control over his emotions.

"Da."

"So track them."

"They cut their wires somehow. Trackers were in their weights."

Unbelievable. Unacceptable.

If Yuri had been in Belarus and something like this happened, the Cowboy would have been executed for incompetence.

"How about radar?" Yuri said.

"I've got the wave set for a square meter. We're getting hits, but the targets are moving surprisingly fast."

"Are the rest of the volunteers secure?"

"Da. Yes."

Yuri clenched and unclenched his enormous hands. Hands that were strong enough to crush a soup can.

But he felt helpless.

This shouldn't be happening. Not now. Not when they were so close to the delivery date.

"Where is the Cowboy?"

"The Punishment Room. Interrogating one of the volunteers."

"Wake up the whole crew. Stay on the radar, give them directions. I want every last prisoner found and returned."

"Da."

Yuri stood up and exited the train car, climbing down the ladder and stepping out into the night. It was cold, which was good; men exhaust quickly in cold weather. He took a moment to curse himself for being too lenient on the workforce. If they had enough strength to run off, they should have been pushed to harvest faster. But the self-flagellation quickly passed, and his wrath centered on the Cowboy.

Yuri was supposed to sell the LeTourneau to the Cowboy when the quota was reached. And Yuri was relying on that money.

But if Yuri's fear enforcer did anything to delay the deadline...

Suffice it to say that the Cowboy wouldn't be pleased with Yuri's response.

Yuri took a moment to cool down, then climbed into Car #12.

As expected, the Punishment Room was occupied. A volunteer, his chin wire still in place, was strung up by his wrists, doing the cattle prod dance as the Cowboy zapped him.

"Stop," Yuri ordered.

The Cowboy stared at him.

"You're asking him how everyone escaped?"

A nod.

"Was he one of those who escaped?"

A slight head shake.

Yuri chose his next words carefully, balancing the rage he felt with the very real fear that the Cowboy could shoot out his heart in a fraction of a second. "If he knew how everyone escaped, wouldn't he be out there with them, running away?"

The Cowboy said nothing.

"Go," Yuri held out his open palm. "Find them all."

The Cowboy hesitated, then handed Yuri the prod and left the car.

Yuri made a huge fist—

—and hit the wall, putting a dent in the metal. He stared at the blood, sprouting out of splits in his knuckles, and then tucked the prod under his armpit and patted down his jacket, locating his pipe.

Smoking during work hours was unwise. Yuri tried to keep his opium habit restricted to the early morning hours, to help with the nightmares. But this unfortunate setback was a reasonable excuse.

He took a puff. Then another.

Calm settled over him like a blanket, tucked in by a loving mother that Yuri had always imagined, but never known.

He regarded the prisoner. Terrified. Half-starved. In obvious pain.

"I have been where you are, comrade," Yuri said, placing his large hand on the man's head. "Sometimes we are the spider. Sometimes the fly. It is always better to be the spider. But…I was the fly once. The things they did to me." Yuri wiggled the cattle prod and snorted. "This is like a child's toy, compared to what they did. Would you like to know how I got away?"

The wide-eyed man stared blankly.

"After weeks of unspeakable torture, I was able to bribe one of my captors. My entire life savings. Every ruble I ever stole while working on the death squad. Over one and a half million rubles. Seven hundred thousand, in American dollars. That pig took it all, in exchange for letting me escape."

Another puff.

"I will confide in you, my friend. When I had money, I lived well. Three apartments, a woman kept in each one. Cars. The latest electronics. I had the huge, flat screen television, larger than the President's, and every Pixar movie on the Blu Ray Discs. *A Bug's Life,* you know this movie? Wonderful American computer-generated comedy movie. I confess, I always sympathized with the grasshoppers."

The captive appeared confused.

"I shall get to the point. I was the fly, trapped in the spider's web. I bribed the spider. That is how I got away. So I ask you; do you have seven hundred thousand dollars?"

The man just stared.

"There is no shame in poverty. I was poor once. But without any money to bribe me, you must remain the fly." Yuri shrugged. "It is the natural order of things. No man rises to the top alone. You must trample upon others, climb over their corpses, and kill anyone who tries to tread upon you."

"Mi llamo Pedro," the man said.

The man hadn't understood a single thing Yuri had said.

Yuri punched him in the stomach for wasting his time, then left the car and headed to the driver's cabin to assist Dmitri with the search effort.

THE COWBOY

With Yuri and Dmitri staying on the LeTourneau, that leaves seven men, plus the Cowboy, to catch the fifteen escapees.

With the exception of the Cowboy, nobody openly carries a gun. It's a rule Yuri insists on to make sure that no slave ever gets hold of a firearm. Yuri does have guns, in a heavy duty lockbox with a combination (can't steal keys to a combination lock), but they aren't normally needed for apprehension.

Instead, hunting down prisoners uses a decidedly *Planet of the Apes* approach, with a modern twist. The guards wield nets and animal control catch poles with wire loops on the ends, tasers in the tips. Rather than horses, they ride ATVs.

After passing out earpieces and doing a quick radio check, the Cowboy climbs on a quad vehicle behind Leonid, a short, thick man who bears a slight resemblance to Herb Benedict's companion. The one the Cowboy shared an intimate moment with, in the Punishment Room.

The one who outshot the Cowboy using only a derringer.

That derringer man is intriguing. His background is no doubt military, probably elite spec ops; Green Berets, Rangers, Delta Force. Perhaps a SEAL. He's short, the right height for submarine duty.

But there's something more to him, other than his obvious skills. That man has secrets. A dark, mysterious past. Beneath the hard shell, the Cowboy senses a deep, permeating sadness.

The Cowboy wants to know more. And the best way to learn about a man is to hurt him until he breaks.

The idea is arousing.

The Cowboy is mostly asexual, due to a combination of past history, unfortunate circumstance, and certain physical issues. But the hormones still occasionally churn, and the Cowboy has the ways and means to take care of those needs while at home.

For this, and other reasons, there have never been any sexual improprieties at work. There are whole swathes of Snuff-X that focus on rape and genital torture, and certainly that will be a part of Usher House 2.0 when it is up and streaming. But the Cowboy never mixes the high of causing pain with the thrill of orgasmic pleasure.

That is, until meeting the derringer man.

And now, the derringer man is missing.

And the Cowboy doesn't even know his name.

Riding bitch on the ATV seat, holding Leonid's stocky torso tight, the Cowboy orders the team to move out.

"Nearest target, three hundred ten meters north northwest," Dmitri says over the headphones.

"We want to start with the farthest targets," the Cowboy tells him. "If we begin with the closest, the others could get out of range."

"Da. Yes. Farthest is...two point two kilometers southwest."

The Cowboy gives Leonid a squeeze. "We'll take that. The rest of you, divvy up the next three."

Leonid hits the gas.

The night is cool and bright. A waning gibbous moon, the centerpiece of a rhinestone patchwork of stars, makes it possible to see for several meters even without the headlamp. As they near the fleeing prisoner, Dmitri micromanages their approach (north, now east a bit, more north, twenty meters ahead), and then they see the man, running ahead, staring back over his shoulder with crazed, wide eyes.

It isn't the derringer man.

Leonid races alongside, then cuts him off, and when the prisoner gobbles the ground the Cowboy dismounts with the catch pole in hand. After two feints, the Cowboy loops the wire over his head, cinches it, and gives him a taser jolt. As the volunteer flops around, Leonid walks over and applies some zip cuffs, and then the Cowboy attaches the swivel on the catch pole's handle to the bracket on the back of the ATV. As the vehicle begins to move, the prisoner is forced to stand up and follow, or else be dragged by his neck and strangled.

It will take at least twenty minutes to return the man to the land train, so the Cowboy radios Dmitri to see if there is anyone else close.

"Two targets. Stationary. Five hundred ten meters west of you."

Is it the derringer man? The Cowboy wonders.

Please let it be the derringer man.

The Cowboy takes the extra catch pole, two pairs of zip cuffs, and the casting net, and sets off on an easy jog.

The easy jog quickly becomes labored. The Cowboy's stamina isn't what it used to be, and crocodile boots, while undeniably cool, aren't the best footwear for chasing prisoners through the plains in the dark. When combined with the constant pain that all the Tramadol in the world can't ever fully mask, the pursuit becomes agonizing.

But the Cowboy doesn't slow down.

Agony and the Cowboy go way back.

"One hundred meters, northwest."

The Cowboy shines the flashlight at a compass—an old-fashioned compass with an actual magnet, rather than a phone app—and adjusts direction.

"Forty meters. Targets still stationary."

The Cowboy kills the flashlight, and the painful jog becomes a walk, the focus on keeping quiet.

Before seeing anyone, the Cowboy hears whispers.

Extending the catch pole, hoping it is the Americans, the Cowboy creeps forward, slowly, silently, controlling every breath, controlling every movement, part of the night, part of the wind, closer and closer and—

Spanish. They're speaking Spanish.

"No te muevas," the Cowboy says.

The men do not move.

Which makes it stupidly easy to shoot them each in the head.

Two more notches for the gun belt. But these two aren't the two the Cowboy wants.

The Cowboy wants the Americans.

Wants the derringer man.

Switching the radio back on, the Cowboy tells Dmitri, "Two attacked me. I had to put them down."

"Two volunteers down?" Yuri has been listening in. "We had better hit our production quota."

Recently, the white Russian has been becoming more paranoid. Less in control.

"We'll hit it, Yuri. Who's closest?"

Dmitri answers, "Six hundred ten meters, west southwest."

"Has anyone found the two Americans yet?"

"Nyet."

The Cowboy feels a buzzing. A text message.

TOMORROW LUNCHTIME.

That's soon. Maybe too soon.

The Cowboy once again resumes jogging.

It hurts.

But pain can be compartmentalized. Managed. And unlike Yuri, who tries to mask his memories with opium, the Cowboy deals with the PTSD in a much healthier way. Prescription drugs can take the edge off the pain, aid in sleep, lower blood pressure, and relax the muscles. But there is only one true way to combat the memories of being hurt.

Forming new memories, of hurting others.

It's a rather obvious, tawdry vicious cycle. The abused becomes the abuser.

But it works ridiculously well.

The one surefire way to vanquish all of the horrors endured in Usher House, is to create Usher House 2.0.

It's not revenge. It's therapy.

So the Cowboy presses onward. With the other creatures of the night.

Hunting prey.

JACK

In the dream, Phin was taking Sam and leaving me. For good.

"Stick to chasing psychos," Phin told me. "You care about that more than us."

"Don't leave," I begged. "You'll destroy me."

"You're destroying yourself, Jack. You want to drag us down, too? We're better off without you."

And then they left, walked off without looking back, and I didn't chase after them. Because Phin was right. I kept making the same mistakes over and over, and I didn't learn from them, and when I tried to change it was always half-assed because something always came up that put me back in the line of fire.

After they left, I started bingeing on bread. Phin's delicious baked bread. And I got fatter and fatter and finally so impossibly huge that I'm all of a sudden an elephant and the main attraction at a circus. Criminals from my past, horrible people who had done horrible things, are pointing at me and laughing and throwing things and I just stood there, fat and humiliated, and I don't do anything. And my husband and daughter were in the crowd, and Sam said, "Daddy, is that Mommy?"

And Phin said, "No, Mommy is right here."

And standing next to Sam, with her hand on Sam's head, is...

Pasha. A woman Phin used to date.

Used to love.

Younger. Prettier. Smarter. Kinder. More affectionate. And no doubt a much better lover than I am.

She deserved him. And Sam.

I deserved to die alone while the world laughed at me.

And then some long dead, leering psychopath from my past spat in my face.

Alex Kork.

"Did you really think I was gone, Jack? You'll never be rid of me."

She laughed, and I'm covered in her warm, slimy phlegm, and I finally opened my eyes to see Rosalina licking my face.

Sleep-groggy, still disoriented and confused, I realized we were no longer moving.

What a shitty night.

All evening I'd been restless, unable to get comfortable, unable to shut my mind off, and whenever REM came it had been some variation of Phin leaving/Me binge eating/Shit I'm an elephant/Alex Kork is still alive/Phin's cheating. In one of the permutations, I actually watched him make love to the impossibly beautiful Pasha, and he was staring at me the whole time saying, "This should be you."

Worst. Nightmare. Ever. If I believed Freud was anything more than a penile-centric misogynist in deep romantic love with his mother, I would have wondered if my subconscious was trying to tell me something.

I sat up in Harry's bed.

Checked my phone.

Phin hadn't returned my call. And why would he? I hadn't left any message.

Checked the time.

It was almost noon.

Checked the GPS.

We were in Nebraska.

I redialed Phin.

He didn't pick up. This time I left a voicemail message, asking if Sam was okay, telling him to call me. I should have also said, "I love you", but I didn't. I didn't, because in my dream he left me and cheated on me.

How much sense did that make? How could I be mad?

Seriously, I was an awful spouse.

After half a second of hesitation, I decided that if I checked on him it would be out of genuine concern, not jealous paranoia. So I accessed Find My iPhone and tried to locate him.

I couldn't. His cell was turned off. According to the app, he'd turned it off hours ago.

There were a dozen legitimate reasons why that could be the case. Maybe it ran out of juice. Or it broke. Got lost. Got stolen. He left it in the car. Sam was playing with it. Duffy ate it. The red ants in the back yard took it deep into their lair to give to their queen, and there is no signal in Ant World.

Or maybe Phin was angry.

Or maybe Phin actually was cheating.

I tried to think like the rational detective that I once was, rather than the shitty wife I'd been since Baja. And I had been shitty. So focused on moving, setting up the new house, my new job, getting Sam situated. Phin and I hadn't had sex more than a handful of times in the past six months.

Shit. I couldn't even remember the last time I blew him.

What had happened to us?

The question was rhetorical. I knew what the problem was.

My macho, bad ass husband had gotten seriously hurt. Trying to help me.

He'd been broken in Mexico.

And instead of helping to fix him, working to restore his confidence, I treated him like a fragile porcelain doll. Because seeing him damaged was a constant reminder of what a terrible person I was, and how it was all my fault.

And now here I was, making things worse. Once again hurting the people I cared about.

But that was bad-partner thinking, not good-detective thinking. A good detective focused on solutions, not placing blame.

We didn't have a land line at the house. I could call my mother. She lived in a retirement community near us. I could ask her to swing by, make sure things were okay. But a call to Mom would mean telling her where I was, and that would be yet another person I loved that I had to lie to.

But there were other ways to trace phones.

From the other room came the yap-yap of McGlade in full patter mode. Must have been streaming again. I caught a few random words and sentences.

"Closing in on the Cowboy…

"Meeting the Sheriff…

"Best friend, Herb Benedict…

"Graphic nature will definitely repulse younger or more sensitive viewers…"

Was McGlade actually going to show the footage of Herb having a tooth yanked out?

Then I heard Herb's screams, and had my answer.

Any groggy self-loathing and jealousy I felt was cast away by a wave of anger. Then my anger was tempered by reality. As much as I wanted to give McGlade a lecture, I didn't want to do it on a live webcast. Heckle and Jeckle might have promised to hide my face and disguise my voice, but I guessed that required some technical set-up and couldn't be guaranteed to work on the fly.

So I kept quiet and hidden in the bedroom, until I heard Harry do his closing.

"…our next episode of Private Dick Live and Streaming In Your Face. I'm Harry McGlade. Keep your lights on and your doors locked."

I exited the bedroom, ready to raise hell.

"Hiya, Jackie. You missed an epic webisode. What's our views at?"

Heckle checked his laptop. "Two point six million."

Harry whistled. "That'll pay a few bills. How are the t-shirt sales going?"

Jeckle checked his laptop. "Eighteen."

"Eighteen? That's it? J-Dawg, wouldn't you buy a shirt that says *Get Streamed In The Face*? They're only forty bucks each."

I stared at him, crossing my arms over my chest.

"How about a thong? Assuming you were younger and slimmer. How many thongs have we sold?"

"One," said Jeckle.

McGlade made a face. "Only one? Is that the one I bought?"

Jeckle nodded.

"How many baby jumpers?"

"Zero the Hero," said Heckle.

"Zilch? What about the mugs that say *I Wake Up To A Private Dick Streaming In My Coffee*?"

"Attila the None," said Jeckle.

Harry rubbed his stubble. "Maybe we need to rethink our merch selection. Broaden our horizons. How about one-of-a-kind stuff? I know a rock star who paints. He's good. Sells art like crazy. J-Dawg, would you buy an original Harry McGlade painting of me, streaming all over your face?"

"You aired that footage of Herb," I stated.

McGlade nodded. "Gotta show the stakes. Viewers need to see the asshole we're taking down."

I moved toward him, in what must have been a menacing way, because Harry's eyes went wide and he leaned back in his chair to get some distance.

"We're not taking the Cowboy down. The authorities are taking the Cowboy down."

"Right. Sure. That's what I meant. But we still need to show the conflict here."

"You're exploiting our friend's pain."

"Exploiting? No way. Herb is going to be a national hero. And by taking the footage off of darknet, we're preserving the evidence.

Now when we—uh, the authorities—arrest the Cowboy, we've got an automatic conviction."

He had a point.

"Can you unclench your fists, J-Dawg? You're scaring Waddlebutt."

I was unaware my fists were clenched. And Waddlebutt didn't look scared. He looked defiant, sitting on his pile of rocks, daring someone to snatch one. Last night, when he'd retreated to his lair in the fridge, Rosalina had eaten Waddlebutt's second nest, the one made of dog treats. Since then, the penguin had been in a mean mood.

Harry stood up. Thankfully, he was wearing pants. A poofy white cloud briefly orbited his pelvis, and I caught the scent of baby powder.

"I'm assuming you have a plan to find the Cowboy," I said. I didn't actually assume this, but Harry had to have some sort of plan. Didn't he?

"We're meeting a dude today. County Sheriff. His sister escaped from the Cowboy. He's been tracking him for years."

"Name?"

"Wyatt Steinhoffer. Middle name is Earp."

"Wyatt Earp?" I got an involuntary, but not unwelcome, image in my head of Kurt Russell.

"Sister's name is Annie Oakley. Parents apparently had a wild west fixation."

"You research these people?"

"Nothing beyond Google. I got the twins on it. You guys turn up any nuggets?"

They both looked up from their laptops in unison, and I got *The Shining* vibes.

"Wyatt Earp is a forty-seven-year-old white male, single, born in San Diego. Currently the Sheriff of Pastor County, the least populated county in Nebraska," said Jeckle.

"Population three hundred and two," said Heckle.

"First elected Sheriff eight years ago," said Jeckle. "Ran unopposed. Was a deputy under the previous Sheriff, who went missing."

"Military record?" I asked.

"No. Nothing in the NCIC database, either," said Heckle.

"Has a balance of $342.31 on his Amex Platinum card," said Jeckle. "Bill from a local mechanic."

"And the sister?"

"Lives with her brother in Ergo, Nebraska. Homestead on a few hundred acres. Not married, no kids. Can't find any evidence of a current job, but Google Earth shows horses, cattle. She was some kind of rodeo star when she was a teenager."

"Anything about her encounter with the Cowboy?"

"Nothing," said Jeckle. "Did a news search, but a lot of smaller papers haven't gone digital yet."

"Did you run the Cowboy through NCIC?"

A double nod. Heckle said, "No concrete hits."

"How about Vicky?" I asked McGlade.

While the National Criminal Information Center was the federal government's attempt at a database for criminals and criminal activity, ViCAT, or the Violent Criminal Apprehension Team, focused on multiple murders. Like NCIC, the information uploaded by state and local cops was voluntary rather than mandatory, so a whole lot of bad things went unreported on a national level. That's why a violent offender could kill someone in Kentucky, and then get picked up in California for assault without there being an automatic link to his out-of-state warrant.

Welcome to the dysfunctional world of law enforcement.

Back when I was still working Homicide, the Feebies had a database they called Vicky, short for the ViCAT computer. Vicky also used her awesome computing power to do some rudimentary suspect profiling. Back then, Vicky's CPU was on par with the chip in my current refrigerator, which sends me a text when we're low on milk. You'd think an appliance like that would be a lifesaver, but we've wound up throwing away four gallons of milk because the fridge is consistently wrong. I've actually begun to wonder if the fridge is doing it intentionally. Taking kickbacks from the dairy industry. Or maybe there's a camera in there, and I'm unwittingly the star of some hilarious Japanese prank show.

My point being, back in those days, Vicky was an idiot.

Maybe's she'd improved since then.

"Vicky did a profile," Harry said. He held up a piece of paper and began to read. "Pegged the Cowboy as organized, thirty-five to fifty, wealthy, narcissistic personality disorder, overly competitive and/or a gambling problem, paranoid, delusional, single."

That was all perfectly rational, and perfectly obvious.

"Is there more?" I asked.

"Suspect is drug addicted, possibly cocaine or meth amphetamine, suffering a chronic health issue possibly related to the addiction, bisexual and possibly incestuous, fixated with childhood things, like toys or television shows, collects stuffed animals, and..." Harry paused.

"And what?" I asked.

"And Vicky thinks the Cowboy has a prosthetic limb."

"That's you," I said. "The Feebies just profiled you as the Cowboy."

Harry shook his head and scowled. "That doesn't match me at all."

I began to tick off fingers. "Narcissistic personality disorder."

"Knowing I'm better than everyone else doesn't make me a narcissist."

"Competitive."

"I'm not competitive."

"You are."

"I'm not. Bet me."

"Collects stuffed animals."

"Those were an investment."

"Fifty years old, unmarried, bisexual—"

"I was only bisexual a couple of times. Fifteen at most. And I'm not drug addicted."

"I've been to your condo. You've got a grow room full of marijuana plants."

"Cool," said Heckle and Jeckle.

"That means I have a green thumb, not a drug problem. And the marijuana is strictly medicinal, to come down after I've snorted too much coke."

I held up another hand. "Paranoid."

"I'm one hundred percent absolutely not paranoid. Wait... does everyone think I'm paranoid?"

"Prosthetic limb."

"That's only one out of, like eight. And how about incestuous? I grew up an orphan, so it was impossible to have sex with a family member, no matter how much I wanted to."

I held up nine.

"That was a joke!" Harry insisted. Then he tried to look calm. "Seriously," he said in his serious voice. "I'm not a serial killer."

"Delusional," I said, holding up finger ten. "I'm out of fingers, and you've hit almost every single trait. The only thing Vicky missed was morbidly obese."

Harry shook his head. "Untrue."

"Does the profile say the killer has enough fat to make three more fat people?"

Heckle and Jeckle chuckled at that. Exactly three chuckles each.

"I'm a little overweight, not morbidly obese."

"You need a bra more than I do."

"I can't be the Cowboy," Harry insisted. "I was here when Herb was getting his tooth pulled out. That was a live stream. How could I be in two places at once?"

"Maybe you have a twin," said Heckle.

Jeckle nodded.

McGlade didn't appear to take the teasing well.

"I left out the most revealing trait," He held up the paper. "Vicky predicts the Cowboy is... wait for it... a female."

I made an *oh really* face. "Are you hiding something from us, Harry?"

"Want me to whip it out right here and prove it?"

"No, Louis CK, no one wants that."

McGlade crumbled up the paper and threw it on the floor, next to Waddlebutt.

The penguin viciously attacked the paper for getting too close to his pebbles.

"We need a different focus for our next webisode, because the FBI is full of shit."

Heckle raised his hand. "Private Dick McDude, we think that you should use that profile."

Jeckle nodded. "The conspiracy geeks will love it. Make yourself a suspect. The Internet will blow up with speculations. Great for pageviews."

McGlade mashed his lips together in thought, then reached for the thrown paper ball. Waddlebutt pecked him in the wrist, drawing blood.

"Do it in a slightly higher pitch," I suggested. "Give them something to talk about."

"You guys are all dicks," Harry said. But I could see the gears turning in his little Harry brain.

As much as the whole exchange really elevated my mood, the unhappies returned when I thought of Phin.

"Harry," I said, lowering my voice. "I actually need your help on something."

"Let me try to guess the fat joke. You took a picture of me but can't print it because there's not enough ink in the state."

"No."

"You're worried my gravity is affecting the tides."

"No."

"You killed someone with a hundred pound chocolate bar and want me to eat the evidence before the cops come."

"It's not a joke, Harry. This is something serious."

"So you don't have any chocolate?"

I hated asking McGlade for anything, but I didn't see any choice. "Can we talk?"

"Aren't we talking right now?"

I glanced at the twins. "In private?"

"Sure. I gotta walk Rosa." Rosalina's ears perked up. "Let's go."

We'd parked at a gas station; go figure because the Crimebago Deux needed gas every ten miles. When I stepped outside, the first thing I noticed was how empty Nebraska was. The day was clear, the sky was huge, and there were no significant land features on the grassy plains, in any direction, except for the gas station, with attached diner, and mountains so far in the distance they looked like a hanging painting.

Air was cool, clean, and smelled like country.

I felt entirely out of my element.

"What's up, Jackie? Tell me you were kidding and your pockets are laden with chocolate. Is that chocolate? Or your fupa?"

"My what?"

"Fupa. Fat upper pubic area."

Normally I ignore Harry's jokes-slash-insults, but the irony was too rich to pass up.

"My fupa? Really? You need both hands to lift your stomach so you can piss."

"I won't lie. That stings."

"Stings like the rash you got from pissing all over yourself?"

"Okay, hitting below the belt here."

"I heard sobbing this morning. Was that your toilet, screaming in pain when you sat down?"

"I think we can call you the winner for this round. Now let's stop the body shaming and pretend we're adults."

I considered giving him a lecture about decency, remembered the dozens of other lectures I'd given him that never stuck, and got back on topic.

"It's Phin."

"He's cheating," McGlade guessed. At least I hope it was a guess.

"Why do you—"

"Because he's a man, and you've been treating him like he's a kid with a peanut allergy who's running around naked at a peanut farm. Not my best analogy. Hey, do you have any peanuts?"

"No. How did—"

"I told you. Phin and I are bros. We talk all the time."

"No you don't."

"Okay, we don't. I drunk text him sometimes, and he ignores me. This is all guessing on my part, but you're confirming it as we speak. You do remember how to be a police officer, don't you, Jackie?"

Rosalina found a spot she liked and proceeded to make a Mount Everest sized deposit.

"We had a fight before I left. I told him he wasn't well enough to come along, and then lied about the reason I was going. Now he won't pick up when I call him."

"That's cruel."

"I know. He's not usually like this."

"Not him. You. What a shitty thing to do. I wouldn't be surprised if he's moving out right now."

"That's the thing. I don't want to be surprised by something like that."

"So what are you saying?"

"How do I track his phone?"

McGlade raised an eyebrow. "Seriously? Rather than try to work things out like adults, you want to secretly spy on him?"

"Yeah."

"No problem. He's got an iPhone?"

"Yeah."

"Got the Find My iPhone app turned on?"

"I did. He either turned it off, or he's keeping his phone off."

"You could activate Lost Mode. It'll show you where he is."

"Won't he know I'm doing that?"

Harry rubbed his chins. "Yeah. Does he use Google?"

"Doesn't everyone?"

"You can sign in as him and track his location history."

"That's actually a thing? Google is tracking us?"

"Stop being naïve. Everyone is tracking us." McGlade stared into the sky and waved. "Hello, spy satellites. Don't laser me."

"How do I do it?" I asked.

"Know his password?"

I nodded. "It's capital I...l-o-v-e...j-a-c-k."

"Ouch," Harry said. "I bet you feel like the world's biggest asshole right now."

"Can you help me?"

"Keep an eye on the dog and give me your cell."

"What if she wanders off?"

"Whistle. She'll come."

Harry took my phone in his robotic hand and began to press, pinch, and swipe.

Rosalina didn't wander off.

The enormous blue sky overhead seemed to get bigger. Or maybe I was shrinking.

"Found him," he eventually said.

"At home? In Florida?"

"Ehhhhh...not quite."

"Where is he?"

McGlade looked at me with pity. Pity from Harry was the worst.

"He's in Chicago," he said.

That didn't make any sense.

"You sure? Right now?"

"As of forty minutes ago."

"Where?"

"O'Hare."

The airport. Ouch.

"Any reason he'd be in Chicago?"

I could think of one. "Can I get a record of his calls?"

"I can pull up numbers. Not recordings. This is Apple, not the NSA. I can pull up his texts, though, if you back-up to iCloud."

I briefly considered the violation of my husband's privacy, weighed it against my own neuroses, and said, "Do it."

McGlade did more phone magic, then winced.

"Did you know he's been in touch with Pasha?" he asked.

I didn't answer. But I felt like I was falling down a deep, dark hole.

"I didn't know that."

"You remember her?"

"From years ago. The clinic in Flutesburg. They used to … date."

"Date? They had it hot and heavy for each other. Phin thought she was the one, until—"

"I know what happened," I interrupted. "What was the text?"

"Last message was from three hours ago. She wrote *C U soon*."

Ugh.

"Want me to read you more?"

I thought about it. Then shook my head. I had my secrets. Phin had his. If he'd wanted to share this with me, he would have.

"Maybe they're just having coffee," McGlade said.

I wasn't good at tuning into my feelings. All of my professional career, I hid them. From my co-workers. From the victims I tried to help, and the suspects I tried to interrogate. Burying my emotions, revealing nothing, gave me an edge.

The problem was, that feature was also a bug. I'd gotten so good at pretending to be in control that I was able fool myself.

If Phin was cheating, what did that mean? Did I deserve it? Was I willing to forgive? Did I still want him in my life?

I didn't know.

How pathetic was that? To not even know what you were feeling?

Rather than tune into it, I excused myself from McGlade and called my mother. My emotional well-being aside, I needed to know if Phin had taken our daughter with him.

Mom picked up on the second ring.

"Hi, honey. Bud and I were just thinking about you. She made you a lovely clay bowl. We're going to put it in the kiln in the activity room after lunch."

And there was my answer. "Can't wait to see it."

"It's so nice that you and Gil are having a romantic getaway. It's been too long."

A romantic getaway. That's the bullshit he told her when he dumped our kid at her place.

"Yeah. Gotta rekindle those sparks. You know how it is."

"Actually, I don't. I've got more boyfriends here than I know what to do with."

"Good for you."

"I just went to my first Viagra party."

"Viagra party," I repeated.

McGlade gave me a thumbs up.

Mom said, "They're all the rage at retirement homes."

"Is this something I need to know?"

"We all gather in the party room, and all the men take a pill, then pick their partner's names out of a hat."

"You're making this up."

"I'm not. Then, while we're all waiting for the pills to kick in, we pass around the bong."

"Of course you do."

"Have you had sex while high? It's delightful."

"And you're watching my daughter?"

"Viagra parties are only on Tuesdays and Fridays, honey. Depending on how long she stays, I suppose I can skip the next one."

"Aren't you being… I dunno… irresponsible?"

"I'm nearing eighty. What responsibilities do I have, exactly?"

"Good point."

"Can you get any cocaine? Mr. Singh in 302 wanted to score some cocaine."

"I'm not entirely comfortable having this conversation."

"He said if you put it on your peter, it stays hard longer."

"Cocaine on penis," I said.

"Makes you stay hard longer," confirmed McGlade.

"Is Bud there? Can I talk to her?"

"She's in the pool, paddling around. Want me to pull her out?"

Much as I wanted to hear my daughter's voice, I didn't want to take her away from pool time.

"Just tell her I love her."

"Is that all? You sound distracted."

I thought about saying more, but settled on, "That's all."

"Have fun with Gil. You two are such a cute couple. I'm glad you're getting some time alone. I was worried you guys were drifting apart. Bye-bye!"

She hung up.

"So..." Harry said, "Sam is with Mom."

"Yeah."

"That's good. It means Phin is going to come back. If he was planning on leaving you, he would have taken Sam with him."

"I guess."

"It's my cheat day, so I'm getting some peanut M&Ms. I got a craving for some reason. You want anything?"

"A gun," I said.

"To shoot Phin? Or yourself? Or the old guy with the coke on his dick whose nailing your mom at Viagra parties?"

I gave him a look.

"The volume on your phone is kinda high," Harry said.

"None of the above. I'm going to focus on the job."

"Good call. That's what I do. Bury my emotions until they start causing health problems. We can find something that goes bang when I get back. I've got all sorts of cool shit to shoot."

HERB

When he woke up, Herb thought he was still a prisoner.

Blessedly, he wasn't. Instead, he and Tequila were clutching each other in the middle of a field, freezing and half-dead from exposure.

Sure dodged a bullet there.

Herb was shivering, but his friend was still. A bad sign. He touched his neck, feeling for a pulse.

Slow. Much too slow.

"Hey, buddy. Can you hear me?"

Tequila's eyelids fluttered. "Hammmmaterma."

"I didn't catch that."

"Hammo…termia."

Hypothermia. "Right. We need to get you warm."

Herb went to stand up, but his joints felt frozen. He took a moment to stretch, squinting at the stunningly bright landscape surrounding him, and heard a bee buzzing.

No. Not a bee.

A motor.

Craning his neck in the direction of the sound, Herb sighted a four-wheeler coming toward them, trailing a plume of kicked-up dirt. He crouched down, hoping he hadn't been seen, but the ATV was beelining toward them.

Are they tracking us somehow?

That question could wait. Herb needed a plan. He looked around for something to defend himself with.

All he saw was grass, and gravel.

During their escape, they'd tripped over dozens of rocks. Large rocks, that would have made decent weapons.

"What do you think, buddy? Grass or gravel?"

Tequila didn't respond.

"Good call. Gravel it is."

Herb gathered up a handful of gravel, then hunkered down and waited for the guy to approach.

Maybe he's friendly. Maybe we're about to be rescued.

The guy turned out to be two guys, and the man behind the driver raised something up over his head.

A net.

So much for friendly.

They came up fast. Herb took five steps to the left, drawing them away from Tequila while also getting the morning sun behind him. The all-terrain vehicle adjusted its course, speeding up, and Herb thought back to every missed opportunity he'd ever had to improve his fighting skills.

"Which activity do you want to take?" Herb's mother asked a ten-year-old Herb. "Karate or baseball?"

"Baseball," Herb had said.

"Dude, self-defense classes at the YMCA," Herb's high school buddy told a sixteen-year-old Herb. "Or do you want to just sit here and watch TV?"

"Green Acres is on," Herb had said.

"You need to improve your hand-to-hand combat skills, as well as your shooting skills," Herb's police academy instructor told a twenty-four-year-old Herb. "What do you want to work on, recruit?"

"Shooting," Herb had said.

"I'm going to the dojang," Jack Daniels had told her partner Herb, dozens of times over the last twenty years. "Want to come with and learn some tae-kwon-do?"

"No thanks," Herb had said. "At this point in my life, why would I need it?"

And just as the flashback ended, the ATV was on him.

Herb whipped the gravel as hard as he could, catching the driver in the face, causing him to turn abruptly.

The ATV flipped, throwing the driver, and his partner, out of their seats and into the air.

A moment later they were cartwheeling across the ground, the ATV tumbling after them, catching up, and rolling over the net guy.

Herb scrambled after the driver, dropping onto his back with both knees, then reaching down and locking his fingers under the man's chin.

Without pausing to think, Herb heaved up with everything he had, and there was a sharp *CRACK!* as the man's head bent backward much further than anatomy intended it to.

Then something was being looped around Herb's neck, and he felt a jolt of electricity that was almost spiritual in the amount of agony it caused.

Herb flopped onto his side, flopped like a landed fish, every muscle spasming, and then it stopped and he saw the net guy standing over him, holding onto a long, metal pole, the wire at the end encircling Herb's head.

Herb looked to the side and yelled to Tequila, "Now!"

Tequila was lying there, passed out. But the net guy didn't know that, and when he turned to defend himself, Herb brought both arms down, hard, on the pole, knocking it from the man's grasp. In a clumsy but effective move, Herb managed to get onto his feet while tugging the loop off his neck, and when his attacker reached for him, Herb swung the pole like a bat and connected with the side of his head.

The guy went down, and Herb, still in adrenaline-surging fight-or-flight mode, dove on top of him, and performed the same move that he had on the first guy. Hands under the chin, quick yank back.

CRACK!

No further movement.

Herb waited for a few seconds, which might have actually been several minutes, shaking so hard he was worried he'd bite his tongue off.

Then there was a brief period of hysterical, out-of-control laughter, mixed with deep sobs, and when Herb's face was thoroughly covered with snot and tears he managed to get his shit together just enough to start stripping the men.

Getting the clothing off of a corpse was much tougher than Herb could have imagined. Even harder was dressing an unconscious Tequila in the man's gear.

Herb then did the same thing for himself, right down to the socks and underwear, which was disgusting but better than freezing to death, and by the time he was finished, he actually felt warm for the first time in hours.

Tequila, however, did not. His hands were frighteningly cold.

Herb walked to the overturned ATV, rocking it upright.

A wheel came off.

Herb found this hilarious, considered the very real fact that he might have gone insane, dismissed the thought because insane people probably wouldn't question their own sanity, then dismissed that thought as insane, then found the gas tank on the vehicle and twisted off the cap.

He spent ten minutes gathering grass, sticks, and flammable parts of the ATV wreckage, made a pile surrounded by gravel, turned the ATV over onto the pile, dumping out several gallons of gas, dragging the ATV away, and then...

Then... what?

He patted down his stolen clothing, looking for a lighter. Or matches. Nothing.

Nothing in Tequila's clothes, either.

Herb began to do that laughing/sobbing thing again. Then he stared at the ATV, wondering how he could use it to make fire.

It had a battery. Hook up some wires, cross them, get a spark and—

Wait. He already had something that made sparks.

Herb picked up the catch pole, stuck the tip in his pile of gas-soaked debris, and pressed the button on the handle.

There was a *WHUMP!* and the instant heat kissed his face like a long-lost lover.

He pulled Tequila closer to the warmth, put one arm around him, and then scanned the horizon for more guards.

They'd see the smoke. They'd be coming.

Soon.

And Herb doubted he'd have as much luck the second time around.

JACK

Heckle and Jeckle had left to check out the gas station diner, and McGlade had a two pound bag of peanut M&Ms up to his mouth like a feedbag.

"Harry, far be it for me to comment on your lifestyle choices."

"What's the gripe? The out-of-control spending? The sex addiction? The obsession with unusual pets?"

"I was more concerned about the binge eating."

Harry stared at me, then stared at his candy.

"You want the long answer, or the short answer?"

I didn't really want either. I wanted a firearm. But there was also a very real possibility that McGlade would suffer heart failure before we found Herb and Tequila.

"How about a mid-length answer?"

"I don't like myself. So to take my mind off that, I distract myself with crap."

"You don't have to do that."

"It beats what you do."

"And what do I do?"

"You channel your self-loathing into hurting the people you care about. I prefer the penguins and M&Ms route."

Wow. That was too on the nose. "I... don't loathe myself."

Harry gave me a look like, *really?*

"Pass the M&Ms," I said.

He handed them over. They tasted like self-doubt and sadness.

"If I liked myself," Harry said, "I wouldn't need a streaming webcast to get the anonymous approval of strangers. And if you liked yourself, you wouldn't need to push Phin away. It's obvious-pants. Since neither of us want to deal with our issues, let's move on."

"You think I push people away?"

"Name a single friend you have that isn't a former co-worker."

I grasped for a straw. "My next door neighbor. Sheila."

"What's her last name?"

"It's, uh, Johnson."

"Johnson is your fake last name. Do you really want to get into this now? Or do you want a gun?"

I opted for the gun.

Harry flipped up a hidden keypad on the wall, pressed a few buttons, and a panel opened in the floor.

"I know," he said, nodding. "This is some James Bond shit."

The revealed arsenal wasn't quite James Bond shit, but it was pretty impressive for a recreational vehicle. Nestled in foam enclosures were two AR-15s, a Remington 870 shotgun, a Marlin 1895 Lever Action rifle, several Glocks, a Springfield M1A, and three revolvers. The revolvers caught my interest.

One was a Smith & Wesson 460, which looked like a .44 Magnum, but about twice as big. It was a ridiculously heavy gun, which shot a ridiculously large .460 cartridge. I'd fired one, once, and it felt like slapping a car speeding by at sixty miles per hour.

The second was a Ruger Super Blackhawk Alaskan. It fired .454 Casull rounds, which were also larger than .44 Magnums. Roughly as comfortable to shoot as catching a swinging baseball bat.

I considered making a joke about McGlade overcompensating for something, decided not to open up the doorway to that discussion, and reached down for the last revolver, a Taurus 66. This was chambered for .357 Magnum, which was a much friendlier round to shoot than .44s and their larger cousins. But .357s also had a cool ability; they could also fire .38s, which were my cartridge of choice.

My go-to gun used to be a Colt Detective Special, a snub-nosed .38. Then I carried a Colt Python, but that was too heavy for an everyday pistol, so I'd given that to Phin and bought a smaller Colt Cobra, which had all of the qualities I was looking for in a concealed carry. It was a revolver, so it never jammed, and it could be easily reloaded with my eyes closed (try loading a 9mm magazine in the dark). It also had a great balance between weight and target damage, and carried well in shoulder, waist, or purse holster.

The Model 66 was bigger than my Cobra. The cylinder held seven rounds rather than six, and the barrel was two inches longer. It also weighed nearly a pound more.

"Really?" Harry asked, eyeing my choice. "Over a Glock 19?"

"Do you really want to compare the two?"

"Bigger capacity with the Glock," Harry said. We'd had the *revolver vs. semi-automatic* argument many times before.

"If I can't destroy it with seven rounds, I shouldn't be carrying a weapon."

"Glock fires faster."

"Bullshit. You want to shoot and see?"

"I still suck lefty."

"You sucked when you were a righty. How do you even chamber a round with a robot hand?"

Harry picked up a Glock lefty, lifted a foot, and then worked the slide by pressing the gun sights against the sole of his shoe and pulling back.

He smiled like a canary-eating-cat, then lost his balance and fell on his ass.

I ignored the chance for ribbing, because he was giving me a gun. "Do you have .38 rounds?"

"I've got a few boxes of .38+P."

Plus P cartridges were the same size as .38s, but had 20% more muzzle velocity.

"Holster?" I asked.

"Paddle."

"Leather?"

"Polymer. Faster draw than leather."

"Sold."

Harry rooted around in his arsenal for the holster and ammo, and I switched the gun from one hand to the other, getting the feel of the cylinder release and ejector rod. The gun was heavy. Maybe too heavy. The loaded Glock 19 was probably ten ounces lighter, and I was considering a swap when Harry found the holster. I fitted the paddle in my waistband on my hip, holstered the weapon, and drew.

Awkward. I was too hippy for a side carry.

"Try it in front."

"Cross draw?" I moved the holster to above my left front pocket, then drew and aimed.

It was smooth. And quick.

"Ammo?" I asked, sighting the gun down the length of the RV.

McGlade took a long, rectangular box out of his hidey-hole, set it aside, and began to look for the .38+P rounds.

"What's in the box?"

"Huh? Oh. AT-4."

"I don't know that model rifle."

"It's not a rifle. It's an anti-tank weapon." He opened the box lid.

I gaped, incredulous. "A rocket launcher."

"Three hundred meter effective range, 84mm exploding projectile, can penetrate fifteen inches of RHA; rolled homogenous armor."

"Why do you have one?"

"Why *don't* you have one?"

Harry found the ammo. I ejected the .357 rounds he'd already loaded, swapped with .38+P, stuck the box in my jacket pocket, then holstered the weapon. McGlade packed everything else up and closed his secret Bond hatch.

"Ready to practice?" he asked.

I nodded. The only way to get used to a new gun was to shoot it.

McGlade led me outside, keeping the animals in the RV, and we walked around to the side. He unlocked a panel door, and wheeled out a large autofeed trap. I tagged behind as he muscled the hand truck-sized contraption fifty meters off road, into the plains. It looked like an old-time generator. Stacked on top were six columns of clay discs.

Trap shooting, a variation of pigeon shooting and skeet shooting, was one of the oldest shooting sports. The skeet were 108mm frisbees that were launched, singly or in pairs, between fifty to a hundred meters. The goal, obviously, was to shoot them before they landed.

The standard firearm for trapshooting was a shotgun. Shotguns had long barrels, usually over eighteen inches, and fired multiple projectiles that spread out, making it much easier to hit a small, moving target.

My Taurus had a four inch barrel, and one projectile, so I wasn't confident this was the proper way to practice. It was unlikely I'd hit anything. An indoor range with a stationary paper target was the right way to train with a handgun.

"You know this is impossible," I told him.

"For you? Naw. You never miss."

"Could you do this?"

"I can't do this with a shotgun. But this isn't about my limitations. It's about yours. Let's send one flying, let you zero out."

He stepped on a pedal and the skeet launched. It landed really far away.

This was impossible.

"C'mon, Jackie. Can't hit the target?"

"Can you even see the target?"

"It's that bright orange dot, about the size of a raisin."

There was no way. I took my stance, gripped the revolver with both hands, and aimed at something much closer; a steer's bleached skull, roughly twenty meters away.

My first shot missed, and the gun kicked hard. While you can't 'zero-out' a revolver, like McGlade said, you can adjust your grip and aim to properly line up your eyes with the sights, in order to get a feel for the bullseye spot. I lowered the barrel a fraction of a degree, and squeezed the trigger again.

The steer's right horn came off.

Then I shot the left horn.

Then I put two between the eyes.

Then I located the orange clay pigeon, ridiculously small in the distance. I let out a slow breath and fired.

Missed. But I kicked up dirt several inches to the right.

"Wind," McGlade said.

Wind wasn't normally a factor in handgun shooting, where targets were sixty feet or closer. But wind, and drop, became important when hitting objects at longer range. To imagine drop, think about dropping a metal slug from shoulder level to the ground. The time it takes for that to happen is the same amount of time it takes a bullet, fired perfectly straight at shoulder level, to hit the ground.

That may sound counter-intuitive, but gravity pulls on stationary objects with the same force as it pulls on moving objects. The way to counter this was to adjust the barrel angle. Shooting higher than parallel meant the bullet would travel in an arc, like a football pass. Some of the bullet's energy is stolen by gravity, but you can shoot farther.

Usually, this requires scopes, rangefinders, and some math. Speed and mass and wind resistance and barrel length all come into play.

Or, you can do what I do, and wing it.

After my small adjustment, I fired again, and the disc kicked up a plume of orange dust.

"Son of a bitch," Harry said. "I would have bet a fortune you couldn't hit that."

"Yet another example of your fiscal irresponsibility," I ejected the spent brass and loaded seven new rounds. "Launch one."

He sent one flying, I fired three times as it zoomed across the sky, missing all three. When it landed, I killed it.

"Again."

McGlade pressed the pedal, and I fired twice, hitting it the second time.

"Again."

He launched. I fired. I hit first try.

"Jesus," Harry said. "Want to try two at once?"

I nodded. The gun, though heavy, was growing on me. I liked the trigger break, liked the slightly longer barrel, and liked packing seven rounds rather than six.

McGlade launched two pigeons, one after the other.

I fired three times, hitting both.

Then he got sneaky and launched two at the same time.

That took me four shots, but I nailed them.

"Is it inappropriate that I'm getting aroused?" he said.

"Extremely."

I loaded seven more, and Harry pressed the pedal seven times in a row.

I got five out of seven.

He did it again.

Five out of seven.

I unbunched my shoulders, took deeper, slower breaths, and blocked out the rest of my surroundings. When I used to do shooting competitions, I could get in the zone. Which meant I lapsed into a kind of tunnel vision, focusing entirely on the target, ignoring everything else around me. I couldn't always hyper-focus like that, but when I could I felt like time slowed down, the firearm was an extension of my arm, and all sorts of other hippie Zen sports bullshit.

"Once more," I breathed.

Harry let the seven fly.

I shot seven down.

When the orange dust settled, I became aware of eyes on me.

Heckle and Jeckle were standing next to the Crimebago Deux, video camera in hand, filming my efforts.

I went from Zen to Super Bitch in point two seconds, and began to stomp toward them.

"J-Dawg, don't kill my crew," Harry said, coming up after me.

"They were filming me. Taping me. Whatever it's called with video."

"Shooting you," Heckle said.

"Do you want to see what my definition of *shooting* is?"

I made an over-dramatic show of flipping out the cylinder with a wrist flick, smacking the ejector rod with my palm to free the spent casings, and reloading as I approached.

"The video's not live," Harry was dragging the autofeed trap behind him, trying to keep up. "Tell her it's not live."

"Chill, Super Cop Chick," said Heckle. "Private Dick McDude is correctomundo. This is B-roll, not live."

"If we use it, we'll blur it," said Jeckle. "That's the dealio."

I finished reloading, holstered the gun, and gave them both a *don't mess with me* stare.

Their return stares were empty. Dead. Like I was looking at storefront mannequins.

"Here's the new dealio," I said. "Neither of you even think about pointing that camera at me until I say it's okay. Got it?"

Heckle and Jeckle exchanged one of their secret looks, then giggled in a way that I didn't like.

I wasn't playing anymore, and I went full pissed-off cop and got into their personal space.

"I asked you a question."

This time I didn't get blank stares.

I got hostile stares.

I'd seen this look a hundred times before, on the faces of perps ready to do something very stupid.

"Hey there," Harry caught up. "Let's deescalate. We're all one big happy. No need to get weird."

The twins didn't back down. Neither did I. McGlade managed to get between us, and he stared at the twins.

"Answer her," Harry told them.

They looked at each other, and Heckle said. "No problem."

I focused on Jeckle.

"No problem," he said.

I walked away, feeling eyes on my back.

Next time I was alone with McGlade, I'd ask him some questions about the twins. In my head, they'd gone from being a nagging doubt to a full-blown concern.

YEARS AGO

TOM AND JERRY

The satanic ritual was for show.
They had black candles. A pentagram drawn on the floor. An altar, draped in a black sheet. Communion wafers, stolen from a local church along with a pint of holy water. A chalice of human blood, thanks to an unwilling homeless donor. And six dead animals; two of them toads, a cat, a squirrel, a puppy, and a stag the twins discovered in the woods, already dead. (The other five animals were alive when they found them.)

They had it all set up in the attic, accompanied by the heaviest heavy metal music they could find, Venom, playing on jam box, burning incense, and strobe lights (which probably weren't a traditional part of a black mass, but looked cool.)

Everything was in place.

All they needed was the maid.

Since MotherBitch's untimely, yet entirely warranted, flameywhiny demise, FatherAss had been having troubledouble performing his duties as a single parent, and had hired a live-in maid named Camila. She was fifty-something, bilingual, fiercely Catholic, and an all-around pain in the ass.

Almost at first sight, Camila had treated Tom and Jerry like delinquents. Tattling to FatherAss every time they questioned her unearned authority. Throwing away a cache of Hustler magazines they'd stolen from the mall bookstore. Cooking shitty food. Acting all full of herself.

But the line had truly been crossed when she walked in on the twins, showering together, engaged in behavior that was in no way related to cleanliness. FatherAss had whipped them both with a belt, leaving welts that lasted more than a week.

Camila had to go.

Going dark, Tom went to get the maid while Jerry hid behind the altar, wearing a mail-order devil mask.

A few minutes later, Camila came stomping up the stairs, grumbling about *niños malos*.

When she turned on the wall switch, it activated the strobe and the stereo, Venom's *Welcome to Hell* playing at full volume just as Jerry popped up.

Camila took a step back, crossed herself, then began to pray in Spanish as she hurried back toward the staircase.

Tom was already on all fours, and Jerry sprinted over and pushed Camila, hard, over his twin on down the stairs.

As they predicted, she hit face-first, then took several cartwheels down the steps until she landed in a bloody, moaning heap at the bottom.

Camila was badly hurt. There was a lot of blood. One leg was at a wrong angle. She had something stuck in her back. But the bitch still had enough strength to crawl for the hallway, praying in rasps to her foreign god, casting panicked glances behind her as Tom and Jerry descended the staircase, mindful of the blood splotches.

"We must figure out some way to kill her, Dear Tom, and still make it look like an accident."

"Truedoo, Dear Jerry. We could bash her head on the floor a few times until her brainybits come out."

"We'll get blood on us, Dear Tom. Plus, the police have ways to figure out that sort of thing."

Camila began to beg for her life. The twins didn't heed her.

"She's breathing really hard, Dear Jerry. See that thing stuck in her back?"

"That, Dear Brother, is not sticking in her back. It's sticky-wicking in her back. That's a rib."

"A ribbyrib?"

"A ribbyribrib. And it gives me an idea."

Shoes and socks off, Jerry stood, barefoot, on Camila's back. Tom followed suit.

"Don't bounce," Jerry warned. "We just want to suffocate her, not break anything else."

They held hands, Tom also touching the wall to keep balance, until Camila's rasps turned to wheezes, and after several very entertaining minutes, a final, rattling gasp.

The twins put on their socks and shoes, went back upstairs, carefully removed all traces of their poorly constructed black mass. Then, wearing gloves, they set Camila's dustpan on the stairs, halfway down, and her broom at the attic entrance.

Afterward, they located Camila's sewing kit, then watched television in the living room until FatherAss came home from work.

"Where's Camila?" he asked upon entering, completely uninterested in their day.

"Haven't seen her," said Tom.

"Heard a noise upstairs a while ago," said Jerry.

FatherAss called the maid's name a few times, cursed when he saw nothing had been prepared for dinner, cursed again at the twins for sitting in front of the television and rotting their brains, and then stomped upstairs.

A few seconds later, he yelped.

Tom and Jerry came running. Each clutched a straight pin.

When they saw Camila's corpse, they each jabbed it into their own hips.

The pain brought moans, and tears, and then FatherAss shielded them from the sight and hurried them downstairs and told them to stay there while he called 911.

The pins hurt. A lot. And the twins kept up the anguish by smacking one another in the hips until the police and paramedics came. When the cop took their statement, they were practically sobbing.

Thankfully, the authorities left before the blood soaked through their jeans.

Later that night, after Camila had been hauled away, FatherAss spoke to them.

"Do either of you have anything you want to tell me?"

Neither did.

FatherAss never hired another live-in maid.

HERB

Tequila twitched, emitting a low moan.

Herb felt his forehead. Some warmth was coming back.

"Sally?" Tequila said.

"No, brother. Just me."

Sally was Tequila's sister. She'd died many years ago. A lifetime ago.

Herb yawned, zoning out of sentry duty long enough to think about his own family. He didn't have siblings. His parents were long gone. Other than his wife, Bernice, Jack Daniels was the closest thing Herb had to a relative. Jack was like a sister.

And Tequila was the closest he had to a brother. Except for a brief bonding period with Jack's old partner, an idiot named Harrison Harold McGlade.

Strangely, like Jack, McGlade had been more or less a constant in Herb's life. Harry was around for a lot of big cases. He invariably showed up at holiday parties. Herb has run into him, unintentionally, dozens of times over the decades.

The man was a self-absorbed, obnoxious ass.

But, perversely, Herb wished he had one more chance to hang out with him.

And with Jack, of course.

And Bernice.

Thinking about Bernice was both medicine and poison. All of his time in captivity, good memories kept Herb going. At the same time, they were a source of terrible longing and pain. It was masochistic. Like imagining a pizza.

Boy, would I kill for a pizza. Deep dish, extra everything, with a frosty mug of beer.

Herb was serious, too.

Well, mostly.

Herb glanced at the naked corpses. Men he'd killed, not for pizza but for self-preservation, lying there and beginning to bloat in the noonday sun.

Or maybe they weren't bloating. Maybe that was in Herb's head.

It made him sick that he'd done it.

Herb had killed before. In the line of duty. And this was practically the same thing. Self-defense, certainly. Plus, they were slavers.

It still made Herb sick.

"Herb?"

"Right here, brother."

Tequila peeked open his eyes. "How long have I been out?"

"A few hours. How you feel?"

"Cold. Tired. Hungry. Injured."

"At least *cold* is a new one. Remember that conversation we had in Mexico? Trying to remember what ice felt like?"

"Their clothes," Tequila mumbled.

Herb didn't follow, then realized Tequila was talking about the guards.

"Yeah."

"Smart. Nice work."

"Thanks," Herb said, though it felt wrong to be complimented on his murder skills. "You warm enough to get going?"

Tequila nodded. Herb got an arm under him, helping the shorter man to his feet.

"Which way?" Herb asked.

Tequila looked up at the sun—

—then fell onto his face.

Herb reached down again, shaking Tequila to get up, and then he heard the telltale buzz of another ATV.

"Come on, brother. They're coming. We gotta go."

"Leebeeee," Tequila said. It came out soft as a sigh.

"Tequila—"

"Leave. Me."

Tequila looked just as dead as the naked corpses. He didn't even open his eyes when Herb slapped him.

But he wasn't dead. He was still breathing. He still had a pulse.

He still had a chance.

"Please," Herb said, getting frantic. "Please get up. I got lucky before. I can't do it again. I need you."

"You... gotta go."

"I'm not leaving."

Tequila's eyes fluttered. "I have to sit this round out, Herb. Go."

Herb looked at the ATV, rapidly approaching.

Looked at Tequila.

Looked at the ATV.

Looked at Tequila.

Herb played out the scenarios.

He could fight back, maybe win again.

Terrible odds on that.

He could run off, and maybe they'd take Tequila, giving Herb a chance to get away.

So-so odds.

He could run off, they could see Tequila was helpless, and then kill him and still chase Herb.

That seemed likely.

Or he could stay with his friend, and help the guards take him back to the land train.

The land train was certain death.

But it was warm.

And it was probably Tequila's best chance at seeing tomorrow.

"Don't be stupid," Tequila said. "Go."

Herb looked away from the ATV. Out into the country.

Into freedom.

Somewhere, maybe somewhere close, was Herb's old life. A life he could have back.

But even closer than that, lying at Herb's feet, was his brother.

Herb knelt down, squeezing Tequila's hand.

"Call me stupid," Herb said. "I'm staying."

Tequila squeezed his hand back, and the two men waited for the guards to arrive.

JACK

"I can't believe it," Harry called through the open cockpit door. "We're out in the middle of nowhere, and I'm still surrounded by my fans."

I peeked out the window, not sure what to expect, and then saw the enormous column of a towering, white, three-bladed wind turbine. It was one of dozens, dotting the grassy plains like silent, alien sentinels.

"Did you shoot that?" Harry asked. "That's one of my greatest puns, ever."

"A windmill isn't a fan," said Jeckle.

"A fan uses electricity," said Heckle, "a turbine generates electricity."

"Did you shoot it or not?"

"No," they said in unison.

"Do a quick set-up and shoot it. Medium shot, then a quick pan to the wind farm."

They exchanged a smarmy glance, then powered up the video camera and went over to Harry.

"I can't believe it. We're in the middle of nowhere, and I'm still surrounded by my fans."

It wasn't any better the second time.

I stared out the window. We'd turned off the main highway an hour ago, and had been following a network of gravel roads that weren't even named on my GPS.

"How close are we?" I asked, making sure the camera had been shut off.

"Technically, we're here. This is all their property."

"They're wind farmers," I said, stating the obvious because I'd never used those words before.

McGlade nodded. "It's a really good investment. Each of these suckers costs about fifty K to build, and generates about three hundred thousand kilowatts per year. Figure they sell electricity back to the grid at twelve cents a kilowatt, that's thirty-six grand annually. So it pays for itself in seventeen months, then makes three grand a month, every month, for the next few decades. Minus maintenance and taxes, of course. And look at them all. Wyatt and Annie are making some serious change. Hey, switch the camera back on."

Heckle came in for the close-up.

"I considered investing in wind power," McGlade said, straight-faced. "But I heard it really blows."

Rosalina made a whining sound.

I patted her head. "I'm right there with you, girl."

I stared at the turbines and felt a sense of unease completely unrelated to Harry's dumb jokes.

Though I wasn't a superstitious person, and tried to maintain a logical, skeptical approach, something about wind farms just felt, well, creepy. Maybe it was the juxtaposition of modern technology in rural settings, sprouting up out of the land like giant, mechanical trees. Cities felt like homes, where human beings shaped their environment to suit them. But being among the turbines made me feel, quite irrationally, like I didn't belong there.

This unsettling, out-of-place sensation was amplified by how quiet everything was.

Waddlebutt squawked. Maybe he didn't like turbines, either. I reached down to give him a reassuring pat on the head, and he nipped my fingers. As I was checking for injuries, I saw Heckle had the camera out.

"Just shooting the bird" said Heckle. "Viewers like the bird."

"It scores high with preteens and middle-aged females," said Jeckle.

Waddlebutt puked a half-digested fish spine onto the floor. He began to peck at it, then picked it up and swung it around, before scarfing it down.

Then he sprayed shit all over the floor.

"We probably won't air that," said Heckle.

"Probably," said Jeckle.

This unimpressed middle-aged female walked around the penguin and the weirdo twins, and went into the cockpit. McGlade, thankfully, was wearing pants. I sat in the passenger seat.

"Seatbelt," he said.

I buckled up and asked, "What's the plan?"

"We're doing two webcasts. Interviewing Wyatt, then interviewing Annie. I could use your help with the questions."

"Sure. Where are they?"

"I haven't done any. But it's just gonna be standard witness interrogation. So if I miss anything, just jump in."

I still had a healthy dose of paranoia about someone discovering I wasn't dead. "You can alter my voice live?"

"This isn't going to be live. I don't know how long these two are going to ramble, so it'll need some editing. I'll weave the taped interviews into the live show."

"What are you plans for finding Herb and Tequila?"

"Hopefully, these two will give us some clues. I've got a few hunches. If they're confirmed, I think we can find a way to track them."

"No way to track through the Snuff-X site?"

"Jack, it's darknet. The Cowboy's stream could be in Bolivia, or Afghanistan, or Sheboygan, Wisconsin. No way to trace it. But, if my research is correct, I think they're somewhere in Nebraska, or a neighboring state. I just need to confirm some things. It'll work out. Always does. Trust me."

My trust in McGlade was a sporadic thing. Sometimes he came through. Sometimes he was full of more shit than Waddlebutt. But even though I had more faith in my ability to roll Harry uphill than I did in his promises, I really had no choice. This was his investigation. I felt like a fifth wheel.

Which, now that I fully focused on it, was the wrong approach. When I was a cop, even back in my rookie days, more cases were solved when I took point. Much as I didn't want to appear on YouTube, I was more suited to questioning Wyatt and Annie than Harry was.

Maybe it's time for the fifth wheel to start load-bearing, I thought.

Then I thought, *not my best analogy.*

"Look!" Harry pointed with his fake hand. "Buffalos! Get a shot of that!"

Technically, there were no buffalo in the Americas, contrary to the popular song. We were driving through a field of bison, which were an entirely different species than buffalo. The half-dozen animals were roaming among the turbines, separated from the road by a short barbed-wire fence. There were also a few heads of cattle, some deep black, some rust-colored, white tags hanging from their ears. And up ahead, at the end of the road—

"Damn," Harry said. "Sheriff Wyatt has got himself a rancher mansion. A *ransion*. Should I use that? Is it clever, or stupid?"

The *ransion*, which had sort of a charming ring to it, was a sprawling, two-story log cabin that had to be over five thousand square feet. The upper and lower decks had wrap-around balconies, there was an attached three car garage, and to the east side of the house was a horse stable and pen.

As we approached, the house began to look even bigger. A huge king post truss with giant windows jutted up like a mountain peak, a front porch bigger than my backyard was furnished with a swing, several rockers, a fire pit, and a dinette set for eight, and three massive, river-rock chimneys stretched up out of the metal roof.

A figure stood up on the porch, and walked out to greet us. He was tall, over six feet, wore jeans and a red flannel shirt, brown boots and a matching brown cowboy hat, and had a mustache that would make Tom Selleck jealous.

"Hot damn," Harry said. "It's the Marlboro Man."

While he wasn't smoking, the man was easily as attractive and well-proportioned as any of the models used in that famous ad campaign.

We parked, and when I opened the side door, he was standing right there. He had the kind of craggy, wrinkled face that looked good on guys my age, with a three day growth of beard that was shaved along his jawline. Eyes were dark brown, almost black. He immediately offered his hand, which was calloused but gentle when he shook mine.

"I'd be Wyatt Steinhoffer." He had a drawl that was more Texas than midwestern. "Welcome to my home, Miss…?"

"Mrs.," I said. "Johnson. Jill Johnson."

He didn't release my hand yet, and I didn't mind too much. Wyatt seemed to be one of those really good looking guys who acted like he wasn't good looking but had to know it.

"Pleasure is mine, Mrs. Johnson. Quite a rig you got there."

"You, too," I said, checking out his side holster. "Colt Python."

His eyes crinkled. Why was it that wrinkles on men were sexy, and women were told they needed surgery or Botox?

"The lady knows her firearms," Wyatt said.

"My husband has a Python." I said. I only realized the innuendo after it had left my mouth.

Wyatt didn't seem to catch it. "He's obviously a man who appreciates the finer things."

I took my hand back.

"I've got a .44," Harry said, coming up behind me. "But those little guns are nice too."

"Mr. McGlade." Wyatt tipped his hat, but didn't offer to shake.

"Mr. Steinhoffer. Thanks for the invite. We'd like to get right to the interview, if you don't mind."

"Did you want coffee first? Lemonade?"

"No thanks. We're in kind of a time crunch. Is your sister home?"

"Annie's out at the moment. She should be back soon."

"Can we set up on the porch?"

"Sure thing."

Harry climbed out, followed by Heckle and Jeckle, who were lugging gear. The twins walked past Wyatt without acknowledging him.

"And who's the grizzly bear?" Wyatt asked.

Rosalina was staring at us.

"That's Rosalina."

"And the obese pigeon?"

"That's Waddlebutt. A chinstrap penguin."

Wyatt adjusted his hat. "I'll bet it was an interesting trip."

"You could say that. Do you mind if Rosa gets some air?"

"Long as she doesn't try to eat the bison. We got some chickens next to the stable, if your little bird friend needs some time with kin."

"Harry?" I called to him as he ordered Heckle and Jeckle around. "Can Waddlebutt play with the chickens?"

"Sure. I'll come get him."

I let Rosalina out, she went off exploring, and Harry came back and scooped up Waddlebutt as I walked with Wyatt toward his house. I wasn't a fan of small talk, so I didn't make any. We approached the front door, then took a right and strolled around the saddle-notch corner of the house, and over to a fenced-in coop, where four or five chickens wandered around. When Waddlebutt was introduced to the flock, they didn't pay him any mind. He ignored them as well, and immediately began gathering pebbles.

"I was hoping for something more," Harry said. "Like penguin-chicken sex. Or a dance fight." He turned to Wyatt. "Only hens?"

Wyatt nodded.

"I can't even make a cock joke," Harry said.

"Give it time," Wyatt said. "Maybe your Antarctic buddy is just waiting to break the ice."

McGlade didn't seem impressed that someone was trying to outfunny him. I paid only half attention, gawking at the horse pen. I was a tomboy growing up, preferring Spider-man to Cinderella and GI Joe dolls to Barbie. But I had a friend who loved Barbie, and she had Barbie's horse, a brown one named Dancer.

I was always a sucker for Dancer. But my experience with real horses was limited to ponies at the petting zoo, and the occasional carriage ride on Chicago's Magnificent Mile.

So my eyes were completely captured by a white horse with brown patches. Or maybe it was a brown horse with white patches.

"Jack," Wyatt said touching my shoulder.

I turned, maybe too fast to appear casual. "Excuse me?"

"The quarter horse. Her name is Jack."

"*Her* name?"

"Ladies can be named Jack." Wyatt was doing that eye-crinkle thing again. I couldn't tell if he was teasing, flirting, or waiting for Big Tobacco to snap his picture.

"A pinto?" I asked, turning away.

"A paint. Quarter horses with that coloring are called paints."

"Fascinating," Harry said, butting in. "Do you have any of those horses that herd chickens?"

Wyatt stopped posing. "Horses that herd chickens?"

"You know," Harry said. "A Clucksdale."

"Why don't we sit down for that interview?" Wyatt suggested.

"Lead the way."

I gave Jack the horse a last look and followed the guys to the porch.

The twins had a two camera set-up, opposite a large piece of white poster board on a stand that was used to bounce the natural sunlight and make the subjects brighter. Two wood-slat Adirondack chairs faced one another. McGlade took one, then motioned me over.

"Think of any questions?"

"You haven't got any?"

"I've got plenty, but if you know any others, jump in."

I stood behind Jeckle's camera, which was focusing on Wyatt. Heckle clipped microphones to each man, and they did a quick sound check. Once they had their level, Harry jumped right in.

"This is Wyatt Earp Steinhoffer, Sheriff of Pastor County, Nebraska. How long have you been Sheriff, Sheriff?"

"Eight years."

"And prior to that?"

"We were venture capitalists."

Harry leaned forward, channeling the practiced concern of Geraldo Rivera. "We?"

"Me and my sister. Annie."

"You've followed an unusual path to become Sheriff in these parts. Can you give me and the millions watching this the quick version?"

Wyatt cleared his throat. "Nine years ago, Annie went missing west of Sioux Falls, South Dakota. She was gone for four months. When she was found, sixty miles east of here, she was practically naked and nearly dead. Annie's an average-sized woman, about five-foot seven, a hundred and forty pounds, but when she was rushed to the hospital she weighed only eighty. Eighty pounds, sopping wet. And the scars..."

"What about the scars, Sheriff?"

"Let's say she didn't have much skin left that wasn't marked up. Worst of all was her teeth."

"What about them?"

"They were gone."

McGlade milked the moment, then leaned even closer. "What happened to your sister, Sheriff?"

"Annie had been taken by slavers. They forced her to work on a poppy farm, harvesting opium. She was beaten with whips and sticks. Raped. Cut. Burned. Starved. Worked to near death."

"And the teeth?"

"Every day, each slave had a quota. If she didn't meet it, he pulled a tooth."

"Who is *he*, Sheriff?"

"The worst human being to ever walk the planet earth."

"And who is that?"

"The...Cowboy."

Again McGlade paused. The story was dramatic in its own right, but I had to say that Harry's pauses made it even more powerful. In the background, dotting the landscape and humming so softly it was almost imagination, half a dozen turbines waved.

"Tell us about...the Cowboy."

"Always wore black. Always kept his face covered with a bandana. He had a ten acre poppy farm, in the Nebraska plains. Used slaves for labor. Kept them chained up so they couldn't get away. Fed them barely enough to stay alive. Deprived them of sleep, shelter, medical attention. And when they didn't perform up to the Cowboy's expectations, he tortured them. There has never been anyone born that was more inhuman. Annie told me stories, some of the things he did..."

Wyatt looked like he was starting to tear up. I snuck a peek at one of the laptops that the twins were using as camera monitors, and Heckle had zoomed in on Wyatt's eyes.

"But your sister escaped."

"She was wearing one of them ball and chains. You know? Like you see on prisoners in a rock quarry, in all them old movies. Annie broke her own foot to get the cuff off. But it wasn't enough. Cuff was still too tight. So she needed to lubricate it."

"How did she do that?"

"With her own blood," Wyatt said. He was breaking up, the tears obvious.

Another dramatic Harry pause. He finally asked, "How did she get away?"

"She crawled off, at night." Wyatt sniffed. "Managed to get a few miles away before she passed out in the middle of nowhere."

"So how was she rescued?"

"Turkey vultures."

McGlade turned to face the camera and he said, deadpan, "Turkey vultures."

"They circle over carrion. Dead livestock and such. Rancher was missing a few heads of cattle, followed the vultures to check. Found Annie there. The birds…they had already begun on her. Poor Annie didn't even have the strength to fight them off."

Wyatt wiped his eyes. I was simultaneously revolted by one of the most horrible stories I'd ever heard, and revolted by McGlade's crass exploitation of it. I'd been hoping for a police interview, but what I'd seen so far was more akin to a badly written infodump on a Lifetime Movie For Women.

"Was the poppy farm ever discovered?" I asked, butting in.

Wyatt sniffled again, then nodded. "Least, the burned remains were found. Few weeks later. Four acres. Only discovered it because of the smoke. Had nothing to do with Annie's investigation. Law enforcement didn't give a shit about her, or the Cowboy."

"Why do you say that?" McGlade asked.

Wyatt folded his arms. "Because nobody did nothing. We talked to the local cops. The state cops. The feds. No one did shit. No searching for the farm. No hunting down the Cowboy. So while Annie focused on getting better, I focused on catching the son of a bitch who did it to her."

"So you ran for sheriff," Harry said.

He gave a single, authoritative nod. "Pastor County is a good county. Good people. But they never dealt with anything like the Cowboy. Previous sheriff was a decent enough fella, but he didn't have the training."

"And you have the training?" I asked.

Wyatt stared at me. The smile lines were gone, and his face had become hard, making him look ten years older.

"I can fight. And I can shoot."

"Where did you get your training, Wyatt?"

He paused, then drew his gun, such an abrupt, shocking thing to do that I also drew mine. But Wyatt didn't aim at me. Instead, he sighted near the horse stable, about forty meters away, and shot at the rooster weathervane on the roof. Wyatt's round hit the arrow, spinning it from north, to south.

A damn fine shot. Especially so quick. Maybe five percent of athletes in the world of sport shooting could have done it.

"I hold my own," Wyatt said, holstering his weapon.

I holstered mine as well, feeling a bit foolish. After a dramatic pause long enough for me to paint my nails, McGlade asked, "What happened to the former sheriff?"

"Few months after I came on as deputy, he vanished."

"Think it was the Cowboy?"

"Coulda been. Old Dan also liked the bottle, if you know what I'm saying. It's a big country out there. Easy to get lost."

"Even if you follow the turkey vultures?" I asked.

Wyatt gave me another cold look. I didn't want to piss off our local contact, especially one who was helping us, and I didn't mean to disrespect a fellow law enforcement officer. But one of my tricks, while interviewing witnesses, was to hit them with the tough questions that a defense attorney would use during a trial. It was a mean thing to do, but it tended to get past all the bullshit and to the root of truth.

"I don't know what happened to Dan," Wyatt said. "My speculation is just that. Speculation."

"But you believed your sister. Her account of what happened."

"Of course."

I pushed it. "You don't think that's pretty far-fetched? Even eight years ago, we had satellites. Google Earth. A nationwide drug enforcement agency. A poppy field isn't an easy thing to hide. Flowers are bright, and grow about three feet high. That's why less than one percent of the heroin in this country is home grown. It's more like point one percent. Because it's much safer to import it, than grow it."

"There are ways to camouflage a farm from satellites. And your Google earth. Netting. Painted roofs. Electronic gizmos."

"But they had workers. It's very tough to hide people. They eat food. Leave waste. Make fires and use machines. You're really saying there was a big poppy farm out there, with many slaves, and no one ever discovered it?"

"Mrs. Johnson, you talk like you've had some police experience."

That threw me off my game a bit. I came back with, "I read a lot."

"I bet you do."

"But would you answer the question, Sheriff?"

"I believe my sister. She didn't do it to herself. And the farm was found, later, burned to the ground. It all adds up. And I stand by her account of things. And *my* account of things."

Harry jumped in. "So, Sheriff Steinhoffer, in eight years of hunting, have you managed to find the Cowboy? Or his newest poppy field?"

"I've had some encounters," Wyatt said.

"Such as?"

"I think the Cowboy figured out what the lady said. That having a poppy farm out in the open is too risky. There are hundreds of thousands of empty acres in the Great Plains, but in order to farm enough opium for it to be profitable, he couldn't chance being discovered. I think he changed his plan."

"How?" I asked.

"I think he took his farm, and his slaves, on the road."

"Like a train," Harry said.

"Farming on a train ain't the worst idea. Poppies are enclosed. Hidden. Train can move from state to state. But there are all kinds of rules and regulations for trains. Plus, they can only go where the tracks go. I think he's using a fleet of trucks. Trucks that can go off-road, but still can tow big trailers. A dozen of those, all growing product, driving through the plains."

"People would still see them," I said. "Cops. Ranchers."

"I tell you what, Mrs. Johnson. Few years ago, some promoters came by, paid me twenty thousand dollars to allow some rock and roll concert out on my property. Twenty grand, for two days. You think I'm the only one who rents out land, time to time? Some come, and squat without paying. Some ask permission, pay a fee. If you owned a hundred acres, paid taxes on a hundred acres, and a guy with a couple of trucks wanted to park on your land, for three days, no questions asked, for a thousand bucks, would you take it?"

"And law enforcement?"

"Mrs. Johnson, I'm sure a pretty thing like yourself has no problem flirting your way out of a speeding ticket. The rest of us make due with a folded hundred dollar bill when we pass over our driver's license. Don't tell me you've never heard of cops looking the other way."

"Have you found any evidence of this?" McGlade asked.

"Every few months, I find tire tracks all around the county. Big tire tracks. I've taken reports from locals who saw a large vehicle moving through the plains. And, of course, there have been bodies."

McGlade was now leaning so far forward his ass was almost off the edge of the seat. "Tell us about the bodies, Sheriff."

"Three found in South Dakota. Four in Kansas. Three in this state. One as far west as Wyoming. Found out in the open. No shirt or shoes. Signs of starvation and abuse. Some dead from exposure. Some dead from a bullet in the head."

"What makes you sure they're all connected to the Cowboy?" I asked.

Wyatt smiled, a thousand watt grin that was Hollywood close-up perfect. Then he raised a finger and tapped his incisors. "No teeth, Mrs. Johnson."

Another lengthy dramatic pause. My feelings were mixed. We were getting good intel, but something felt off to me. I'd gone from being slightly intimidated by Wyatt's good looks and wealth, to slightly flattered by his charm and flirting, to slightly skeptical of his version of this story.

Sheriff Wyatt Earp Steinhoffer was hiding something. Or withholding something.

Or, maybe, outright lying.

"Have you ever run into the Cowboy," McGlade asked. "Face to face?"

Of course, the answer would be no.

"The answer is yes," Wyatt said. "Two years ago. South of Norfolk. I was tracking the Cowboy's vehicle, riding Jack."

"Your horse," McGlade interrupted. "Not my dead best friend."

I barely restrained my eyeroll, and made a mental note to prevent Heckle and Jeckle from using that footage.

"We'd been riding for three days." Wyatt had already learned how to ignore McGlade's vocal diarrhea. "Trail wasn't easy to pick up, lots of rocks and grass, but I knew I was following something big. Never saw tire tracks like that. Each wheel was wide as a pickup truck. We'd settled in for the night. I had dinner, fire was about to die, and was just stretching out in my bag to sleep. It was quiet. Crazy quiet. Not even the crickets out. That's when he snuck into camp."

Now Wyatt did the dramatic pause. It lasted so long, Harry had to ask, "What happened?"

"He wore all black. Except for that bandana over his nose and mouth. It had some sort of Halloween face on it. A ghoul or a witch or something. Jack and I didn't even hear him coming, until he was standing right next to me."

Pause. The turbines behind Wyatt stood out like lighters during a rock ballad.

"We both drew and shot. The Cowboy was faster. So fast it was... inhuman."

"And?" McGlade asked.

"His first shot hit my gun." Wyatt held up his arm, and unsnapped a large TAG Heuer watch. "Knocked it out of my hand. Ricochet nicked my wrist."

He showed the scar.

"Then his second shot..."

Wyatt lifted up his flannel shirt.

Of course he had a six pack.

He also had a bullet hole, a few centimeters above his navel.

"Did you hit him?" McGlade asked. He'd somehow gone from aggrandizing talk show host to awed fanboy.

Wyatt chuckled, shook his head. "I did. In his boot."

Now Wyatt began to unbutton his shirt. I didn't see the point, but saw no reason to stop him. Three buttons down, he exposed his necklace. It was the rowel—the star-shaped pointy part—from a spur, hanging from a strip of leather. Two of the points were missing.

"He left me to die. Gut shot. Bad way to go out. But I managed to mount Jack, and she carried me fifty miles to safety. Just before my stomach acid ate through my diaphragm."

"You didn't call for help?" Harry asked.

Wyatt shook his head. "No signal out there."

"And the spur?"

"Sterling silver. No prints. No marks. No way to ever trace it to the Cowboy. Except…" Wyatt's voice trailed off.

McGlade ate it up like Wyatt's words were peanut M&Ms. "Except…?"

"Except when I match it with its twin."

I watched the laptop as Heckle zoomed back in for the close-up. Then Harry said, "Cut!" and stood up with a huge grin on his face.

"That was hella awesome. Have you been on camera before, Sheriff? Because my viewers are going to love you, buddy. What did you think, J-Dawg?"

"I have a few more questions."

Wyatt leaned forward and hefted himself to his feet. "Happy to answer. But right now I need a whiskey. How about you folks?"

"Twins and I need to do some editing." Harry gave me a look. "Holler if you need me."

I gave him a curt nod, and then he and his crew headed back to the Crimebago Deux, Rosalina tagging behind them. Then Wyatt was all of a sudden standing too close to me, his eyes twinkling.

"How about you, little lady?"

I wasn't sure I'd ever been called *little lady*. But Wyatt was so much taller than me, I actually felt a bit dainty.

"Sure," I said. "A drink sounds good."

He actually crooked out an elbow, offering me his arm.

I quickly considered all the ways I could play it. Aloof. Friendly. Professional. Interested. Annoyed. Curious.

I went with friendly, lightly took his arm, and let him lead me into his ransion.

THE COWBOY

The text reads, ARE YOUR EARS BURNING?

The Cowboy knows not to respond. There are scheduled times for texts, and now isn't one of them. Besides, why restate the obvious?

After deleting it, another one appears.

IT'S HER.

The Cowboy stares at the words, and blinks.

First comes a surge of adrenaline, and something akin to joy.

Then comes trembling.

With a shaky finger, the Cowboy texts, REALLY?

There's no immediate answer.

Five seconds pass.

Ten.

Then, a picture arrives.

An old newspaper clipping, showing a face that the Cowboy has memorized.

Jacqueline Daniels.

SHE'S ALIVE, comes the follow-up text.

The Cowboy's thumb hovers over the delete button, but pauses to savor for another few seconds.

Incredible.

Beautiful.

Intoxicating.

Jack Daniels.

Among the living.

Not for long.

The Cowboy breaks into a rare, painful grin, then draws the Ruger Vaquero.

I'm faster. I'm deadlier. I'm better.

And I'm going to show her.

I'm going to maim her.

Hurt her.

Kill her.

After she's spent a good long while begging for death, of course.

It's so tempting to drop everything, and rush to her. Right now.

But after waiting this long, the Cowboy can wait a bit longer.

For the deal to go through.

For the LeTourneau to be handed over.

For Usher House 2.0 to be live.

Jack Daniels and Harry McGlade, live on darknet. Being slowly taken apart, agonizing piece by agonizing piece.

The ratings will be spectacular.

After deletion, one more text appears.

i'm on it.

The Cowboy is tempted to immediately reply don't touch her she's mine!!!, but knows the person on the receiving end is well-aware of this.

He won't dare do anything on his own.

The Cowboy deletes it, then gets Dmitri on the radio.

"What's our count?"

"Four still out there, not including two you dispatched. Closing in on two more."

"Where's Yuri?"

"Yuri," said Yuri, "is listening in. Is there something you need, Cowboy?"

"I need to leave for a few hours."

A pause. Then Yuri says, "Are the workers back at work?"

"They've all been fish-hooked, and are harvesting. We'll make the weight quota by the meeting tomorrow."

Even with all the opium you smoke yourself, the Cowboy thinks.

"How about the two Americans? Have they been found?"

"Nyet," says Dmitri. "But we have two teams out, there are more pings."

"We still have no idea how so many volunteers managed to escape at once," Yuri says.

The Cowboy doesn't like his tone. Wonders if he's high again.

"The quota will be met," the Cowboy repeats.

The escape was an aggravation, and no one is more upset over losing the Americans than the Cowboy is, but Yuri isn't focusing on the bigger picture. Once the transaction takes place, Yuri is planning on killing the prisoners anyway. Why should it matter how they got away? They'll all be dead within twenty-four hours. The man is losing his grip.

"I'm working on it," the Cowboy says, instead of going there. No need to tempt fate this close to the finish line.

"Working on it, by leaving for a few hours?"

"Would you like to discuss this in person, Yuri?"

There's no immediate answer, and the Cowboy wonders if a face-to-face meeting might actually be required. The Cowboy knows Yuri's reputation. His past. The things he's done, and the things that have been done to him.

Being tortured changes a man. Warps him into a funhouse mirror version of himself, enlarging some important parts while reducing others.

The Cowboy knows this, exquisitely well.

"No," Yuri finally says. "Alert me when you return."

"Contact me when the Americans are found. Don't kill them until I've had a chance to interrogate them."

"I wouldn't think of starting without you, Cowboy. Dasvidaniya."

JACK

Material things usually didn't impress me. The handful of times I'd gone to McGlade's various domiciles, he puffed and crowed while showing me expensive gadgets and rare objects, bragging about how much he paid for some work of art, or how old his single malt scotch was. I was a simple woman, with simple tastes, and didn't need my own Ms. Pac-Man machine, or a signed first edition of *The Big Sleep*. Especially when my Kindle Fire adequately replaced both.

But walking into Wyatt's house was like a trip through the looking glass.

Immediately upon entering, I was in the great room; a ridiculously enormous open space with a twenty-foot high log-lined cathedral ceiling, a river stone fireplace on each end, a full bar, a rustic, twelve person dining room table made of oak limbs, a red felt pool table, four gigantic leather sofas, a dozen matching easy chairs, an overhead ceiling fan network with a single belt that connected and turned all ten of them, and various full-size taxidermy animals including two grizzly bears, a puma, and a timber wolf. And there were logs everywhere; walls, beams, arches, and they even formed a grand staircase at the far end of the room.

It had a ski lodge vibe, with enough room to land a private plane.

I sat on a barstool at the bar, gaping at everything, and Wyatt returned from the bathroom and situated himself behind the elongated, rough-hewn countertop.

"Jack Daniels?" he asked.

I blinked. "Excuse me?"

He pulled a familiar, rectangular bottle from behind the bar and set it next to me.

Jack Daniels whiskey.

"Rocks?" he asked.

"No."

"Water?"

"A few drops."

He nodded his approval, as if adding water to open up a whiskey and release its flavors and aromas was some closely guarded secret. After setting two rocks glasses in front of me, he poured a few fingers in each and then produced a glass bottle of Acqua Panna. We each got a splash, and then Wyatt raised his glass.

I lifted mine as well.

"To friends," he said, "old and new."

We clinked. We drank. Jack Daniels tasted reassuringly familiar in this odd setting. I wanted to ask him more questions about the Cowboy, but for the moment I kept it congenial.

"Do you hunt?" I asked, my eyes falling on the stuffed wildcat behind the bar.

"No. The animals are all Annie's."

I took another sip. So did he.

"So, your friend Harry is a private detective. Do you work with him?"

"My husband does. I'm more of a secretary."

Wyatt winked. Of course he was a winker. It was an alpha male thing. "Do all secretaries pack a .357?"

"Around Harry? Yeah."

Wyatt finished his drink, then looked at mine, silently encouraging me to catch up with him. I made no effort to sip any faster. Rather than wait, he poured himself another.

"Tell me—" we both said at the same time.

Wyatt winked again. "Jinx." He raised his glass, and we clinked. "You first."

I took another small sip and said, "Tell me about your sister."

"Annie? We grew up with a bit of money, but our parents were... emotionally unavailable. They substituted expensive gifts for affection, and our dad never cottoned to the bible saying *spare the rod, spoil the child*. So she grew up tough. Even tougher than me."

"What did she do before the abduction?"

"A bit of everything. You could call her a Jack of all trades. She was into rodeo for a long time. Riding and roping. Bull riding. Girl could stick to a bull or a bucking bronco like super glue to your thumb. She was a WPRA star, won a lot of events."

"WPRA?"

"Women's Professional Rodeo Association. The PRCA, Professional Rodeo Cowboys Association, that's the big one that everyone knows. But when Annie was into rodeo, women weren't allowed to compete against men."

"How do you feel about that?"

Wyatt snorted. "It's bullshit. She would have whooped all their asses. Treat a person like a person. Everyone wants to divvy people up. This group, that group, my group, their group. You don't feel good about yourself, so you gotta separate yourself from other folks so you can feel superior."

He killed his second glass, and these weren't small glasses. I killed mine as well, only to encourage him to refill us both. The more he drank, the more he'd talk.

Wyatt gave an even more generous pour. He added water to mine, but didn't bother with his own.

"So, Annie—"

"Uh-uh," he said, wagging a finger. "Your turn. Tell me about your husband."

"He's..." What best described Phin? "He's a bad ass."

"Bad boy, huh?"

"Yes. No. He can be, but that's not what I'm saying. He's the kind of guy who you want on your side when the heavy shit goes down. Slow to anger, but quick to calm."

"So why are you riding with McGlade, instead of your bad ass husband?"

"He's...recuperating."

"Sorry to hear that. Nothing serious, I hope."

I shrugged. "He's tough. He'll get over it."

At least, that was my hope.

"You guys got kids?"

I considered the truth, discarded it. "No. You?"

"Naw."

"Is there a Mrs. Wyatt Earp Steinhoffer?"

He downed his third drink. "I don't believe in marriage."

"Why's that?"

"Because Jack Daniels is nice, but easy to get sick of," Wyatt said. He hefted another bottle onto the bar top. "Sometimes you also want Jägermeister."

He poured one for himself, and I took a tiny sip of my whiskey.

"Can I see your necklace?" I asked.

He nodded. I expected him to take it off. But instead he pulled it out of his shirt and leaned close to me.

He was too close, but I wanted to see it. I took it in my hand, Wyatt's whiskey breath in my hair. There was a divot in the rowel, and a few of the points were missing, but I couldn't tell if a bullet had done the damage, or something else had.

"I've never worn spurs," I said. "Do they make noise?"

Wyatt grinned at me. "Spurs are musical. Like a tinhorn jingling his pocket change in a Dodge City whorehouse."

I released the rowel and leaned back, crossing my legs to put some distance between us. Wyatt put his palms on the bar, and it looked like he was getting ready to vault over. I wasn't enjoying the way he was looking at me. It was a horny stranger stare. The stare of a man who wanted something, but didn't care what you wanted.

"What are you kids drinking?" McGlade had come in, and he was walking pretty fast for a fat guy. "Shit! Jäger? Do you have any Red Bull, Sheriff? A Jäger Bomb would really hit the spot."

As Harry sidled up on the stool next to me, and Wyatt reached under his magic bar and came up with a can. He pushed that, and a glass, over to Harry, who poured himself a shot of Jägermeister and topped it off with the energy drink.

McGlade raised it up. "To the Cowboy," he said. "Don't care if he's six feet under, or serving ten life sentences, as long as the son of a bitch is in a hole."

We all clinked glasses.

Harry downed his drink.

I sipped mine.

Wyatt, for some reason, didn't lift his glass to his lips.

HERB

This time, they came with guns.

Guns trumped a shock pole, and Herb surrendered on behalf of himself, and Tequila, who'd passed out again.

Herb expected to plead for Tequila's life, but the guards showed no intention of shooting the unconscious man. Instead, they had a wagon on the back of the ATV. Tequila was hoisted onto that, and Herb was pulled along behind them, a wire loop around his neck. Luckily, the added weight of Tequila meant the vehicle crept along at walking speed. As long as Herb didn't trip over something and fall, he was able to keep up without strangling.

If he had any doubt he was back in the USA, the doubt vanished when he and Tequila were taken over a slight slope, and Herb kicked a beer bottle.

The faded label was instantly recognizable.

Old Style.

Old Style was a cheap, mass market beer, like Budweiser or Miller. But it didn't have the nationwide reach of those brands. Old Style was regional. A Midwest thing.

Could they actually be in Illinois?

The landscape didn't seem familiar. Herb knew Illinois, even the southern part that consisted of a thirty million acre cornfield. And it didn't have the woodsy terrain of Wisconsin or Minnesota.

Iowa, maybe? One of the Dakotas? Nebraska?

The thought that Herb might be less than five hundred miles away from his home in Chicago was the most depressing thought he ever had. He felt like crying.

What was that Greek myth?

Tantalus. Condemned to stand for eternity in a pool of water with a fruit tree over his head. When he reached for the fruit to eat, it pulled away. When he stooped to drink, the water receded.

A mile or so later, gasping for air as they crested an endless, gradual slope, Herb was able to get his clearest look at his surroundings since his escape. Off in the distance, to the east, there was a house. And to the west, dotting the plains, a speckling of white dots.

Turbines.

A wind farm.

So close. And so far away.

Herb yelled. Loud as he could.

He didn't expect to be heard.

He didn't expect to be rescued.

Herb yelled to prove he was still there. Still alive. Still relevant.

He yelled for his friend, Tequila, who against all odds was still defying death.

He yelled for injustice. For bad luck. But also for the opportunity and privilege of being born. For living, up until this point, a damn fine life.

Herb Benedict took all that made him human, that made him *him*, and let it loose in a single, soul-baring, heartbreaking cry to the universe.

The universe didn't notice.

Then his catch pole shocked him, dropping Herb to his knees, and he was dragged for a few meters before the ATV stopped and he was able to stand up again, neck and throat aching, palms skinned.

Herb kept going. But he knew it didn't matter.

After that yell, he was empty.

He had nothing left.

YURI

"Vehicle, approaching from the south," Dmitri said.

Yuri checked the time. It was early. He pressed the intercom button. "Is it them?"

"Da. Yes."

Yuri set down the opium pipe. He was feeling no pain, but still judged himself clear-headed enough for this transaction. After a quick check of his desk, he located the battery operated disc sander, and then went to meet the arrivals.

They came in a large grapple truck; a construction vehicle that resembled a dump truck, but with a mechanical arm and crane attached to the cab, allowing it to load itself.

Yuri approached, flanked by two of his men. None of them were armed. And why would they be? There was nothing illegal about what was about to transpire. And Yuri didn't care what these people thought of his land train. In a few days, Yuri will be across the ocean, five thousand miles away.

No, this wasn't the transaction he had to worry about. That will come later. That's the big gamble.

This was nothing more than a side bet. Albeit, an essential one.

Yuri had never met the man he's dealing with, a metal scrapper named Melvin who owned a company called TungCore. He approached the truck with a practiced smile. Yuri wanted to foster a good relationship. One that might well continue into the next decade.

A man exited the cab. He was short, stout, wearing overalls and a weary face. MELVIN was stenciled on the left breast of his blue work shirt. He took a long look at the LeTourneau, then acknowledged Yuri and extended his hand.

"Welcome, my friend," Yuri said, shaking it enthusiastically.

"Ain't that the damnedest thing. A train with no track." He looked at Yuri. "You George?"

George was the Western equivalent of Yuri, in case Melvin had some prejudice against dealing with a Belarusian.

"I am."

"I'm Mel. This is my associate, Greg."

Greg was tall, lanky, and looked every bit as tired as Melvin.

"How was your trip?" Yuri asked, ever the cordial businessman.

"Long. And confusing. Never traveled by latitude and longitude before."

"Sorry for the trouble." Yuri was trying his best to sound as American as possible. "Damn train broke down here, we're still doing repairs. Thanks for meeting us."

"No problem, buddy. For an order this big, I would have driven all the way down to Brazil. Where do you want it?"

"In the last car, on the end. My guys can help. But do you mind if I..." Yuri raised the grinder.

"Of course. This way."

Melvin led him to the rear of the truck, to the tailgate. It had a pin lock in it the width of Yuri's wrist. The man Melvin brought along, Greg, pulled the pin and the two men lowered it, revealing the payload.

Yuri was surprised by how shiny the rods were. And how small.

"This is twenty tons?" Yuri said.

"Yes sir. It's a heavy sucker. Twice the weight of lead. Almost as tough as diamonds. You need a hand up there?"

Yuri was only paying half-attention, and already climbing up the rear ladder, into the dump bed.

The eight rods were each six feet long, thick as a tree, and the sun reflecting off them seemed even brighter than the actual sun.

Yuri crawled to the end of the nearest rod, switched on his grinder, and touched the sanding disc to it, leaning in hard.

There were sparks, but not many, and the color was dark orange. The grinder could cut through a crowbar in less than a minute. But when Yuri turned it off, there wasn't a scratch on the rod. He checked the grinding wheel, and saw that much of it had worn away.

This was the real thing.

"This is…perfect," Yuri said.

"Glad to hear it, George. As you can guess, it isn't the easiest metal to work with. Especially making rods this size."

"I'm aware of that."

"And the price per pound has gone up since we took the order, but of course I'm honoring our original agreement. With delivery, we're looking at four hundred and sixty thousand dollars."

Yuri nodded. He climbed out of the truck bed, and snapped his fingers. One of his men, Grigori, brought over his laptop.

It took five minutes to make the bank transfer. Normally, the process took less than three minutes, but Yuri kept hitting the wrong keys.

His mind was elsewhere. Back in Belarus.

"Thank you for your business, George. Put them in the last car, you said?"

Yuri nodded, unable to take his eyes off the rods.

"I gotta ask this. What in the world do you need eight, two and a half ton tungsten carbide rods for?"

Yuri smiled, thinking of President Lukashenko. "They're a surprise. For an old friend."

Melvin scratched his head. "Oooookay. Well, I hope your friend likes them."

"Melvin," Yuri said, "these are going to absolutely blow him away."

JACK

"All I'm saying," I told Harry, "is I don't trust the guy."

Wyatt had left us, yet again, to go to the bathroom. Yet again.

"Because he keeps going to the shitter?" McGlade said. "Maybe he has irritable bowel syndrome. Or has to put out a fire."

"Huh?"

"Wring the zinger. Uncap the mushroom. Make the bladder gladder. You know. Piss. All that booze has to go somewhere."

McGlade had a point. Wyatt had made some serious dents in the whiskey, the Jägermeister, and a recently introduced bottle of Cuervo.

"What about the spur?" I asked. "Spurs jingle, and in Wyatt's gunfight story he said it was crazy quiet that night. Not even the crickets out. Remember? So how could the Cowboy have snuck up on him? Wyatt would have heard him coming."

McGlade poured more Red Bull. "Brilliant deduction, Holmes. The jury is sure to convict and recommend the death penalty, based on that rock solid evidence." He took a sip, made a sound of approval, and drained it. "C'mon, Jack. Guy slips up once, and he's automatically the villain? That only happens in trashy thriller novels."

I wasn't convinced. "It's more than a slip-up. It's a lie."

"Everyone lies when telling stories. It's called taking creative embellishment liberties. Or something. You don't just tell your buddies you scored. You tell them you scored with the hottest chick ever, who was amazing in bed, and then her twin sister joined you. Which actually happened to me. Twice."

"So you believe him?"

"I believe everyone. And I believe no one. But most of all, I believe I'll have another Jäger Bomb. That would be a good title for something, wouldn't it? Maybe I'll pitch it to my agent."

Harry got up and walked around the bar, hunting for more Red Bull. While his head was down he said, "Holy shit, Jack. I think you may be right about him."

"What?" I stood up to see what Harry had found.

With dramatic flourish, Harry set a bottle of beer on the counter.

"Old Style," he said. "You can't trust anyone who drinks Old Style."

I wasn't impressed. Harry shrugged and pinched off the cap with his robot hand, then took a swig.

"I hate this beer. Have I ever made you try Sam Adams Utopias? Two-fifty a bottle, but worth every penny. Best beer ever."

"You pay two hundred and fifty dollars for a bottle of beer, and then wonder why you're broke."

"I don't wonder at all. I know exactly why I'm broke. I have impulse control problems and I make bad decisions."

"Speaking of," I said. "Heckle and Jeckle. What's their story?"

"You mean, why do they seem like creepy, telepathic serial killers in training?"

I nodded.

"They answered an ad. Knew who I was. Were willing to work for free. I ran their backgrounds. Sealed juvee records, but nothing recent. You got a bad feeling about them, too?"

I shrugged, and drank more whiskey.

"You don't think I'd notice if I hired two lunatics to work for me?"

"You married a lunatic."

"I explained that. Impulse control and bad decisions. But it's not really my fault. I didn't think women could be serial killers, because; sexism."

"I think you're the first guy to use sexism as a defense."

"*Equal* doesn't mean *same*. I'm a feminist, but there are some big differences between the sexes. Men tend to be more violent."

I'd heard this argument before. "Women can be violent."

"I said *more* violent. You don't see women starting wars, torturing prisoners, or grabbing an AR-14 and firing into a crowd."

"Putting women on a pedestal is its own shitty kind of sexism."

"I'm not saying women aren't horrible. They are. Look what you just did to your poor husband. But there's a big difference between being an asshole and ethnic cleansing. Yes, there are female serial killers. Yes, there are women in prison, many for violent offenses. But there are twelve times as many men in prison. That's not sexism. We're just worse than you."

As a rule, I didn't like to agree with Harry. But considering the number of men I arrested, vs. women, I understood his point.

"I still think there's something going on with Wyatt."

"Sure there is. It's called chemistry. He's really hot. And I'm betting Phin hasn't tapped that in a while."

At the other end of the great room, Wyatt was coming back. A woman on his arm.

"Why do you say that?" I asked Harry.

"Because there are no men's magazines called *Fupa*."

"You're a dick."

"I know. I hate myself, remember? But it's always good to be reminded how much I suck."

"Jill," Wyatt said on approach, "Harry, I'd like you to meet my sister. Annie."

Annie was brunette, long hair that hung past her collarbone, and much shorter than her brother. Like Wyatt, she wore jeans and a flannel shirt, though hers was green, and she filled her clothes out in an angular, rather than curvy, way. Unlike Wyatt, she wasn't wearing a belt or gun holster, and she approached as if walking wasn't something she did much of.

Harry actually stood up—I'd never seen him stand for a woman before—and immediately stuck out his hand. "Miss Steinhoffer, it's a pleasure."

Her eyes lit up when she saw him, and she shook enthusiastically. I also took her hand, and found her grip to be firm and assured, but a bit moist. And there was something...odd, about her face. Then I remembered her ordeal with the Cowboy, and all the pulled teeth. She must have had some major orthodontia work done, and it left her jawline somewhat asymmetrical.

"Nice to meet you both," she said. Her voice lacked the energy of her handshake.

"Thank you for agreeing to this interview," said Harry. "I can only guess how difficult it is for you."

So Harry was attempting charm to make sure she'd go on camera.

"Anything I can do to catch that psychopath, I'm willing to do."

"Is now a good time? I can call my guys in."

Annie nodded. "Actually, I'd like to get it over with. Not just because of the bad memories, but I've had a long day."

Harry stepped away to use his cell and Wyatt said, "Annie volunteers at the dog shelter in town."

Annie smiled, which unfortunately looked distorted and scary. Poor thing. "Chasing after dogs all day can wear a girl out."

"You're an animal lover?" I asked.

"Of course."

"And you hunt?"

Annie stared at me like I'd asked her to lasso the moon.

"These stuffed trophies," I said, indicating the nearest taxidermy bear. "Wyatt said they were yours."

Annie nodded. "I bought them. I didn't hunt them. They're antiques."

"Ah, I see. I was under the impression you shot them."

She smiled that creepy smile again. "What fun is shooting something that can't shoot back?"

What an odd thing to say. I excused myself to go to the bathroom, and Wyatt asked if I needed help finding it.

"I'll manage," I said, not wanting him to come along.

Or did I secretly want his company?

Was my suspicion actually just a cover for a crush?

I considered it as I walked off, alone. I prided myself in being self-aware, so I was self-aware enough to know that I wasn't self-aware enough. Among my navel-gazing habits was second-guessing, third-guessing, and fourth-guessing myself, and an inability to understand what my motives were.

Truth was, Phin and I hadn't had sex in a while, and really good sex for even longer. And that made me feel hormonally, and emotionally, bereft. I knew Wyatt was flirting with me. At least, I think he was. Maybe my adverse reaction was my fault, not his. And now I was getting an odd vibe from his sister.

What seemed more likelier? That Heckle, Jeckle, Wyatt, and Annie were all hiding deep, dark secrets, and were actually terrible people? Or that I was the terrible person, trying to hide that from the world and overreacting?

Odds were on me being the crazy one.

Leaving the great room, I walked down a hallway decorated with plaques and medals. Ann Steinhoffer won a whole lot of competitions. Roping. Shooting. Riding. Racing. And one for Steer Wrestling, which is apparently a thing.

Tough chick.

Wyatt, though he didn't mention it, also had his share of awards, including a trophy shelf. Seems the guy was an amateur boxer. Heavyweight. And he'd won more than a few bouts.

Wyatt and Annie were probably good people. And Heckle and Jeckle were probably harmless, socially awkward nerds. The problem was me, angry with the world because I'd driven my husband into the bed of his ex-girlfriend.

McGlade, though, really was a dick.

I found the bathroom, and it was lush, all mirrors and granite and brass, large enough to work-out in. The rustic touch was a toilet with a pull chain flush. When I was finished I whipped out my cell and called Phin, rehearsing my apology in my head.

It didn't matter. He didn't pick up.

I tried to locate his phone, but it was turned off. Google's last checkpoint was Chicago, hours ago.

Even though I'd gotten no alerts, I double-checked to see if I'd gotten any texts or voicemails.

Nada.

Fix it when you get home, Jack. Do whatever it takes to win him back. Right now, focus on finding Herb.

I washed my hands, tried to shake off the whiskey in my system, and strolled back to the group. Heckle and Jeckle had set up next to one of the fireplaces, Harry and Annie facing each other in two of the deep leather chairs. As I approached, they were already in the midst of the interview. I stood behind the cameras, next to Wyatt, who was holding a fresh drink.

"I'm horrified," McGlade said. "And I hesitate to bring this up. But all those things that were done to you; I'm sure some of my viewers won't be able to believe you went through all of that and still survived. Is there any sort of evidence to support your claim?"

McGlade, the dick, went straight for the sensationalism. I felt awful for her.

Annie hesitated, and then she stood up and began to unbutton her flannel shirt. This stunt apparently ran in the family.

A moment later, I was sorry I had that thought.

Annie wasn't showing off a scar.

Annie *was* a scar.

Every bit of her front that wasn't covered by her sports bra was scarred. Shiny, off-white, raised, gnarled streaks of tissue. A giant scar mosaic. Then she turned around, and her back was even worse. It looked like someone had stapled spiced ham to her back.

McGlade was quiet. I don't think he was doing his dramatic pause nonsense. I think he was just as shocked as I was.

When he finally found his voice, he asked, "And this was all the Cowboy?"

Annie nodded. "And that's not all." She put her face in her hands, and when she looked up again, her face had—

Deflated.

It seriously looked like someone had pulled her jawbone out of its socket. Her cheeks were sunken in. Her lips flapped, like a chimpanzee. It took me a moment to realize she'd taken out her false teeth, and whatever other orthodontia she'd been wearing.

"Whoa," Harry said.

Annie put her mouthpieces back in, then sat down and began to button her shirt. I tried to imagine the courage it would take to show myself on the Internet if I were scarred like that, and didn't think I'd be able to do it.

"Are you assisting your brother in searching for the Cowboy?" Harry recovered enough to ask.

"No. I appreciate what he's doing. But I've done my best to put it all behind me." Annie looked away from Harry, speaking directly into the camera. "The past can consume you, if you allow it. I don't have control over what was done to me. But I have control over how I go forward. If I was seeking justice, or revenge, then the Cowboy would still have the power. The best advice I can give anyone who has had any sort of tragedy is: move on. If you let it define you, you've let the bad guys win."

That was something to chew on. I was definitely hiding from my past. Pretending it didn't happen. Pushing away my husband. Keeping all of my scars hidden from everyone, including myself.

What defined me?

My daughter?

I hadn't even spoken to my daughter since I left Florida.

My friends were few and far between. My husband was probably cheating on me. My job at the gun range was just something to do.

What defined me?

Chasing criminals?

If that was the case, I was an idiot. Because chasing criminals brought me, and those that I cared about, untold amounts of pain.

"So you're saying, after the Cowboy did all of this to you, you wouldn't shoot him if you had the chance?"

"Shoot him?" Annie guffawed. "There's no way I could shoot him."

She held up her right hand—

—and pulled her index and middle fingers off with her left hand.

Then she held up her left hand and did the same.

"The Cowboy cut four of my fingers off," Annie said. "Once upon a time, I was pretty good with a pistol. Now, I'd have a better chance of hitting a target if I threw the bullets."

I hadn't even noticed she had rubber fingers when I shook her hand. Some sleuth I was.

"My hand is fake," Harry said, holding it up. "It also vibrates."

Awkward.

When no one reacted, Harry said, "We can cut that. Let's see…uh…okay. What do you think about your brother's theory, that the Cowboy has made his opium farm portable?"

"I agree," Annie said. "One hundred percent."

"What makes you so sure he's right?"

"I've seen the tracks. There are fresh ones nearby."

"Fresh ones?" Harry said.

"They're on the edge of our property," she replied. "Want to see?"

HERB

Left.
    Right.
Left.
Right.
So tired.
So very, very tired.

Herb remembered the fatigue that came from working tough cases. Sixty to eighty hour work weeks. No sleep. Constantly on the go.

Left.
Right.

Those were his younger days, before Bernice lost her patience and demanded he work sensible hours. He could clearly recall one investigation, it might have been Charles Kork, where he was so exhausted he actually fell asleep standing next to the office coffee machine. His partner, Jack, had woken him up, startling Herb so badly he almost lost his balance and fell over.

That was nothing compared to how tired he was right now.

Left.
Right.
Left.

Trudging after the ATV, practically sleepwalking, Herb was ready to give up. All he had to do was fall down. He'd choke to death in a matter of minutes. Probably black out long before it became unbearable. Or he might even get lucky, and his neck would snap.

Right.

Left.

Right.

Left.

It was so tempting.

So, so tempting.

So, so tired.

Beyond tired.

Herb was so beyond tired, he had begun to hallucinate.

Not anything particularly trippy, like dragons or aliens or talking clouds.

Herb's hallucination was based on an old memory, of an old friend.

Right.

Left.

As he plodded along to his death march, he thought he saw a road in the distance. And on that road, clear as if it had been real, was an obnoxious, bright red recreational vehicle.

Harry McGlade's motorhome. He'd named that technological, gas-guzzling monstrosity the Crimebago Deux.

What a stupid thing to imagine.

Right.

Left.

Right.

Why couldn't Herb have a vision of his wife? Or angels, welcoming him into the pearly gates?

Maybe that happened to luckier guys. Herb's misfiring brain had to imagine, of all things, obnoxious Harry McGlade. Driving through a landscape dotted with white windmills. Of all the stupid—

That was pretty stupid.

Very stupid.

The stupidest thing ever.

Left.

Right.

Left.

So stupid, that Herb began to question if it was all in his head.

Of all the things he could conjure up? A whole lifetime of pleasurable activities? Vacations, food, love, sex, friends, holidays, and the thing Herb was seeing was the Crimebago Deux?

It didn't make sense.

And because it didn't make sense, maybe it did make sense.

Maybe it wasn't a hallucination at all.

One way to find out. And Herb really had nothing to lose.

In fact, another jolt to the neck might snap him out of his stupor.

As the RV passed in the distance, no more than two hundred meters away, Herb shouted, "HARRY!"

As expected, he got shocked. But he managed to keep his feet, and the pain gave him a fat dose of reality.

The RV was still there.

It was real.

Could it be that McGlade was actually looking for them? That he knew he and Tequila were close?

"HARRY!"

This time the jolt went on and on, silencing the word in his throat, dropping Herb to his knees.

Then he was being dragged again.

Dragged, as the RV drove on, not even slowing down.

THE MAN

Jack Daniels is ridiculously easy to track.
For someone who is so cautious that she faked her own death and is living under the name Jill Johnson, she doesn't seem to have any awareness of her surroundings whatsoever.

And neither does her rotund partner in crime, Harry McGlade.

Both former cops. Both with successes in the private sector. And neither take any precautions to make sure they aren't being tailed.

He follows until the bright red motorhome—real inconspicuous, McGlade—comes to a stop in the middle of a field.

The man picks up speed—

—and drives right past them.

He watches the rearview, wondering if they'll follow. Almost hoping for it.

But they stay parked.

There's a rolling hill ahead. He drives the rental car just past the crest, pulls over, and gets out. Unlike his blissfully unaware target, the man takes a long, hard look in all directions to make sure there's no one else around, before going into the trunk and taking out the rifle case.

It takes three minutes to assemble the takedown Kel-Tec SU-16A. He pauses several times during the rifle's assembly, to peer through a Leupold scope.

To look at Jack.

To look all around him.

Nothing but wind turbines and prairie dogs.

He has three magazines, each loaded with ten rounds of .223 Remington cartridges.

Sniper bullets.

Jack, Harry, along with another man and woman, are walking through the grass, apparently searching for something. With them is an absolutely gigantic dog, which takes off, bounding up the road.

In the man's direction.

Can that dog scent me from this far away?

He stares through the scope, watching the beast break into a run.

Then McGlade lets out a shrill whistle, and the dog returns to him.

The threat averted, the man hunkers behind the side of the car, and pulls on the forestock of the weapon, releasing the integrated bipod. He gets on the ground, scopes in on Jack, and wonders how she'd react if she knew he was there.

The thought brings a smile to his lips.

JACK

Heckle and Jeckle lugged out the gear and began to shoot the gigantic tire tracks as we all gathered around. Then they focused on McGlade, who had taken a knee next to the tracks, his expression grim as he stared into the camera.

"What kind of vehicle could make tracks this large? I can think of only one. At one time, it brought joy to children and inebriated blue collar workers from red states. But now, a beloved symbol of American ingenuity has shown its dark side. I speak, of course, of the irrepressible... *monster truck*."

I rubbed my eyes, feeling a McGlade-sized headache coming on.

"Could the Cowboy be roaming the Great Plains in a fleet of 4x4 monsters?" he babbled on. "Sheriff, have you spotted any monster truck evidence?"

"Like what?" Wyatt asked.

"Like... a trail of crushed cars?"

That went straight to the top of the dumbest things Harry ever said.

"Can't say that I have," answered Wyatt. Props to him for keeping a straight face.

McGlade tried to stand up, and it took a lot of effort because; fat.

"Maybe it's monster trucks. Maybe it's a ghost train. Maybe ghost monster trucks, or a train with monster truck wheels. Or maybe, like crop circles, it's ancient aliens, returning to earth to claim the abandoned souls of the pharaohs. The possibilities are double infinite. Whatever it could be, we're going to get to the bottom of this bizarre, possibly ghostly, possibly alien, possibly even alien ghostly, torture slash murder mystery. Be sure to check out our previous episodes, and click below to subscribe. And tune in for our next episode of Private Dick Live and Streaming In Your Face. I'm Harry McGlade. Keep your lights on and your doors locked."

"Aliens?" I said when the cameras stopped rolling.

"You missed the ancient alien episode?" McGlade frowned. "That was one of my favorites. Why does the Cowboy wear a bandana on his face? Could it be to cover his weird, alien-shaped head? Heckle, show her the artist's interpretation."

Heckle took a piece of paper out of his pocket and unfolded it, revealing a poorly done pen sketch. It looked like ET in a balaclava.

"I drew it myself," McGlade said.

I turned away from all the stupid, and walked over to Wyatt, who was studying the tire impressions. "Can you follow these tracks?"

He nodded.

"When can you start?"

"Tomorrow."

"How about now?"

He shook his head. "Gotta pack my camping gear. Food. Water. Get my horse ready. Plus, I need to go up to Mulford, for supplies. Best to start first thing in the morning. I assume you folks want to come along?"

"Yeah."

"Why don't we invite our new friends to stay the night?" Annie said. "There are plenty of rooms. You can entertain, and I'll go to Mulford."

"I can go," Wyatt said.

"It's a fifty mile drive," said Annie. "And I wouldn't trust you to drive a lawnmower right now."

I watched them stare each other down, and assumed Wyatt's alcoholism was a point of contention in their household.

"Fine," Wyatt said. "I can use another drink anyway. Harry, you got any beer on board?"

"I should have a six pack of Zombie Dust in the pantry. It's warm, though."

"No problem. I'd drink hot piss if it was over five percent alcohol."

"Good to know next time I'm out shopping."

We lined up to pile back into the Crimebago Deux, and McGlade came over and whispered, "I got this."

"Got what?"

"I know how to follow the tire tracks. We don't need Wyatt."

"Why are we whispering?" I whispered.

"Because I've warmed up to your over-bloated, crazy paranoia. I think something is going on with Wyatt and Annie. I'll tell you when we're alone."

He left me that nugget and walked on ahead, followed by Heckle and Jeckle, who were giggling.

As they climbed into the motorhome, I stopped and stared out over the plains.

Inexplicably, I felt a chill.

I hugged myself.

"Cold?" Wyatt asked, taking the opportunity to sidle up and put an arm around my waist. "Gets nippy out here this time of year."

I gently disengaged. "I'm fine."

But I wasn't fine. Though it was cool out, that wasn't the reason I shuddered.

Being outside, surrounded by all the turbines, made me feel spooked.

Like we were being watched.

YURI

"We have the Americans," Dmitri announced over the intercom.

"Bring them to the Punishment Room," Yuri ordered. "How long before we're able to move?"

"Two hours. Three. Bank 6 battery working fine now."

"So what's the problem?"

"Bank 5."

These delays were unacceptable. "I want to be in Wyoming for the launch on Saturday."

"Da. We make it."

"See that we do."

Yuri drummed his fingers on his desk, reviewing the timeline in his head for the hundredth time.

Make the promised weight.

Deliver the opium.

Get to the launch pad.

Pay the outstanding balance.

Load the tungsten rods onto the satellite.

Launch.

Rain hell.

There were still many things that could go wrong. If they didn't deliver their promised weight, *Solntsevskaya Bratva*—the Russian mafia—would not be pleased. Even if they met their quota, drug deals were always risky, especially with tens of millions of dollars at stake. There were also launch contingencies. The permits were all in place (And why shouldn't they be? What Yuri was doing was perfectly legal) but shooting a rocket into low earth orbit always came with risks. If it exploded, the payload could be recovered; the high melting point of the rods would ensure their safety. But another satellite would need to be built, and Yuri's funds were stretched to the max.

Unless…

The Cowboy was buying the LeTourneau, and Yuri was giving him a deal. But maybe there was a way to extract more money.

It would be delicate. Yuri had noticed the rising tension between the two of them, especially in the last few days. The Cowboy was wise enough to not want Yuri as an enemy. But Yuri was wise enough not to push his fear enforcer too hard.

Somewhere, in the middle, there might be some room to renegotiate their deal. The prisoner escape, and the Americans, were the key.

Yuri would have to tread carefully.

After another quick hit of the opium pipe, Yuri was climbing into Car #4. The Americans were kneeling side-by-side, their ankles and wrists chained to bolts in the floor. They wore guard uniforms, taken from the men they'd killed, and Yuri bit back a flare of rage.

"How did you escape?" he asked.

Neither answered. The short one looked barely alive.

Yuri squatted next to them, taking the short one's face in his massive hand.

"I know it was you. The Cowboy turned off the cameras when you were in here. Tell me what was said."

The man's eyelids fluttered. "You're a big man," he softly said.

"Yes. Yes I am."

"I've killed bigger."

Yuri slapped him, knocking him over. Then he stood and went to the tool board, his eyes locking onto a cordless drill.

Out of the many tortures Yuri had endured at the hands of his former comrades, the drill into the femur was one of the worst.

He picked it up, and placed the long, rusty bit against the short man's thigh.

"I want to know what was said."

"It wasn't him," the other man blurted out. "It was me. I stole a pair of wire clippers."

Yuri ignored him. He grabbed the short man by the hair and peered into his droopy eyes.

"You seem a bit sleepy. Let me wake you up."

"No!" screamed his companion.

Yuri pressed the trigger on the drill.

Nothing happened.

He looked over at the nearest guard. "Why isn't the battery charged?" he barked.

The guard shrugged.

Yuri stood, going back to the wall to look for something that didn't require eighteen volts. He picked up a small, butane-fueled blowtorch. Rather than embarrass himself again, he pulled the trigger to make sure it worked.

It didn't. Out of fluid.

"Seriously?" He threw the torch onto the floor. "Who's job is it to keep this room stocked?"

"Anton's."

"Where's Anton?"

"They killed him."

Gritting his teeth, Yuri sought out another implement. He was trying to decide between an icepick and some vice-grip pliers when the short man mumbled something.

"What was that?" Yuri asked.

"Sex," the man mumbled again.

Yuri approached. "What are you talking about?"

"The Cowboy. Turned off the cameras. Then we had sex."

The man didn't seem to be joking around.

"You had sex?" the other American asked. "With the Cowboy?"

"It wasn't consensual," the man said. "Entirely."

"So how did you get away?" Yuri asked.

"Cowboy gave me wire cutters. Said you were going to kill me. Didn't want me to die."

"The Cowboy...wanted you to escape?" Yuri couldn't believe it.

The man shrugged. "It was good sex."

Yuri considered the icepick again, then rejected the idea. Something about this man's words rang true.

"Can you prove this?" he asked.

"Sure," the man said. "I can show you."

"How?"

"Unchain me and bend over."

Rather than anger at the insult, Yuri began to formulate a plan. If this were actually true, then he had more bargaining power over the Cowboy than he thought.

"Unchain them," he told the guard. "Put them back to work in Car #12. And bring them food. And blankets."

The guard hesitated. "Yuri, they killed Anton. And Peter."

"Do you want to be next?" Yuri snarled.

"No. My son, he's in Little League. I'm coaching next season."

"Then do as I said." Yuri turned to the Americans. "If you're lying to me, your deaths will be more horrible than you can ever imagine."

Then he left the car.

If he played this the right way, it could be the best of all possible outcomes.

But he needed to think.

To plan.

Yuri took out his cell phone, and texted the Cowboy.

WE HAVE THEM. COME RIGHT AWAY.

TOM AND JERRY

They snuck out of the rear exit door of the nearly-empty movie theater before the opening credits were over, then double-checked to make sure they had the ticket stubs in their pockets. They'd seen the film the night before, so they were ready to answer any and all questions about the stupid characters and silly plot when the police asked.

Before they walked out the exit, they shoved matchsticks into the lock mechanism of the door into the alley, so it wouldn't lock.

Their bikes were already parked there. It took thirty-eight minutes for them to get home, riding as fast as they could.

Even though it was a long film, two hours and eighteen minutes, they would be cutting things close.

The ski masks, latex gloves, plastic shoe covers, and disposable rain ponchos were hidden in a garbage bag, in the bushes outside the dining room window.

So were the aluminum bats. They'd bought one at a sporting goods store, a week earlier, paying cash. The other was a gift from FatherAss, years ago.

After putting on the masks, ponchos, shoe covers, and gloves, they entered through the front door and found FatherAss in the living room, asleep in front of the TV.

That wouldn't do.

They wanted him to see it coming.

Jerry shook him awake and said, "Hello, Father."

Tom hit him first.

Beating a man to death was easier than the twins would have guessed. It only took three or four solid hits to the head.

Since it went so fast, they were able to spend an extra five minutes busting up the living room, kitchen, and upstairs bedrooms.

The last thing they broke was the living room window. From the outside, of course.

Then they removed their protective gear, shoved it back into the garbage bag with the bats, made sure the top was tied good and tight, and tossed the bag into the pond as they biked past, on their way back to the movie theater.

The twins parked in the alley, let themselves into the back door, pulling out and discarding the matchsticks, and took their seats five minutes before the credits rolled. No one saw them.

In the lobby, they refilled the sodas and made elaborate fun of the cashier, being such jerks that she threatened to call her manager. Afterward, they immediately went to the Denny's around the corner, demanded needlessly complicated orders, and sent their food back, twice.

They would be remembered.

For a while, it looked like the rain that had been forecast days before wasn't going to come. But the skies did open up, and the twins called their father's car service to get a ride, because who would want to bike all that way when it was pouring out?

When the limo driver pulled up to their house, he noticed the broken window and told them to stay in the car as he went to go check it out.

The twins clutched each other and began to giggle, letting their guard down for the only time that night.

"Congratulations, Tom-boy," said Jerry. "We just inherited twenty million dollars."

JACK

With another beer in him, courtesy of McGlade, Wyatt became loudly insistent we join him in the hot tub when we returned to the ransion. I hadn't brought a swimsuit, but the twins and Harry were down for it. To try and convince me, Wyatt brought us to the tub area, a cedar-lined room next to the kitchen.

Calling it a *hot tub* was probably a misnomer. It was more like a *hot pool*; five feet deep, large enough to do laps in, with a riverstone fireplace at one end and his and hers washrooms at the other.

I wasn't really a hot tub fan; sitting around, doing nothing, always struck me as a waste of time. But the sheer novelty of actually trying out a hot tub that large won out over the fact that I'd have to soak in nothing but a sports bra, panties, and one of Harry's XXL t-shirts. I changed in the Crimebago, his black MONSTER MOVIE shirt hanging to my knees.

"What do you think, Rosa?" I asked, modeling for the dog. "Can you tell it isn't Gucci?"

Rosalina couldn't seem to tell.

I wondered what I was supposed to do with my revolver, and decided to lug it, and my clothes and phone, in a pillowcase.

As I exited the RV, I ran into Annie, who was behind the wheel of a Chevy Silverado. She pulled up next to me and rolled down the window.

"Wyatt likes you," she said.

"He told you that?"

"I can tell. We're close."

Her expression was tough to read. If they weren't siblings, I would have guessed she was acting jealous.

"I'm married," I told her.

"Have you ever been with a woman?"

That came out of nowhere.

"I haven't."

"You'd like it," she said.

"Well, as I said, married."

Annie shrugged. "It wouldn't have to be with me. The scars, the fingers, the teeth...I know I'm repulsive."

"I believe, when it comes to attraction, it's what's inside that counts."

"Sure." She unclipped some sunglasses from the sun visor and put them on. "If you lay Wyatt, make him wear a rubber. He's been with *everyone*."

Annie winked, then sped off.

The men were already in the hot tub. Wyatt had a metal martini shaker, and was pouring a round of something into plastic cups. I set my pillowcase on one of the molded chairs, and descended the stairs into the pool.

Wow. It felt amazing.

I waded in perfectly clear and warm chest-deep water over to the group, and Wyatt held out a cup.

"I'm good," I said, not taking the drink. "Headache."

"Try it. It's called a *Hot Blooded*."

"I have this rule about not accepting a beverage that I didn't see poured."

Wyatt's eyes crinkled. "Did something happen to you once? Drugged? Raped?"

"This hot tub is incredible," I said, ignoring the creepy question. "Is it saline?"

"Yeah." Wyatt downed the drink he'd offered me, then went to the side of the pool and pulled himself out of the water. Then he made a show of opening up the martini shaker and adding ingredients he had lined up, poolside. A Hot Blooded was made with Jack

Daniels, blood orange juice, agave nectar, and a jalapeno pepper, snapped in half. He poured two and brought one over to me.

I took it, smiling like I enjoyed having pushy alpha males make up my mind for me, and had a sip.

It was actually really good. Maybe a bit too much heat, but when I made one for Phin I'd limit the pepper.

Phin.

What the hell am I going to do about that situation?

"Ready for the bubbles?" Wyatt asked.

I didn't know what he meant, so I didn't answer. Turns out, Wyatt wasn't waiting for an answer, because he was already pressing a button next to the drain basket.

The calm, warm waters immediately began to churn. A massage jet hit me at exactly the right spot between my shoulders, and I leaned against it, letting out a sigh.

McGlade, who'd been discussing edits with the twins, bounced over to me, raising up his cup. "Hey! It's my Rainmakers shirt! Looks good on you."

"Thanks."

"If it fades, you bought it."

Wyatt was mixing himself another drink, his hand getting heavier.

"So," McGlade said, leaning in closer and speaking under the sound of the tub jets. "I heard a convo between the Steinhoffer siblings. Laugh like I just said something funny."

"I don't find you particularly funny."

"Do it for Wyatt so he doesn't get suspicious."

"If I laughed at one of your lame jokes, that would make him suspicious."

"Whatever. Guess what they said?"

I waited.

"They said they'd love to take turns with you."

"And that made you suspicious?"

"They were talking about doing something to you, Jack. And I can guess what it is."

"Sex?"

"What? No. Torture. Killing you. Wait, why did you say sex?"

"They've both been hitting on me."

"Seriously?"

I sipped my drink and nodded.

McGlade's plum face scrunched up in thought. "Hmm. That might make sense. I had some alone time with Annie, and she didn't seem interested in me in the slightest. So being a lesbian fits."

"She's not into you, so she must be queer?"

He made a *no duh* face.

I glanced at Wyatt. He grinned and winked.

I glanced at the twins. They were giggling amongst themselves.

There was enough toxic masculinity in that hot tub to cause a skin rash.

Wyatt began to wade over with the martini shaker, and McGlade said, "I'm going to go check on Waddlebutt. I don't give unsolicited advice—"

"You're constantly giving unsolicited advice."

"—but I'd caution against having revenge-sex with Wyatt to get back at Phin. He's a player. Trust me, takes one to know one."

"I know. And I don't need to be one to know that."

"Just be careful. But if things do get serious, try to get a naked pic of him. That guy is *built*."

McGlade tried to pull himself out of the water like Wyatt had done, couldn't get his fat ass up on the pool ledge, and waded over to the stairs. He said something to Heckle and Jeckle, and they nodded.

When Harry got out of the water, the level dropped three inches.

"Another Hot Blooded?" Wyatt asked me, standing too close.

"Still haven't finished this one."

He topped me off anyway.

I smiled pretty. "Where would I be without a big, strong man showing me what I want?"

If Wyatt caught the sarcasm, he didn't show it.

The guy was ridiculously cute. And built. But what I'd said to Annie was true. Personalities, not looks, was what did it for me. Unlike Wyatt, Phin treated me like an equal and a friend. He didn't pour me drinks. He asked first.

God, I missed him.

And I should have let him come along.

It took Wyatt's Neanderthal act to make me realize that I'd been treating Phin the same way. Like the alpha who knew better. Forcing him to do what I wanted.

"Thank you," I told Wyatt.

"For what?"

"For helping me realize that I married the right guy."

I pulled up out of the pool, took a towel off a hook, wrapped it around my body, and then grabbed my pillowcase and headed for the women's washroom.

The interior looked like it belonged in a health club, complete with subway tile, benches, and lockers. The shower looked big and inviting, and my skin was tingling from the salt water, but I wasn't sure I wanted to get naked in that house.

I gave it a quick inspection, looking for peepholes. None that I could see, and goosebumps were forming because I was getting really cold, and the showerhead was massive, about eight times the size of my rain shower at home.

I decided to risk it, putting the pillowcase with the gun and my clothes on the floor next to the shower, setting my wet shirt and underwear next to the case, then turning on the spout.

Wow.

It was like being under a waterfall.

I had no idea how we could fit one of these into our bedroom at home, but we needed to get one. As amazing as the hot tub was, this shower was even better. There was a fresh bottle of shampoo on a wire shelf, and I lathered up and fantasized about being rich.

I'd just finished rinsing off when the lights went out.

In the pitch blackness, I immediately dropped to all four and crawled over to the shower curtain, reaching underneath for the pillowcase and the Taurus.

The pillowcase was gone.

HERB

They were brought back to the farm car and locked inside with a pile of blankets and two paper plates stacked with pancakes.

They were microwave pancakes, some still frozen in the center, and absolutely drenched with artificial blueberry syrup.

It was the greatest thing Herb had ever put in his mouth.

"Quick thinking," he told Tequila, who had cocooned himself in blankets. "That worked out pretty good."

"When in doubt, tell the truth."

Herb paused in mid-chew. "Wait... the truth?"

Tequila nodded.

Herb tried to wrap his head around it. "You didn't actually have sex with that psychopath. Did you?"

"I did."

"No."

"Yeah."

"No."

"Yeah."

"How could you?"

Tequila shrugged. "The Cowboy pulled down my pants, and I put my—"

"I know how it works," Herb interrupted, not wanting to hear the details. "I want to know how you could do that with someone who shot off half your ear."

"You would have done the same thing."

"I can tell you, absolutely, I would have not."

Tequila ate another pancake. "What if it was a choice? Get tortured, or get laid?"

"Was it a choice?"

Tequila shrugged. "Not really. But we're still alive."

"What's your endgame? The Cowboy falls in love with you, lets us go, and you move in with her and have a couple of kids?"

"Of course not. She's a psychopath."

"That's what I'm saying," Herb says. "Why would you sleep with a psychopath? She is, quite seriously, the absolute worst woman I've ever met in my life. And I'm a cop. I've met some people."

"She reminds me of someone," Tequila said. "A woman I knew in Italy."

Herb shoveled another pancake in. He knew the food was too rich, that'd he'd probably be sick, but he couldn't stop himself.

"You got any sort of plan?" Herb asked. "Yuri is going to talk to the Cowboy and find out she didn't give you the wire snips."

"That's what I'm hoping. Maybe they'll save me the trouble and kill each other."

"And if they don't?"

Tequila stretched, shaking off the blankets.

"I'm warm, I'm rested, and I'm full, for the first time in months," he said. "Next person who opens that door, I'm breaking their fucking neck."

JACK

During my fifty years of life I'd been in danger, serious danger, too many times to count.

But this was the first time things had gone to shit while I was naked.

I considered my options.

Yell?

For who?

McGlade wasn't past playing a practical joke, but he knew not to mess with a person's firearm. Besides, I'd watched him leave.

That left Wyatt, and Heckle and Jeckle.

I could imagine Wyatt attempting to get into the shower with me, but flicking lights off and stealing clothing didn't seem his style.

Could it have been the twins?

If so, calling for Wyatt's help would probably get him to come running.

Come running to me while I was naked.

Besides, if he was in the pool, he would have seen the twins go into the ladies room.

Unless he was too buzzed to notice.

I couldn't hear anything with the shower still on, so I felt around for the handle and turned off the water. After a few seconds of dripping, the bathroom was quiet.

"I'm not scared," I said, loudly and firmly. "But I am getting pissed. Turn on the lights and leave my clothes on the floor."

No one answered.

I spent a millisecond blaming myself for getting into the situation, remembered that those kinds of thoughts were why we taught our daughters to carry pepper spray rather than teach our sons not to assault women, and chose to act rather than react.

I came out of the shower, fast and low, arms spread to tackle anyone standing close. After not running into anyone, I stopped, held my breath, and listened.

I didn't hear anything. And the bathroom felt empty.

Working by memory, careful of my wet feet on a tile floor, I made my way to the door and fumbled around for the light switch.

I flipped it on and spun—

—finding myself alone.

The pillowcase was missing. So were my wet clothes, and the towel I'd brought in.

I padded back to the shower, tore off the curtain, and folded it in half, winding it around my body in a makeshift tube dress. Cinching it by tucking the end under my armpit, I approached the bathroom door, grabbed the handle, and tugged it open in one quick motion while staying in a crouch.

The hot tub was empty.

If this was a prank, I would have expected the practical joker to be standing there, holding my clothes, and maybe a camera.

The towels were gone, too. So was the Jack Daniels bottle and martini shaker.

I considered breaking up one of the plastic chairs to use as a weapon, dismissed the idea as near-useless, and instead went to the nearest towel hook. It was stainless steel, solid five inches long. I used both hands, and with a quick downward jerk, tore it off the cedar wall, taking two long screws with it.

Not quite brass knuckles, but I sure wouldn't want to be hit in the face with it.

I opened the spa room door the same way I'd done with the bathroom door, quick and low. The hallway was empty. I thought about trading my towel hook with one of the framed pictures of

Annie winning a CAS medal, or Wyatt in the ring wearing boxing gloves, decided to stick with the hook, and crept toward the great room.

I heard something.

A clinking sound.

A familiar, clinking sound.

Wyatt was at the bar, wearing jeans and a blue flannel shirt, pouring himself a tequila into a glass. That was the sound, glass on glass. When he noticed me, he grinned.

"Now you didn't have to go and get all dressed up just for me, little lady."

"Where are my clothes?" I demanded.

"Where did you leave them?" He eyed the hook in my fist. "Are my hangers not to your liking?"

I walked up to him, more pissed than cautious. "No bullshit, Wyatt. Did you take them?"

Wyatt's eyes narrowed slightly. "You know I'm not the only person in this house, Mrs. Johnson."

"Where are the twins?"

"When I left, they were still in the hot tub."

"Why did you leave?"

He lifted the tequila. "Saddest thing in the world is an empty glass. Don't you think?"

"Someone took my clothes."

"Apparently."

I folded my arms across my shower curtain dress. "And my gun."

"Now that's downright improper, taking a lady's firearm. How close are you and that McGlade fella?"

"Close enough that I know it wasn't him."

"Well, I'm happy to help you look for your items. Unless…"

"Unless?"

"Since you're already close to naked, we could go back to my room. I got a few ideas on how I can dry your hair."

"Enough with the flirting bullshit, Wyatt. I'm not interested. Got it? I can write it down and staple it backwards, to your forehead, in case you forget."

Wyatt put on an innocent face. "Message received, no stapling required. You...do like men, right? Because my sister seems to think—"

"You and you sister need to keep those thoughts to yourself."

He nodded, then stood up. "Okay, then. Let's see if we can find where your things went."

We did a quick search of the great room, Wyatt taking not-so-subtle glances my way whenever I bent down to check under something.

Striking out in the great room, Wyatt suggested the kitchen. It wasn't anywhere in the open, so I began checking cabinets. He went into the refrigerator.

"Looking for a mixer?" I asked, annoyed.

"Old gag from school days. Stealing clothes and putting them in the—"

He opened the freezer, and sitting there was my pillowcase.

"Real funny," I said, walking over.

"Wasn't me." He was smirking. "Gag is, you're all wet, and the clothes are cold."

The pillowcase was heavy, and I checked to make sure the gun was still there. It was. Along with my clothes, my wet underwear, and McGlade's rock and roll shirt.

I headed back to the bathroom.

"You can dress here. I'll turn my head."

I bet he'd turn his head.

In the bathroom, door locked, I quickly dressed in my earlier clothes, leaving the wet undies and shirt in the bag. Then I checked to make sure the Taurus was still loaded, and adjusted it in the paddle holster until it felt right.

When I came back to the great room, Wyatt wasn't around. I headed to the Crimebago Deux, to get some dry underwear. As I walked around its length to enter the side door, I saw Harry talking to someone with her back to me. A woman, with short, red hair. I approached, and McGlade saw me coming and said, "Oh, shit."

The woman turned around, and I felt my blood pressure spike.

Chandler.

Chandler was a spy. I didn't know much about her past, or her training, but she was one of the deadliest people I'd ever met.

She'd been there, in Baja, when we'd left Herb for dead.

Leaving him had been her idea.

I could remember the scene like it had just happened.

Chandler reached over, feeling under Herb's pant leg. "He's gone."

"Phin," I said, "take his legs. We're bringing him home."

"Leave him," Chandler said. She was bleeding pretty bad.

I shook my head. "I can't leave him!"

"Then figure out how you, Phin, and Harry can carry both me and Herb."

"We can call Val and Fleming. They can drive in and—"

Chandler grabbed my shirt and pulled me close. "And risk their lives, too? How many people do you want to die for this rescue attempt, Jack? Tequila's dead. Herb's dead. I'm down two pints of blood and counting. And you want to risk my sister and your friend, just to bring a corpse back home? We need to blow this place and get out of here before we're all dead."

My rage became a razor focus, zeroing in on her like a rifle scope.

"You," I said, my teeth clenched.

Chandler had one arm in a sling. She extended the other, holding her palm up. "Jack, I did what needed to be done."

"You're the one who checked Herb's pulse. You're the one who insisted we leave him."

My hands clenched into fists. Harry, obviously knowing what was good for him, backed the hell away.

"I came to help," Chandler said. "Let's find Herb and Tequila. We can settle this later."

"We can settle this now."

"I don't want to—"

"I do," I said, and threw the first punch.

Chandler slipped it, shuffled to my right, and I threw a left that she ducked away from.

"Jack, if we didn't leave him there, we'd all be dead."

"We don't leave our friends behind, you asshole."

"Fine." Chandler put down her arm and stood still. "You want to kick my ass? Go ahead and—"

I hit her so hard I spun her around.

She spat blood, then looked at me, her lower lip beginning to swell.

"Feel better?"

"I watched some maniac yank a tooth out of Herb's mouth."

"So what do you want from me?"

"I'll start," I said, "with a tooth."

I swung, and she dodged it, slipping her arm out of the sling and raising both fists. I danced in close, threw a right and left combo, and she blocked both punches, wincing as she did.

Pivoting my hips, I brought my leg around, snap-kicking her in the side, and then Chandler threw a punch, grazing my nose.

It was on.

I jabbed, missed, jabbed again, threw up my forearm to block a kick, and then caught her jaw with a left uppercut. Before she could center herself I lunge-kicked her chest, and then she was on the ground, whipping her leg around, trying to sweep me.

I hopped away, and Chandler spun crazy-fast, doing some sort of capoeira shit, her other leg extending up out of nowhere and connecting with my shoulder.

I absorbed the blow, threw a knee that missed her face, and then brought my hands up and gave the universal *bring it* gesture, beckoning with my fingers.

"We've done this dance before," Chandler said. "You lost."

"I remember. I won't make that mistake again."

"You're good, Jack. But you don't have the training to—"

I punched that thought right out of her goddamn head.

Chandler rolled with it, using momentum to launch her spin kick, but I saw that coming and caught her leg, pinning it, and then threw an elbow into her nose.

She tried to grab me, and I pushed her away and assumed my fighting stance.

"You guys are acting stupid," Harry said, keeping his distance. "You both need to stop this pointless jackassery."

I moved in, feinted with a right, then did a double-roundhouse kick, smacking her left side, then her right side, snapping my hips so each kick hit hard. Chandler came up with a flying knee strike, but last time I was in the *dojang* I'd sparred with a muay thai guy who was good at those, and he showed me how to get above it and push down. I knocked her off-balance for a fraction of a second, and as her head came forward my head was already down, smacking her in the face.

In top of head vs face situations, top of head always won.

Chandler staggered back, found balance, and raised her fists. "Okay," she said, blood trickling down her nose. "I've had a shitty week, and you're pissing me off. You really want to do this? Let's—"

I went in, left, right, left, Chandler putting up her arms and taking the shots, but her left arm was low, weak, and I tagged her in the ear.

"You're fighting like a girl," I said dancing away. "What happened to your arm?"

Chandler didn't answer. But her face got really dark.

"Harry? What's up with her arm?"

"This pointless jackassery is between you guys," he said. "I'm not taking any sides."

"Is it broken?" I asked. "Because if it isn't, I'm—"

Then I was on my ass, my head ringing, and Chandler was on top of me, twisting to wrap her legs around my arm.

If she'd been in perfect shape, she would have clinched the arm bar, and I would have been forced to give up.

But she wasn't in perfect shape, and I got my leg up and mule-kicked the side of her head once, twice, and she released me and rolled onto all fours.

I came at her, no longer trying to block, leaving myself open as I threw wild haymakers, channeling all of the anger at what she'd done into a flurry of hard punches.

She took the knocks and slipped inside my swings, popping me in my left eye, then my forehead, but leaving her legs open just enough for me to hook an arm beneath her, scoop her up, and pile-drive her lying, betraying ass onto the ground.

I heard one of her ribs crack, but that wasn't enough for me, and I grabbed her by her dyed red hair, stretching her head back, raising my fist to make her choke on her teeth—

—and then the barrel of my Taurus Model 66 was pressing into my throat.

Chandler had taken my gun.

That took the fight right out of me.

I opened my fist and slowly lowered my hand.

"Get off," Chandler said, sounding hurt.

I nodded, slowly climbing off of Chandler, raising up my hands.

"Don't shoot her, Chandler," Harry said. Not as an order, or a plea. He said it neutrally, but I noticed his jacket was open, his Magnum shoulder holster exposed.

Chandler sat up, wincing. I didn't think she'd kill me. But I wondered if she'd wound me, out of anger.

Instead, she did something I totally didn't expect.

"I'm sorry," Chandler said. "I'm sorry, Jack. I'm sorry about Herb."

The anger fell away, and my eyes got wet.

"You left him there. He was still alive, and you left him there." A sob came out of me. "*We* left him there."

"I'm sorry. My training... I was trained to survive. At all costs. I made a call. It was a bad call. I really didn't think there was any way we could have—"

Then came a gunshot.

I froze, unable to comprehend what had just happened.

The revolver fell from Chandler's hand, and she looked confused, then pained, as a spurt of blood gushed from her shoulder.

"Sniper!" I heard McGlade yell.

I looked at Harry, saw him pointing into the distance, behind me, and without thinking I grabbed Chandler by the shirt and dragged her to the Crimebago, Harry and I pulling her underneath.

THE MAN

He hit the redhead. Then Jack bolted, taking the redhead with her. She, and McGlade, yanked the woman under the RV, and then the man couldn't see them anymore.

Didn't matter. He'd given away his position when he fired, so it was time to move.

Hurrying back to the rental car, he set the rifle in the passenger seat and fired up the engine, racing for the back-up lookout spot he'd scouted earlier. It was a hundred yards further away, but that was no problem.

The spot was still well within shooting distance.

JACK

"Do you see him?" I asked Harry. He had his .44 in his hand, and was looking sweaty and pale.

"Are you kidding me? I'm not sticking my head out there."

I had my palm pressed to Chandler's shoulder wound, so I couldn't look for the sniper myself.

"What did you see, Harry? Anything at all?"

"I saw a muzzle flash. From the plains. Maybe two hundred meters out."

"See the person? Man? Woman?"

"It happened too fast," McGlade said. "I was busy watching you guys working out your pointless jackassery."

"Vehicle?" I asked.

McGlade's face scrunched up. "Yeah. I saw ... something."

"Make? Color?" I was thinking of Annie's black Silverado.

"Dunno what kind. I think it was blue. Or green."

"How bad?" Chandler asked, craning her head up to see her injury.

"Don't worry," I told her. "No one is leaving you behind."

I looked toward the ransion, and saw Wyatt on the porch, a rifle in one hand, field glasses in the other, scanning the area.

"Stop wiggling," I told Chandler.

"Back pocket. Celox."

"You keep blood clotting powder in your pocket?"

"You don't?"

Keeping pressure on her wound, I reached around and fished out three packets of the hemostat. I tore open one with my teeth.

"Harry, when I say *three*, pull up her shirt."

"Really?" He looked at Chandler. "Is that okay? I'm all about consent."

"Gimme your gun and do it."

Harry handed her his weapon, and I counted to three.

I took my hand away, Harry pulled, and I dumped the whole two grams of Celox on the weeping wound.

Like magic, the bleeding stopped.

"Other side," Chandler grunted. "It went through."

We carefully turned her over and McGlade exposed the injury. Like many exit wounds, it was bigger and uglier than the entry.

I dumped a pack of Celox on it, and it was still oozing, so I used the last one.

"Caliber?" Chandler asked.

"Too big for a twenty-two," Harry said. "But smaller than a three-oh-eight or thirty-ought-six. I'll call it a two-two-three."

"I think it ricocheted up off the shoulder blade," I said, pressing down. "Doesn't feel shattered."

"Good to know. I like my shoulder blades."

"How's the pain?"

"Want to see? I'll shoot you in the shoulder."

"Pass."

"Sounds like you ladies have worked out your pointless jackassery," Harry said. "You want to kiss and make up?"

"Do you want to get smacked around next?" Chandler asked him.

Harry didn't answer. He seemed to be considering it.

"You folks okay?"

Wyatt, calling from the porch.

"Got one wounded," McGlade said. "Spot the shooter?"

"No. Where'd the shot come from?"

"Southeast," said McGlade. "Maybe two hundred meters. Green or blue car."

"I'm going to check it out," Wyatt said. "You folks stay put."

I looked at McGlade. "Where are the twins?"

"In the Crimebago Deux, with Rosa and Waddlebutt. We were editing the next webcast when Chandler showed up."

"How did you get here so fast?" I asked the spy.

"I called her a few days ago," McGlade said. "In case we needed some help."

Of course he did. And of course he didn't tell me.

"I've been in Nebraska since this morning," Chandler said. "McGlade just sent me pictures of the tire tracks. I can help."

I checked around. "Where's your car?"

"Bike. Ducati, parked about a click away."

"You rode a motorcycle with a bad arm?"

Chandler shrugged. "It's just pain. Might be tougher now, though. Either of you guys want to buy a Ducati?"

"The answer is yes," said McGlade. "Those things are panty peelers."

I looked at Chandler. "Does the bike have a weight limit?" I asked.

Chandler chortled. McGlade made a face.

Wyatt, on Jack the horse, galloped past us, into the plains.

"What's up with the Marlboro Man?" Chandler asked. "He's hot."

"I know, right?" said McGlade.

I'd had enough of being under the RV, and crawled out. If the sniper was still out there, he or she would be watching Wyatt.

Squatting, I helped get Chandler out, and McGlade tried to follow, but he needed more help than Chandler did. He was huffing and puffing when he stood up.

"Whew. Missed breakfast. Feeling weak."

He led us through the side door of the Crimebago. Heckle and Jeckle were on their laptops and didn't acknowledge our presence. No snickering when I entered made me wonder if it was them, or

Wyatt, who stole my clothes. Rosalina came in from the bedroom, and Chandler lifted up her leg and did the fastest ankle draw I'd ever seen, a Beretta Px4 sub-compact in her hand.

"She's Tequila's," I told her.

"Careful," McGlade said. "She doesn't like guns."

Chandler put her foot on the sofa and holstered her weapon, and McGlade went into a pantry and broke out white bread, a plastic squeeze bottle of grape jelly, and Fruity Pebbles. He used all three ingredients to make himself a sandwich.

"It would be quicker if you just injected sugar straight into your heart," Chandler said. "But not by much."

"The NSA called earlier," he told her. "They're revoking your license to bitch."

"I don't have a license," Chandler said. "I bitch in an unofficial capacity."

"Harry, where's your first aid stuff?"

"Bedroom closet, behind the other emergency supplies."

I went to look. Apparently McGlade considered six boxes of Twinkies and a case of SpaghettiOs "emergency supplies". I grabbed the substantial med kit, and returned to the living area. Chandler was sitting at McGlade's computer, holding something that looked like a cell phone, but not quite.

"I ran the tracks through the Google database," said Chandler, using her thumbs on the device's touch screen. "They belong to a LeTourneau LCC-1 Sno-Train."

"Google has a tire track database?" McGlade asked. He had jelly on his chin, with Fruity Pebbles stuck to it.

"Google has indexed over a trillion URLs. My sister wrote a program to match and compare tire tracks."

"Which sister? The one in the wheelchair who's hot for me? Or the crazy psycho who I've tapped on multiple occasions?"

"The one in the wheelchair who thinks you're sleazy."

McGlade nodded. "She wants me."

"I'm cutting off your shirt," I said to Chandler, using some non-stick medical scissors.

Chandler didn't seem to notice. "It's a big vehicle. They call it a train for a reason. I assumed they were using some sort of roof camouflage to keep it invisible to satellites. I confirmed that doing a quick check of the surrounding two hundred square miles. The computer didn't locate anything. But something that big will still leave a signature."

"Fuel exhaust," McGlade said.

"That's the scan I ran. Nothing came up. But while I was letting Jack slap me around, I had an idea."

"You weren't letting me do it," I said, "and your full attention was on me the whole time."

"With only about ten percent of my attention focused on Jack—"

"Liar."

"—I realized that a vehicle that big would use a ridiculous amount of fuel. No way it's going to fill up at the local Amoco."

"This is going to sting," I said, pouring isopropyl alcohol on Chandler's bullet wounds.

Chandler didn't flinch.

"What are you thinking?" McGlade asked. "Hybrid? Solar?"

"It's probably some combination of energy sources. So I asked the computer to look for a range of heat signatures."

"And?" I asked.

Chandler checked her watch. "And the next satellite flyover is in four minutes. We'll know if it worked then."

"You own a satellite?" said Heckle.

"No. I hacked a satellite," Chandler looked at McGlade. "Who are these guys?"

"My videographers."

"They're creepy. Tell them not to talk to me again or I'll kick their asses."

"Do you want stitches?" I asked.

"Am I still bleeding?"

"No."

"Then just bandage me up."

As I applied gauze pads and tape, McGlade made himself another sandwich. This one with Nutella and Frosted Flakes. When he noticed us staring, he asked, "You guys want one?"

Chandler and I declined.

I finished taping her up just as her phone-thingy beeped.

"Okay, we should know in just a few seconds," she said, looking at the screen.

We waited, and I hoped so hard that this was going to work.

Another beep.

"Got them," Chandler said. "They're seven kilometers away."

"Run the edited footage!" McGlade ordered the twins, dropping his sandwich on the floor. "We need to go live in three minutes! Go, guys, go!"

Here we come, Herb.

Here we come.

YURI

"Fixed," Dmitri said over the intercom. "We can go when you give the order."

It was coincidental timing, because Yuri's men had just finished inventory of the packed buckets of raw opium.

They were two hundred and fifty-five kilos shy of quota.

Bratva was paying US thirteen hundred dollars per kilo. Which meant Yuri would be out over three hundred thousand dollars.

Yuri was furious. The money wasn't the main issue. He could get the money. The problem was coming up short on the promised amount. Bratva didn't play around.

He swore, Russian obscenities spitting form his mouth like dragon fire.

All of these years. All of this work put in. Acquiring and running the land train. The payoffs. The risks. The technology. Plus the diplomacy. Besides Bratva, Yuri had made promises to other organizations. To other *countries*. They'd invested, heavily, in Yuri's plan to assassinate the reigning president of Belarus.

It might all fall apart now, over a few hundred kilos of paste.

"Vehicle approaching. It's Cowboy."

The Cowboy.

It was the Cowboy's fault.

And she expected to buy the LeTourneau at the agreed-upon price? When failing to keep up her end of their agreement?

Yuri left Car #7 and walked to Car #9, where the Cowboy was parking.

"We are short," Yuri said as the Cowboy exited the vehicle.

The Cowboy stared for a moment, then asked, "How much>"

"Almost three hundred kilos."

The Cowboy didn't say anything.

"You know the meeting is tomorrow. You know the consequences."

Still no response.

"I've told you the cost of launching a satellite into space, with ten tons of cargo. You expect me to sell you the train. Tell me, Cowboy, why your dreams should come true, when mine do not."

The Cowboy just stared. Eyes as dead as coals.

"I also know about your... *thing*. With the American."

"That's my business."

"Finally! A reaction! Allow me to explain your business. Your business was to ensure we met quota. If you think that—"

"I'll cover it."

"Cover it?"

"I'll cover your loss."

Yuri guffawed. "Of course you'll cover the loss. But this is about more than that. Losing face in front of Bratva is unacceptable."

"Give them a discount. The quota is short, sell it to them under the agreed upon price."

Yuri raised an eyebrow. "Discount?"

"It's called capitalism, Yuri. Offer them five percent, they'll demand fifteen, settle for ten."

"If I do that, I lose..." Yuri did a quick mental calculation. "Over two million dollars."

"I'll cover it."

"You have that kind of money?"

The Cowboy didn't answer. Yuri tried to think it through. While that plan could work, Yuri was unsure if the Cowboy would actually be able to make good on her word.

"For me to trust you," Yuri said, "I need assurances."

"What are you suggesting?"

"A show of... solidarity. To prove you are still loyal to me."

The Cowboy waited. After almost ten seconds, she asked, "What is it you want, Yuri?"

"The Americans," Yuri said. "Kill them both."

JACK

I had the gas pedal pinned on the unwieldy, unfit-for-off-road Crimebago Deux, and behind me Heckle said, "On in three... two..."

Harry spoke into the camera. "With my good friend, and sometime lover, C-Dawg, shot in the chest and nearly dead, we're less than half a mile away from the land train where the Cowboy may be running a portable opium farm and the biggest slavery ring in modern US history. I've called the police and the FBI, but they're hours away. But we won't wait. There's nothing that will delay me from saving my best friend, Herb Benedict."

There was nothing that would delay me, either. But I called it. I knew, from the very beginning, that Harry's intent to involve the authorities was bullshit. I made a mental note to listen to myself more often.

Except when it came to Phin. In that case, I needed to start doing the opposite of whatever my initial thought was. No more trying to protect him. No more telling him what to—

"Holy shit," I said, interrupting my own thought as I gazed into the distance, spotting an impossibly huge vehicle. "There's the train."

THE COWBOY

The Cowboy has Yuri's money. It will mean a financial hit, but Usher House 2.0 will make up the loss within a year.

As for killing the Americans, in particular the derringer man, that will be a shame. He would have been a fun playmate for the website grand opening.

But business is business.

"Of course," the Cowboy says. "When?"

Yuri, looking more unhinged than usual, smiles.

"Do it now."

HERB

"I didn't say thank you," Tequila said.

As expected, Herb was feeling nauseous. He'd eaten too much, and the shitty, cheap food was too rich. The pancakes felt alive in his gut.

"For what?"

"You could have left me there. You didn't."

"We're in this together, brother."

"I..." Herb could sense Tequila was struggling with something. "What?"

"If the roles were reversed, I would have left you."

Herb shook his head. "No, you wouldn't have."

"I really think I would."

"How about Mexico?" Herb asked. "You broke that kid's leg. So I wouldn't be alone."

"I broke that kid's leg, to give me a chance to escape."

He didn't like Tequila ragging on himself. Herb knew him. Knew him well. Knew he was a decent person.

"I don't believe you. You're a good man, Tequila Abernathy. You wouldn't leave me behind."

Tequila didn't look convinced.

Herb clapped him on the shoulder. "Trust me. You're not the betraying type."

"Self-preservation isn't betrayal." He stared at Herb. Hard. "Promise me something. If you get another chance, to run, you'll take it. Whether I come with or not."

"I can't make that promise, brother."

"That's stupid."

Herb shrugged. "As I said, call me stupid. But after all that's happened to us, the biggest tragedy of all would be if we lost our humanity."

"I don't think I ever had any humanity," Tequila said.

"I think, if given the chance, you might surprise yourself."

JACK

"Holy shit is right," McGlade said, coming into the cockpit with me. He had that ridiculous camera rig strapped to his forehead. "That is one really big boy right there. Good thing it isn't moving. I don't know how we'd stop it."

"They'll be armed," Chandler, aka C-Dawg, said. She was wearing one of McGlade's Rainmakers t-shirts. Apparently he had several. "You mentioned you have weapons."

"Does a fish piss in the water?" Harry grinned, wide as a zebra's ass. "Hell yeah I have weapons."

YURI

Da. Eto khorosho.

The Cowboy seemed to be falling into line, Bratva should be pleased, and the launch can go as scheduled.

Yuri relaxed, just a bit. After being so obsessed, for so long, things looked like they were finally going to—

"Vehicle approaching," Dmitri said over the intercom.

Yuri frowned. "What kind of vehicle?"

"It looks like…" the driver's voice trailed off.

"Like what, man?"

"Like a…motor home."

What could it be? A tourist?

Yuri couldn't take that chance.

"Get moving." He looked at the Cowboy. "Do you know the M60E3 machine gun? Rambo used it in the American movie *First Blood Part 2*."

The Cowboy nodded. "I *love* the M60E3 machine gun."

JACK

As we approached the land train, its size grew from impressive to ridiculous. The tires were as tall as the Crimebago Deux. It had a dozen, no, fourteen cars, each larger than a semi-truck trailer. The vehicle made me appreciate how large our country was, if it could traverse the land without being detected for this long.

Our storm-the-castle plan, conducted in haste, seemed foolish. Chandler had a bag full of zip ties on her belt, and a Glock in each hand. She was going to tie up the guards that surrendered, and shoot the ones that didn't, while Harry freed the slaves and I searched for Herb and Tequila.

But I didn't even know if we'd be able to get inside. This train looked big and strong enough to weather a siege from a small army.

"How close are we, J-Dawg?"

"A hundred meters out, and— oh, hell."

"What's wrong?"

"Big boy," I said, "just started moving."

HERB

"We're moving," Herb said, stating the obvious.

YURI

"Motor home closing in," warned Dmitri.

Yuri stared at the numerical combination on the weapons locker.

He was coming up blank.

How could he not remember it?

It was the opium. The opium he'd been smoking lately, to calm himself, had clouded his memory.

"Fifty meters and closing," Dmitri announced.

Three numbers. What were the three numbers?

"Did you forget the damn combination?" the Cowboy asked.

"Just give me a second."

"Time's up." The Cowboy drew her sidearm and pointed it at the lock.

JACK

"McGlade!" I yelled, wrestling with the steering wheel, "this is the stupidest idea you've had in a long history of stupid ideas!"

"Bullshit," McGlade said, kneeling next to the open side door. "What's the point of owning a rocket launcher if you can't use it?"

"Aim for the front car," Chandler told him. "And you, creepy twin guy, if you stand behind it the blowback is going to burn your face off."

"We clear?" McGlade said. I watched him try to turn around to check, but he was too fat.

"Clear," Chandler said, kneeling with Rosalina. Waddlebutt was in Rosa's mouth.

"Firing in three ... two ... one!"

There was a *WHOOSH!* and a wave of hot air, and I watched the rocket leave a smoke trail as it beelined for the lead car of the LeTourneau LCC-1 Sno-Train.

I expected some kind of gigantic explosion, something with huge flames and a giant *BOOM!*, but instead there was a metal-on-metal clang, and a big *whump* of instant smoke as the car rocked up on two wheels, threatening to tip onto its side.

But it didn't. The gigantic wheels came back down, and the train continued moving forward.

HERB

"Something just happened," Herb said, stating the obvious.

JACK

"Got another one?" I asked McGlade.

Chandler said, "Give it a second."

Slowly, inexorably, the first car cut sideways, and the wheels stopped turning. But the second car kept pressing forward, and with the first car blocking its path, began to push it sideways.

"Domino effect," Chandler said.

The second car veered left, nowhere to go, and the third began to lift off the ground. Then the fourth twisted the opposite way, making a zig-zag that had nowhere to go but up and over. I was witnessing the world's slowest crash, one train car after another climbing over its predecessor.

"Each car has its own drivetrain," Chandler said. "It's going to fold up like an accordion."

THE COWBOY

"The front engine blew!" Yuri wails.

"We're under attack, you idiot," the Cowboy tells him.

And she has a pretty good idea who it was.

The Cowboy takes aim at the locker again, and the train begins to creak and shake, and then tilt as the front of the car lifts up.

"No," Yuri shakes his head. "No no no no no no."

The Cowboy shoots the locker, then pulls the handle.

It wouldn't open.

"You fool!" Yuri shouts. "You fused the lock! I knew the goddamn combination!"

The Cowboy hurries to her parked vehicle, but the train is already too lopsided to attempt getting in. Instead, she leaps out the side door, hitting the ground with ankles pressed tight together, doing several painful rolls until coming to a stop in the dirt.

She still has her gun. Still has her hat.

Getting her bearings, the Cowboy looks up and she sees a red motor home putting on the brakes.

Jack Daniels is driving.

Harry McGlade is standing at the open door.

They are less than thirty meters away, and the Cowboy brings up her gun. Not to kill. At this distance, she can wound. Then deal with them later, in a more relaxed setting.

She takes aim at Jack's arm, and then hears the groan of shearing metal and turns to see the land train, digging a furrow into the earth, plowing right at her.

HERB

The car turned onto its side, but it did it so slowly that Herb and Tequila were able to walk up the wall as it became the floor, Fred Astaire *Royal Wedding* style.

The poppy plants didn't fare as well, uprooting as all of the soil shifted, becoming a rolling, dirt-spewing, mini avalanche.

Herb and Tequila managed to stay on top of it, and then the car began to scrape sideways along the ground, metal screeching like a wailing child.

"The door," Tequila said, pointing up.

The side door was now on the ceiling, but Herb could see the crack in the frame.

It was open.

It was also too high to reach.

"Start piling up dirt," Herb said. "We'll make a hill."

The men began piling.

JACK

I saw her.

The Cowboy.

Running away as the land train continued its slow-motion pile-up.

Caution and common sense cast aside in my overwhelming concern for Herb, I threw open the door and jumped out of the Crimebago Deux, sprinting after her, the Taurus in my hand.

She darted through the space between two overturned cars. I followed, stopping fast as I came up to the corner, in case she was waiting to shoot me, cautiously peeking around with my gun ready, trying to spot where she—

BANG!

It was like a punch to my fist, my gun spinning to the ground as I instinctively brought up my stinging palm, sure she'd shot me.

But she'd only shot the gun from my hand.

It had fallen between my feet, and in the fraction of a second it took to decide between reaching for it and diving for cover, another shot grazed my cheek.

I raised my hands and stared at her, less than ten meters away.

"Hello, Jack," she said, over the grinding of train metal from the ongoing wreck behind us.

She was getting up from a sniper position, lying on her belly with her gun forward. As soon as she'd run around the side of the train, she must have dropped down to ambush me.

And in my adrenaline-fueled haste to save my friends, I'd fallen for it.

"I like you better with the bandana," I said. "Annie."

The Cowboy reached up, and pulled the skull balaclava down. Her face cracked into that lopsided smile.

"When did you know?" Annie asked.

"Just a minute ago. You lost one of your fake fingers."

She nodded. "I wear them to look normal. Can you imagine? A woman who looks like me, still appealing to vanity."

"I said it earlier. It's the inside that counts. And you are one ugly bitch."

Annie assumed a gunfighting stance. "I've been dreaming about this moment for a long time, Jack."

"Sounds like you've got a crush."

"Oh, Jack. It's more than a crush. It's a hunger, that's been devouring me for more than fifteen years."

Gunfire. On the other side of the train. Chandler and McGlade, storming the castle.

"Can I ask why?" I asked, trying to buy some time.

"You and Harry, you took something from me."

This. This was the reason I faked my own death. Because there was always one more lunatic, with some perceived grudge, trying to harm me for something I did on the job.

If I had the chance to do it all over, I wouldn't have ever become a cop.

"Did Harry and I kill one of your little psycho friends, Annie?"

She laughed. "No, Jack. You did the opposite."

And then she proceeded to tell me exactly what I did.

SIXTEEN YEARS AGO

ANNIE

It had taken months of false starts, dead-ends, and useless bribes to finally get an invitation to Usher House.

To say Annie was excited was an understatement.

Up until that point, murder had been a carefully planned, methodical, worrisome thing. You had to constantly be aware of evidence, witnesses, alibis, police; it was enough to make a girl consider a less stressful hobby.

But Usher House, an urban legend that was actually real, was an all-inclusive club for those with Annie's particular tastes. For a price, she could kill without even the slightest concern. No mess. No fuss. No repercussions.

It would be the best vacation ever.

The invitation came via an unmarked, hand-delivered envelope. Typed using some kind of special ink that began to disappear the moment it was exposed to light. But Annie memorized the time and place, along with the password, and the next day she was on a plane, anxious to fulfill some dark, bloody fantasies.

To say it exceeded her wildest expectations was an understatement. The event coordinator kindly gave her a tour of the facilities, and offered custom scenarios for clients with special requests.

Annie could torture a person of her choice, choosing by race, gender, and age, in a practically endless variety of wonderful ways.

She could hunt humans in a wide selection of exciting environments.

There were portions of the house devoted to rape and genital mutilation, and to the production of snuff films, and to gambling, betting on two people fighting to the death.

Annie spent far too much money, indulging in one atrocity after another, a glutton for it. After a lifetime of being careful not to get a speck of blood on her, she was finally able to bathe in it.

She also met a lot of interesting people. Well known politicians and media celebrities, buying sex slaves. Rich oil sheiks, shopping for transplant organs. And others like herself, who roamed the world, looking for prey.

Annie was on the Usher House firing range, counting how many .22lr bullets she could put in a screaming man before he died, when she met the Korks.

A brother and sister serial killer team. Charles was dark. Handsome. Mysterious. His sister, Alex, was poised and statuesque, and a ridiculously good shot.

"What a lovely game," Alex said. "Did you make it up?"

Annie nodded. "My record is two hundred and eight. You have to avoid all the vitals, but eventually the blood loss gets them."

"Can we play with you?"

It was always more fun to play with others, so naturally, Annie said yes.

After a day of playing and drinking and eating together, the blossoming friendship turned into a competition. They had the concierge create a device that restrained a target's hand, so Annie and Alex could take turns shooting off fingers. There were moving targets, victims tethered by a wire going through their chin.

The best event, the one that brought them both to tears with laughter, was called the Toddler Run.

Alex considered herself the better markswoman. Annie disagreed. They competed on the range, over and over, neither the clear victor, until the rivalry became less fun and more heated.

The last night of her stay, when Annie was ahead by more than ten points, she decided to call it quits and go to bed.

Alex was gracious in her defeat, paying off her debt, ending the evening with a long hug and a promise they'd get together soon.

It was sooner than Annie expected. That night, while she slept, the Korks broke into Annie's room.

They subdued her and brought her to a private part of the dungeon. Chained her up. And began to do all of the horrible things Annie had been doing to others over the past week.

The torture went on for days.

Annie went insane. Several times.

And when she was begging for death, pleading for it to finally be over, the Korks, who had been teasing that they'd let her go after 'just one more thing', actually let her go.

"We like you," Alex told her. "You're tough. But we can't have you coming after us with your little six gun."

So they took four of her fingers.

The owners of Usher House apologized profusely once they found out what happened. They also graciously got her medical attention.

It took Annie over a year to heal. During that time, she lapsed into drug addiction. To fight the pain. And the nightmares.

First came prescription opioids. Then harder things.

Cocaine. Bath salts. Meth.

Annie loved meth. It made her feel strong, even as it ate away the few teeth Alex and Charles had left her with. She smoked it and snorted it and even shot it into her veins, week after week, month after month. A pathetic, drug-fueled death seemed inevitable.

Wyatt was the one who rescued her.

Forced her into rehab.

Forced a gun back into her useless hands.

With her brother's help, and love, she slowly recovered.

It took her another year to learn how to draw and shoot with only two fingers and a thumb on each hand.

Annie had the purest motivation ever.

She thirsted to pay the Korks back. In kind.

After a lifetime of mostly motiveless murder, Annie finally had a reason. A cause.

In a way, the Korks had done her a perverse favor. Rather than aimlessly picking victims, sleepwalking through the murder life, they'd given Annie a purpose.

There had always been something missing from killing. Something that Annie had to supplement with rodeo, and Cowboy Action Shooting, and Gunslinger Showdown.

The Korks had taught Annie that serial killers need goals, too.

And the Cowboy was born.

But Annie's thoughts of vengeance were shattered when that asshole, Harry McGlade, took Charles Kork away from her.

Then, years later, Jack Daniels took Alex.

All of the training. The fantasies. The ache for vengeance.

Gone.

And the hatred that burned inside Annie didn't just go away. It was too strong. Too raw.

So she transferred her hatred to two new targets.

The two who robbed Annie of her biggest, most important goal.

Jack Daniels and Harry McGlade.

They were going to suffer. And they were going to die.

And The Cowboy was going to make sure the whole world bore witness to their long and messy deaths.

HERB

"I hear gunfire," Herb said, stating the obvious.

"Keep going," Tequila said.

They got the mound of dirt and poppies up to shoulder level, and then carefully climbed to the top.

"Can you boost me?" Tequila asked.

Herb locked his fingers together, lifted Tequila's foot, and heaved hard.

Tequila missed the crack in the door by a few inches, then fell on top of Herb and rolled down the mound.

"We need more dirt," Herb said.

Tequila shook his head. "Won't work. To make the top higher, we have to make the base wider. We don't have enough. Let's try again."

He climbed up the mound, placed a foot in Herb's hands, and his hands on Herb's shoulders.

"I know you're tired, Herb. We can actually get out of here. Get home. What's the one thing you want most of all?"

Herb didn't hesitate, his wife's lovely face instantly popping into his head.

"Bernice. I want to see Bernice."

"Then do this for your wife. C'mon. Throw me."

Herb closed his eyes, bracing himself, picturing a reunion with the woman he loved, and Tequila shouted. "Now!" and Herb put everything he had into the throw.

Tequila went up—

—and didn't come down.

Somehow, his friend had gotten his hand in the door, and he hung there with one hand, while the other slid the door back just enough to chin up through the opening and get a leg over.

Herb had never done a chin-up in his life. But Tequila was a one-time Olympic gymnast, and apparently age, captivity, and injuries weren't enough to keep the diminutive man down.

Herb waited, staring at the door, for Tequila to stick down his hand and help Herb up.

He waited.

And he waited.

"Tequila?" he called.

Tequila didn't answer.

JACK

That was one seriously effed-up story.

"I was so upset when I thought you were dead," the Cowboy continued. "I almost started doing meth again."

"Thank goodness for your self-control," I deadpanned. Jack Daniels, snark under stress.

"Self-control? When I first saw you, earlier today, I was almost star-struck. Do you know the self-control it took, not to shoot you right then?"

"Why didn't you?" Where the hell were Chandler and Harry? I kept hearing gunshots, but they were nowhere to be seen.

"You were both armed. Both had your guards up. It was safer to wait until you were asleep." Annie got a faraway look in her eyes. "People are so vulnerable when they're asleep."

"You should thank me," I said. "When I took care of Alex, I did you a favor."

"I intend on thanking you. And I'm going to thank you, again and again, over and over, for days and days. You think I have a lot of scars? You won't even be recognizable as human when I'm done with you. Now pick up your gun. Slowly. And holster it. I've heard about your skills with a firearm, Jack. We're going to have ourselves a classic Western stand-off. And I'll even give you an advantage."

"And what's that?"

The Cowboy smiled. "I'll let you use all five fingers."

HERB

"Did you think I left?" Tequila asked, peeking his head down.

"Not for a second," Herb lied. "What were you doing?"

"Taking off my pants."

"Of course you were."

Tequila lowered said pants into the car, low enough for Herb to jump and grab them. Then, hand over hand, Tequila began to pull him up.

"I can't hold on," Herb said, his grip slipping.

"Hold on."

"I'm not as strong as you are."

"Do it for Bernice," Tequila grunted.

Inch by inch, Herb got closer to the opening. But it might as well have been a mile high. He was too exhausted. Too weak. Every muscle fiber in Herb's body was vibrating with pain, ready to let go, and then he passed his endurance limit and his hands released the pants and he began to fall and it didn't matter how many times he tried this there was no way it was ever going to work and—

—Tequila caught him by his collar.

"We need to have a talk about improving your upper body strength," Tequila said, hauling him up out the door.

The men sat there for a moment, both of them breathing heavy, and Tequila put his pants back on.

"We still have the same problem," Herb said. "We have no place to go."

"Yeah we do."

Tequila pointed.

And Herb saw the most beautiful thing he'd ever seen. Parked in the distance.

The Crimebago Deux.

It hadn't been some messed-up hallucination. Harry McGlade was actually here.

Also surrounding the crumbled land train, prisoners were running free, and guards were kneeling with their hands in the air as Harry with an AR-15, and some redhead packing two semi-automatics, rounded them all up.

"Over here!" Herb shouted, a burst of happiness threatening to make his heart pop.

And then he felt it. The car he was on shook with an impact, accompanied by a *CLANG*.

Herb turned and saw the man who had jumped from the connecting car to this one.

It was that huge Russian guy. All two hundred and eighty pounds of him.

And the man looked seriously pissed.

THE COWBOY

This is it.
 The culmination of a third of her life.
 Distilled to this one moment.
 Gunslinger Showdown. High Noon.
 For real.
 With Jack Daniels.
 "Here's what's going to happen," the Cowboy tells her. "I've never needed more than six bullets. I have four left. With you, I only need three. With one, I'm going to shoot the gun out of your hand again. Then I'm going to shoot both of your knees. Are you ready?"
 Jack doesn't answer. She looks scared.
 "Wyatt and I have a room, all prepared for you, Jack. In our basement. Welcome to the beginning of your hell."
 She slowly holsters her Vaquero.
 The anticipation is electric.
 "Your move," the Cowboy says.

HERB

"Can you jump over the side?" Tequila said as Yuri approached. The drop is at least fourteen feet. That didn't sound like much, but people have died falling off roofs a lot lower than that.

"I'll break something," Herb said.

"Go back into the car. Jump on the dirt pile."

Herb looked down. "I'm not going back in there."

"Then we only have one option left," Tequila said, putting up his fists. "We fight."

Herb stood next to his friend, his brother, and raised his fists as well.

JACK

I'd been in a quick draw situation before.
　　I'd lost.
To say I was terrified was an understatement.
I didn't know how good Annie actually was, but if she'd beaten Alex Kork, she was better than me.
Push away the negative thoughts, Jack.
Focus.
I thought about Herb. I'd come here to save him and Tequila, and I would never know if they were freed.
Come on. Get in the zone.
I thought about Samantha. She'd grow up without a mother, exactly as I feared.
Concentrate on the draw. On the shot.
Tune out everything else.
I thought about Phin. How I'd never get the chance to apologize.
You'll have the chance to apologize, you idiot.
Just win.
Shoot this crazy Cowboy bitch and find Herb and Tequila and go home to your family.
Focus.
You can do it.
Focus.
Focus…

Time slowed down.

Tunnel-vision took over.

The world became me, and the Cowboy.

She's fast.

But so am I.

My hand was lightning as I yanked the Taurus from the holster and fired three times, aiming at her center mass, shooting her three times in the chest.

YURI

Gone.
Everything gone.
The only thing left was rage.
Yuri lowered his head and charged at the Americans, determined to rip their limbs off of their screaming bodies.

HERB

"Go high," Tequila said. "I'll go low."

The Russian came at them, arms wide, and Tequila moved in and punched the huge man in the stomach. Herb wasn't sure what *go high* meant, but he took a swing at Yuri's head. It was like hitting a mailbox. The Russian swatted him aside like Herb was a child, and Herb rolled across the car and barely slid to a stop before falling off the side.

He looked, as Tequila was doing some insanely fast karate moves, attacking the bigger man with fists and feet like he was a heavy bag at the gym.

The Russian took the blows, then made a grab for Tequila.

Tequila ducked inside the grab, working the man's body, then hitting him with an uppercut that was so hard the Russian staggered back.

Herb got to his feet.

"Go high again?" he asked.

"I'll go high. Try low this time."

Herb went low, and got a size fifteen combat boot to the face.

The world went blurry and Herb's knees turned to jelly.

When he was able to see again, he was on his ass, and Tequila was still throwing, and connecting, punches. But Herb could see that his friend was tiring. The Russian kept taking everything that was thrown at him, and Tequila's blows were getting weaker and weaker.

And then it happened. The big man reached for Tequila, and Tequila was too slow to duck away.

A millisecond later, Tequila was on his back, the Russian on top, strangling him.

Herb got up to his feet, and began to hammer the man in the face, punching as hard as he could.

The Russian didn't let go.

Herb tried to get behind him, to pull his head back like he'd done with the guards.

But the Russian was too strong.

Finally Herb realized there was only one thing left to do.

"Sorry, Bernice," he whispered to the winds. "I love you."

His own safety be damned, Herb took a running start and body tackled the Russian, knocking him off Tequila, and they both tumbled over the edge of the train car, falling to the unforgiving earth fourteen feet below.

JACK

The pain came suddenly. My gun was gone, and my hand was bloody.

I looked up at the Cowboy.

She was still standing there.

Vest. She's wearing a vest.

Annie touched her chest. "God DAMN, that hurts. You're better than I hoped, Jack. That is going to leave a mark for sure."

I looked around for the gun, saw it a meter away. I could grab it lefty and—

Annie shot again, kicking my gun across the ground. Not only was it farther from me, but she'd shot the cylinder out of it. The gun was trashed.

"Don't worry," she said. "I saved the last two bullets. One for each of your knees. You can brace for it if you want, but it isn't going to help."

Instead of bracing myself, I chose to dive to the left, launching myself into the air, ready to come up in a roll and rush her before she had a chance to reload.

She fired just as I made my move.

The first bullet hit my left thigh.

The second hit my right calf.

When I tried to come up in a roll, my body wouldn't obey. I could only get to my knees.

"How about that, Jack. You made me miss."

Annie rubbed her chest again, then fished a bullet out of her pocket.

"I never need more than six bullets," she said, holding it up and walking over. "But I keep a spare on me, just in case. And a promise is a promise. Which knee do you want it in?"

"My friends will come after you," I told her.

"After I shoot you, I'll take care of your friends. We'll have a big party in my basement. Have you ever smelled your own flesh cook, Jack? It smells exactly like—"

Gunshot.

Annie's hat flew off.

And she dropped right in front of me, her head spurting blood.

I looked around, expecting to see Harry, or Chandler, ready to thank them for saving my ass.

But it wasn't Harry or Chandler walking up to me with a Kel-Tec SU-16A rifle.

My Kel-Tec SU-16A rifle.

"Phin."

THE MAN

The man, Phineas Troutt, slings the rifle and grins. "When we discuss this moment later, remember that you tried to leave me at home."

"You followed me," Jack says.

"Of course I followed you. I've been following you since you left."

Realization comes to Jack's eyes. "You. It was you who shot Chandler."

Oops. He'd only met Chandler briefly, but she's on their side. "That was Chandler? She changed her hair. And she was holding a gun to your neck."

"She was losing the fight, so she cheated."

"Is she okay?"

"She'll live."

"Tell her I'm sorry."

Jack's eyes got glassy. "Phin... I know you were in Chicago."

"You were tracking my phone?" He nods. "Figured you would. I kept it off most of the time."

"I thought... maybe..."

"Maybe what?"

"Maybe you'd gone back to Pasha."

"Reading my texts, too?" He laughs, and it feels good. "I had a layover at O'Hare on the way to Omaha. We met for coffee. She gives you her best. You really thought...?"

Jack nods. She's crying now.

"I'm sorry. I should have taken you with me. I'll never leave you behind again. I swear I'll never—"

The shot enters Jack's back, and comes out of her stomach in an eruption of blood.

Phin brings up the rifle, fires at the man who is running over as the man shoots back, diving to the side as bullets stitch across his Kevlar. They feel like whacks with a sledgehammer, and Phin lands on his rifle.

He tries to turn onto his back, and then the man is on top of him, whacking him in the head with the butt of his revolver.

"Name is Wyatt," the man says. "You must be Jack's husband. Heard you're a bad ass. Don't look like such a bad ass to me."

And then the gun comes down again, and the world winks out.

HERB

Something was broken.
Maybe everything was broken.
Herb looked around, saw that his arm was all crooked.
So was a leg.
The pain hadn't hit yet, but when it did, he knew it would be bad. Real bad.
Herb saw movement. To his right.
The Russian. He was somehow able to stand up.
And he was coming over.
Herb tried to sit up, to scoot away, but he knew he wasn't going anywhere.
He looked up, expecting to see Tequila sailing through the air, leaping off the land train in a flying tackle.
But Tequila didn't appear.
Then the Russian was towering above him, filling Herb's vision, lifting up his huge foot over Herb's head.
"Mu'dak!"
Herb lifted an arm to protect himself. Knew it wouldn't do any good.
And then he heard it.
A voice.
An angelic voice.
"Hey! Asshole! Don't you dare stomp on my best friend!"
That was no angel.
That was Harry McGlade.

PHIN

When the world spins back into focus, Phin's gun is gone.

He sees Jack, face down in the dirt, not moving. He can't tell if she's breathing or not.

There's a sobbing sound. He see the man, Wyatt, cradling the head of the woman Phin had shot.

"Tom-boy, Tom-boy, don't be murderdead, girl. Don't be murderdead. Jerry's here. Jerry's here. It'll all be okeydoke. I promiseswear. I promiseswear."

Wyatt has a gun in his holster, and Phin has no idea if he's reloaded yet. He shot Jack once, and Phin thinks he's been shot five times.

There's a slim chance that Wyatt is out of bullets.

A slim chance is better than none.

Head pounding, body aching, Phineas Troutt manages to twist up onto his stomach and get his legs under him, and then he staggers toward Wyatt, picking up speed, and just as the man notices Phin manages to slug him in the face.

Phin falls to all fours, and Wyatt shakes off the punch, stands, and plants a cowboy boot into Phin's armpit.

Phin rolls, the world spinning helter-skelter, his head feeling like it's about to pop.

Then Wyatt was aiming another kick at Phin's head, and Phin manages to get an arm up to block, and then, somehow, gets up on his feet.

He stares, groggily, at Wyatt, his eyes lowering to the man's gun holster.

"Not loaded," Wyatt says. "Don't matter. Don't need it for you."

Wyatt puts up his fists, dances forward, bobbing and weaving, and Phin immediately realizes this guy knows how to box.

He covers up, taking four punches on the shoulders, and then Wyatt finds an opening and tags Phin on the chin.

"Do you even know how to fight, boy?" Wyatt says, landing another one-two combination. "I just killed your wife. Doesn't that piss you off?" One-two.

"And I killed your Tom-boy," Phin says. "Doesn't that piss *you* off?"

Wyatt narrows his eyes. "She was my sister. And my lover. And I'm going to beat the skin right off your body."

He comes in fast, throwing a flurry of punches that drop Phin to his knees.

Jack was right.

Phin wasn't fully recovered from Baja.

He was damn near useless.

"Come on," Wyatt says. "Get up. Don't wuss out on me, bad ass. I'm just getting warmed up."

Wyatt feints a punch.

Phin flinches.

Wyatt laughs.

Phin manages to get up on his feet.

He raises his fists.

Wyatt easily moves in, clocking Phin on the chin.

Phin staggers, but stays on his feet. Everything feels wrong. He's awkward. Can't find his rhythm. He throws a left, which Wyatt dodges, and then Wyatt feints a right.

Phin flinches.

"Look at you, bad ass. You're scared. And you should be. Because when I'm done beating you, I'm gonna make you watch me lay some pipe in your dead wife."

Wyatt feints again.

Phin flinches.

And seeing himself flinch, he accepts it.

Accepts that he's not one hundred percent.

Accepts that he might never be.

But Phin knows two things, for certain.

I'm tired of being afraid.

And even if I'm not at my best, I'm still a bad ass.

Wyatt feints.

This time Phin doesn't flinch. He throws a roundhouse, catching Wyatt on the shoulder, and then popping the jab on his chin.

Wyatt dances away, grinning. "Well, look who showed up. I like that fire in your eyes right now. But don't get too excited. I'm a Golden Gloves champ. You can't outbox me."

"I know. I'm not going to box you." Phin tucks his chin down. "I'm going to kill you."

He charges.

Wyatt throws two punches, hitting Phin on both sides of his aching head, but Phin has a target in mind and nothing was going to stop him. He reaches up, going for Wyatt's neck, grabbing the man's thick leather necklace and yanking down, hard, while bringing up a knee.

Wyatt's face bounces off of Phin's patella, and Phin throws him, face-first, into the ground. But he doesn't let go of the leather. He sits on Wyatt's back like he's busting a bronco, the necklace tight in both fists, and chokes the son of a bitch for all he's worth.

HERB

"That's right, you giant sack of shit," Harry McGlade said. "Step away from Herb, and put your hands over your head."

The Russian lowered his foot and raised his hands.

"Harry?" Herb said. "That's really you?"

"It's me, buddy."

"You're..."

"I know. I'm a hero."

"You're... enormous."

Harry's fat face became pinched. "Okay, I get it. You're all broken up. You're obviously delirious from pain."

"It looks like someone stuck a tube up your ass and inflated you."

"Herb, be nice. See the camera on my head? We're streaming live. Ten million people are watching this on YouTube."

"You're too fat to fit on YouTube," Herb said.

"Well you're also... uh... geez, Herb, you lost a lot of weight."

"And you found it. You're like two fat guys, wearing the same blazer."

"Words hurt, Herb."

"I bet sit-ups hurt, too."

Harry tried to cross his arms, but they were too fat. "I can do a sit up."

"How do you fit in the gym? Is it in an airplane hangar?"

"Just because I've gain a few pounds shouldn't make me an object of ridicule."

"You've got a Fruity Pebble stuck to your chin," Herb said. "It's stuck there with jelly. The ridicule is justified."

Then everything suddenly and dramatically went very, very wrong. The Russian lunged at McGlade, and Harry shot him five times, but the big man didn't even slow down, piledriving into Harry, knocking him down, tossing his gun away, and bringing down his huge fists, over and over.

Herb again tried to move, again failed, and let out a faint cry for help as McGlade was getting beaten to death.

Help came.

Just as Herb had expected, Tequila leapt off the land train, sailing through the air, landing on the big man in a flying tackle.

They rolled across the ground, and Herb was ready to cheer his brother on when he saw the Russian pin Tequila down and resume the choking that Herb had interrupted earlier.

"McGlade!" Herb bellowed "Get your fat ass up!

Harry managed to rock up to a sitting position, then crawl at the Russian.

The big man swatted McGlade away as easily as he'd done with Herb.

Tequila was being murdered, right in front of them.

And neither of them could do a damn thing to stop it.

THE COWBOY

A nnie opens her eyes.
Sees red.
It's blood.
Her blood.
Head shot. Came out of nowhere.
She raises up a hand, feels her scalp. Can't tell what the damage is, but her vision is blurry.
Concussion.
Or worse.
She scans the area, looking for her own brains, and sees two people struggling.
Jerry!
Someone is on top of her brother, strangling him, and Annie tries to get up and the whole world tilts sideways.
But as it tilts, the Cowboy notices two things.
Her Ruger Vaquero.
And the last bullet.
The Vaquero is within reach, and the Cowboy snatches it up, then stretches for the dropped ammo, winking there in the dirt.
It's close.
So close.
She reaches further, nudging it with her ring finger.
Almost... almost...

And then she feels a stabbing pain as something black attacks her hand.

Something black. And white.

Is that... *a penguin?*

The penguin pecks her again, then picks up the bullet—*her last bullet!*—and waddles off as the lights go out of Jerry's eyes.

No.

No!

White hot rage courses through the Cowboy, and with it comes clarity.

My derringer.

In my ankle holster.

She reaches for it.

There are two shots.

One for the guy who killed her Jerry.

And one for that goddamn penguin.

HERB

"Harry!" Herb yells. "Do something!"

Harry looks at Herb. Looks at Tequila and the Russian. Then raises his good hand to his mouth.

For god's sake, is he eating something?

No, McGlade wasn't eating.

He was whistling.

And five seconds later, the biggest dog Herb had ever seen was bounding up to them, barreling into the Russian, and tearing out his throat.

Then the beast's gigantic muzzle, dripping with gore, turned on Tequila—

—and began to lick his face.

"Good girl, Rosa," Tequila moaned. "Good girl."

That's the last thing Herb saw before the pain took hold and he blessedly passed out.

PHIN

Phin gets off of Wyatt's dead body, tries to stand, almost falls, and then staggers over to Jack.

He feels for a pulse.

It's there, but faint.

He looks around, searching for help, and sees movement.

A penguin.

And next to it.

The woman that Jack shot in the head. She's struggling to reach inside her boot.

Phin walks over, slaps her hand away, and fishes a gun out of her ankle holster.

A derringer. Phin opens the breach. Two rounds of .22lr.

The woman rolls onto her back, reaching up for the weapon, a fake finger falling off.

"I'm sick of you assholes coming after my family," Phin says.

A head shot is risky with a twenty-two. The bullets could deflect off the skull. So Phin reaches down, tears her shirt, and tugs the Velcro off her bulletproof vest.

Then he shoots her twice through the heart.

Throwing the gun away, he hurries back to Jack.

"Phin..." she whispers.

"You're going to make it, babe," he tells her. "*We're* going to make it."

He kisses her, so softly, and then the next words that come from her beautiful lips tear him apart.

"I can't feel my legs, Phin. I can't feel my legs..."

THE NEXT DAY

HERB

Herb awoke and immediately sat up, searching for Tequila.

His friend was in the hospital bed next to him. Rosalina was on the floor, sprawled out like a giant, wrinkled bear rug.

"Jack out of surgery yet?"

Tequila shook his head.

"I still can't believe we're here."

Tequila nodded.

"I told you so," Herb told him.

"Told me what?" Tequila's voice is hoarse. A double-strangulation will do that to a guy.

"That you were a good man. That you wouldn't leave me when you had the chance."

"I never..." Tequila whispered.

"What's that?"

"I never... had a friend before."

"We're not friends," Herb said. "You're my brother."

Tequila nods, and the morphine drip puts Herb back to sleep. When he wakes up again, someone is holding his hand.

"I can't stop crying," Bernice said, tears running down her cheeks. "I keep putting on make-up, and it keeps coming off."

"You're beautiful," Herb starts crying as well. "You're the most beautiful thing I've ever seen."

"I never stopped believing you were alive, Herb. I never stopped. Your funeral, we buried an empty casket. I knew you were still out there. I could feel it."

"I love you," Herb told his wife. "I love you so, so much. And I need a really big favor."

"Name it."

"Kiss me," Herb said. "And never, ever stop."

JACK

Phin was there when the anesthesia wore off.
"How'd it go?" I mumbled.
He patted my hand. "Good."
"Will I walk again?"
"Too soon to say. Do you... feel anything?"
I shook my head. "I'm sorry, Phin."
"It's okay."
"You saved me."
"Of course I did. I love you."
"I love you, too."

• • •

Phin was there when I woke up.
"Herb's okay?"
"He keeps asking about you. You up for visitors?"
I nodded.
Phin calls him. Turns out Herb was waiting in the hallway. His wife pushes his wheelchair in.
"Hiya, partner," Herb says, reaching out to hold my hand.
"Herb...I...I didn't know you were still alive."
"I know. Chandler told me. It wasn't your fault, Jack."
"You're okay?"
"I should make a full recovery. It's Bernice I'm worried about."

I looked at Bernice, a question on my face. She gave her husband a slap on the arm and blushed.

"What am I missing here?" I asked.

"She can't get enough of my trim new body. So she promised me sex every day for a full year," Herb said. "She's got three hundred and sixty-four days to go."

"Your arm and leg are broken," I said.

"Everything else works fine," laughed Bernice.

"I'm glad you're back, Herb."

"Glad to be back. Why don't you guys stop in Chicago before you go back to Florida? First beer is on me."

• • •

Phin was there when I opened my eyes.

So was McGlade. He had bandages on his face.

"Hiya, Jackie."

"Harry. Where are Heckle and Jeckle with the cameras?"

"Good news and bad news. Good news, I've hit over four hundred million views. My thongs and coffee cups are selling like crazy."

"And the bad news?"

McGlade handed me his iPhone and pressed the screen. A video started.

It's of the land train. There was general commotion, as prisoners milled about and Chandler subdued some guards. Then Heckle came into frame, and he and Jeckle, who was obviously running the camera, moved away from the crowd and went behind the land train. They came up to Annie's Silverado, tipped on its side. They walked past it, and over to two bodies.

One was Wyatt. Eyes open. Obviously dead.

The other was the Cowboy.

Heckle felt for a pulse, and then lifted her up.

They brought her back to the Silverado. It took them a few minutes to attach a tow chain to the undercarriage, and pull it back onto all four wheels. They put Annie into the cab, and drove off. Then the video ended.

"I put two in her chest," Phin said.

"Right here?" Harry patted his left side.

Phin nodded.

"You can see that in the video, if you pause it. You can also see her breathing. I had a hunch. So I pulled some strings, paid a few people, to do Wyatt's autopsy early. He was born with his heart on his right side. It's called dextrocardia. It's genetic, happens one in twelve thousand people. I'm betting his twin sister inherited the same anomaly."

"Where did the twins take her?" I asked.

Harry shrugged. "Authorities are looking for them, and the truck. Nothing's turned up."

I sighed. "I knew those guys were bad news."

"You should have said something to me," Harry said.

• • •

Phin woke me up, holding out my phone. "You should take this."

I expected it to be Sam, or my mother.

"Heard you still can't walk."

It was Chandler.

"Bullet hit my T-11 thoracic nerve. I have no feeling below my belly button."

"I'm sorry."

"If you're feeling bad, you can come and change my diaper."

"Pass. Meant to visit, but I had business out of the country. I thought that you should hear something. Might make you feel a little better."

"You've got some secret government serum that can regrow nerve tissue."

"No. I've been doing some digging into the land train and its owner. His name was Yuri Morozov. Former KGB, head of a death squad in Belarus. Real first class asshole. On board the train were eight tungsten rods, two and a half tons each. You ever hear the term *rod from god?*"

"No."

"It's a kinetic bombardment weapon. In a nutshell, you put the rods on a low earth orbit satellite, then drop them on your target. They hit going Mach 10. Each one has the explosive force of twelve tons of TNT. I did some digging, and Yuri actually had a satellite ready to go."

"There are agencies that stop that sort of thing. Right?"

"Wrong. The Outer Space Treaty bans WMDs in orbit. But tungsten carbide isn't considered a weapon of mass destruction."

"You're kidding."

"Welcome to diplomacy. Yuri would have launched, and he could have killed tens of thousands. Maybe hundreds of thousands. And who knows what that would have led to."

I couldn't quite wrap my head around it.

"You did good, Jack. You and McGlade prevented the biggest terrorist attack in history. Something that may have caused World War 3. How do you feel about that?"

"Numb."

"Interesting."

"Interesting?"

"I feel the same way, every time I save the world. I gotta run. Do everyone a favor and get better."

Chandler hung up.

"We saved the world," I told my husband.

Phin said, "Cool."

• • •

Phin was there when I woke up.

So was Tequila.

"Thanks," he said.

I nodded.

Not one for conversation, Tequila left, Rosalina trotting along behind him.

• • •

Phin was there when I opened my eyes.

I began to cry.

"I might never walk again," I said.

"You won't need to," he assured me. "I'll carry you. Everywhere."

• • •

When I opened my eyes, Phin was there.

Phin was always there.

It took me too damn long to figure that out, but I finally did, and the feeling of being so loved overwhelmed me.

"I love you," I said, holding his hand. "I love you so much."

• • •

I opened my eyes, and Phin was there.

So was Mom. And Sam.

Without asking, Sam hopped up onto my hospital bed and threw her arms around my neck.

"I missed you Mommy I love you so much!"

I winced. "I love you too, Sammy. But you're hurting Mommy's legs."

Phin's eyes got wide.

I was confused, then I realized what I just said.

And I knew, I just knew, that everything was going to be okay.

EPILOGUE: SOMEWHERE, SOMEWHEN

THE COWBOY

Jerry is dead.

    Murderdead.

And Annie is going to kill everyone responsible.

The ache for vengeance is more powerful than ever.

"We hacked McGlade's office computer," says Heckle.

"We need to search the data dump, but we should be able to find where Jack and Phin live," says Jeckle.

Annie smiles. "My guardian angels. Saving my life. Nursing me back to health. What did I do to deserve you? I owe you both so much."

"We only want one thing in return," says Heckle.

"Only one thing," says Jeckle.

Annie knows what it is. But they say it anyway, in perfect unison.

"Teach us to be like you."

THE END

JOE KONRATH'S COMPLETE BIBLIOGRAPHY

JACQUELINE "JACK" DANIELS THRILLERS
WHISKEY SOUR (Book 1)
BLOODY MARY (Book 2)
RUSTY NAIL (Book 3)
DIRTY MARTINI (Book 4)
FUZZY NAVEL (Book 5)
CHERRY BOMB (Book 6)
SHAKEN (Book 7)
STIRRED with Blake Crouch (Book 8)
RUM RUNNER (Book 9)
LAST CALL (Book 10)
WHITE RUSSIAN (Book 11)
SHOT GIRL (Book 12)
CHASER (Book 13)
OLD FASHIONED (Book 14)
BITE FORCE (Book 15)
JACK ROSE (Book 16)
LADY 52 with Jude Hardin (Book 2.5)

JACK DANIELS AND ASSOCIATES MYSTERIES
DEAD ON MY FEET (Book 1)
JACK DANIELS STORIES VOL. 1 (Book 2)
SHOT OF TEQUILA (Book 3)
JACK DANIELS STORIES VOL. 2 (Book 4)
DYING BREATH (Book 5)
SERIAL KILLERS UNCUT with Blake Crouch (Book 6)
JACK DANIELS STORIES VOL. 3 (Book 7)
EVERYBODY DIES (Book 8)
JACK DANIELS STORIES VOL. 4 (Book 9)
BANANA HAMMOCK (Book 10)

KONRATH DARK THRILLER COLLECTIVE
THE LIST (Book 1)
ORIGIN (Book 2)
AFRAID (Book 3)
TRAPPED (Book 4)
ENDURANCE (Book 5)
HAUNTED HOUSE (Book 6)
WEBCAM (Book 7)
DISTURB (Book 8)
WHAT HAPPENED TO LORI (Book 9)
THE NINE (Book 10)
SECOND COMING (Book 11)
CLOSE YOUR EYES (Book 12)
HOLES IN THE GROUND with Iain Rob Wright (Book 4.5)
DRACULAS with Blake Crouch, Jeff Strand, F. Paul Wilson (Book 5.5)
GRANDMA? with Talon Konrath (Book 6.5)

STOP A MURDER PUZZLE BOOKS
STOP A MURDER – HOW: PUZZLES 1 – 12 (Book 1)
STOP A MURDER – WHERE: PUZZLES 13 – 24 (Book 2)
STOP A MURDER – WHY: PUZZLES 25 – 36 (Book 3)
STOP A MURDER – WHO: PUZZLES 37 – 48 (Book 4)
STOP A MURDER – WHEN: PUZZLES 49 – 60 (Book 5)
STOP A MURDER – ANSWERS (Book 6)
STOP A MURDER COMPLETE CASES (Books 1-5)

CODENAME: CHANDLER
(PETERSON & KONRATH)
FLEE (Book 1)
SPREE (Book 2)
THREE (Book 3)
HIT (Book 4)
EXPOSED (Book 5)
NAUGHTY (Book 6)
FIX with F. Paul Wilson (Book 7)
RESCUE (Book 8)

TIMECASTER SERIES
TIMECASTER (Book 1)
TIMECASTER SUPERSYMMETRY (Book 2)
TIMECASTER STEAMPUNK (Book 3)

EROTICA
(WRITING AS MELINDA DUCHAMP)

Make Me Blush series
KINKY SECRETS OF MISTER KINK (Book 1)
KINKY SECRETS OF WITCHES (Book 2)
KINKY SECRETS OF SIX & CANDY (Book 3)

Alice series
KINKY SECRETS OF ALICE IN WONDERLAND (Book 1)
KINKY SECRETS OF ALICE THROUGH THE LOOKING GLASS (Book 2)
KINKY SECRETS OF ALICE AT THE HELLFIRE CLUB (Book 3)
KINKY SECRETS OF ALICE VS DRACULA (Book 4)
KINKY SECRETS OF ALICE VS DR. JEKYLL & MR. HYDE (Book 5)
KINKY SECRETS OF ALICE VS FRANKENSTEIN (Book 6)
KINKY SECRETS OF ALICE'S CHRISTMAS SPECIAL (Book 7)

Jezebel series
KINKY SECRETS OF JEZEBEL AND THE BEANSTALK (Book 1)
KINKY SECRETS OF PUSS IN BOOTS (Book 2)
KINKY SECRETS OF GOLDILOCKS (Book 3)

Sexperts series
THE SEXPERTS – KINKY GRADES OF SHAY (Book 1)
THE SEXPERTS – KINKY SECRETS OF THE PEARL NECKLACE (Book 2)
THE SEXPERTS – KINKY SECRETS OF THE ALIEN (Book 3)

MISCELLANEOUS
65 PROOF – COLLECTED SHORT STORIES
THE GLOBS OF USE-A-LOT 3 (with Dan Maderak)
A NEWBIES GUIDE TO PUBLISHING

OLD FASHIONED

Former Chicago Homicide Lieutenant Jacqueline "Jack" Daniels has finally left her violent past behind, and she's moved into a new house with her family.

But her elderly next door neighbor is a bit… off.

Is he really as he appears, a kind old gentlemen with a few eccentricities?

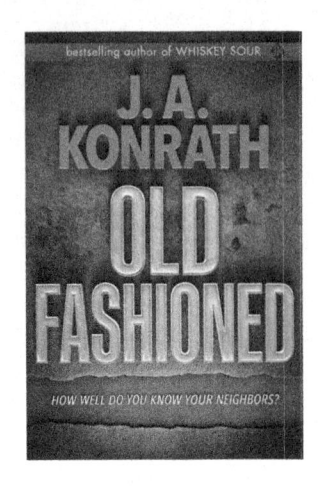

Or are Jack's instincts correct, and he's something much, much darker?

And what is it he'd got in his basement?

Jack Daniels is about to learn that evil doesn't mellow with age.

OLD FASHIONED by JA Konrath
How well do you know your neighbors?

DEAD ON MY FEET

His name is Phineas Troutt. He's a problem solver.

If a woman is being stalked by her ex-husband, Phin can convince him to stop. If a union is being squeezed, Phin can squeeze the squeezer. He's not a mercenary. He's not a bodyguard. He's not a private dick. He's a guy who takes cash for solving problems with violence.

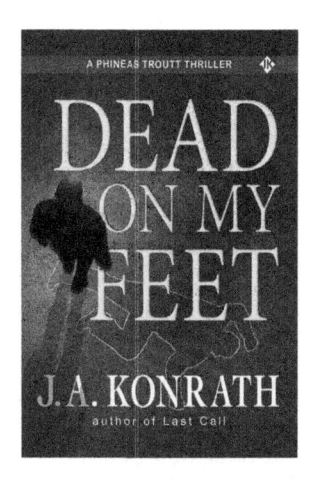

When a doctor at a suburban women's health clinic is being harassed, she hires Phin to make it stop. But the situation proves to be larger, and more dangerous, than even he can handle on his own. So he calls in some friends to help out; a P.I. named Harry McGlade and a female cop named Jack Daniels…

DEAD ON MY FEET by J.A. Konrath

Set in 2007, Konrath turns up the noir and gives leading man status to his favorite tough guy. Phin has appeared in the bestselling novels WHISKEY SOUR, RUSTY NAIL, SHAKEN, RUM RUNNER, LAST CALL, and many others, but now he's the main character. Filled with the same action, humor, and intrigue as the Jack Daniels series, but with a grittier, hardboiled edge, DEAD ON MY FEET is the first in a Phin Troutt trilogy, which also includes DYING BREATH and EVERYBODY DIES.

STOP A MURDER

This is unlike any mystery or thriller book you've ever read before. You play the sleuth, and try to follow the clues and solve the puzzles to prevent a murder from happening.

In this five-book series, you'll be tasked with decoding the mind and motivations of a nefarious killer who is plotting to commit an unspeakable crime.

Each book contains an epistolary collection of emails, texts, and letters, sent to bestselling author J.A. Konrath, by a serial killer. This psychopath is leaving detailed, cryptic hints about who will be murdered, why, when, where, and how. Some of the hints are easy to figure out. Others are much more devious.

Do you like solving mysteries? Do you enjoy puzzles or escape-the-room games? Are you good at spotting clues?

Only you can stop a murder.

Are you smart enough?

Are you brave enough?

Let the games begin...

#1 STOP A MURDER - HOW: Puzzles 1-12

#2 STOP A MURDER - WHERE: Puzzles 13-24

#3 STOP A MURDER - WHY: Puzzles 25-36

#4 STOP A MURDER - WHO: Puzzles 37-48

#5 STOP A MURDER - WHEN: Puzzles 49-60

Sign up for the J.A. Konrath newsletter. A few times a year I pick random people to give free stuff to. It could be you.

http://www.jakonrath.com/mailing-list.php

I won't spam you or give your information out without your permission!

Made in the USA
Las Vegas, NV
05 February 2025